DELILAH DEVLIN

Silver Shadow

ELLORA'S CAVE
ROMANTICA PUBLISHING

An Ellora's Cave Romantica Publication

www.ellorascave.com

Silver Shadow

ISBN 9781419956577
ALL RIGHTS RESERVED.
Uncovering Navarro Copyright © 2005 Delilah Devlin
Silver Bullet Copyright © 2006 Delilah Devlin
Edited by Briana St. James.
Cover art by Syneca.

This book printed in the U.S.A. by Jasmine-Jade Enterprises, LLC

Trade paperback Publication June 2007

Content Advisory:

S – ENSUOUS
E – ROTIC
X – TREME

Ellora's Cave Publishing offers three levels of Romantica™ reading entertainment: S (S-ensuous), E (E-rotic), and X (X-treme).

The following material contains graphic sexual content meant for mature readers. This story has been rated E–rotic.

S-*ensuous* love scenes are explicit and leave nothing to the imagination.

E-*rotic* love scenes are explicit, leave nothing to the imagination, and are high in volume per the overall word count. E-rated titles might contain material that some readers find objectionable — in other words, almost anything goes, sexually. E-rated titles are the most graphic titles we carry in terms of both sexual language and descriptiveness in these works of literature.

X-*treme* titles differ from E-rated titles only in plot premise and storyline execution. Stories designated with the letter X tend to contain difficult or controversial subject matter not for the faint of heart.

Also by Delilah Devlin

80

Arctic Dragon

Desire 1: Prisoner of Desire

Desire 2: Slave of Desire

Desire 3: Garden Of Desire

Ellora's Cavemen: Legendary Tails III (*anthology*)

Ellora's Cavemen: Seasons of Seduction I (*anthology*)

Ellora's Cavemen: Tales from the Temple III (*anthology*)

Fated Mates (*anthology*)

Jacq's Warlord *with Myla Jackson*

Lion in the Shadows

My Immortal Knight 1: All Hallows Heartbreaker

My Immortal Knight 2: Love Bites

My Immortal Knight 3: All Knight Long

My Immortal Knight 4: Relentless

Nibbles 'n' Bits (*anthology*)

Ride a Cowboy

Silent Knight

The Pleasure Bot

Witch's Choice

About the Author

සෙ

Delilah Devlin dated a Samoan, a Venezuelan, a Turk, a Cuban, and was engaged to a Greek before marrying her Irishman. She's lived in Saudi Arabia, Germany, and Ireland, but calls Texas home for now. Ever a risk taker, she lived in the Saudi Peninsula during the Gulf War, thwarted an attempted abduction by white slave traders, and survived her children's juvenile delinquency.

Creating alter egos for herself in the pages of her books enables her to live new adventures. Since discovering the sinful pleasure of erotica, she writes to satisfy her need for variety—it keeps her from running away with the Indian working in the cubicle beside her!

In addition to writing erotica, she enjoys creating romantic comedies and suspense novels.

Delilah welcomes comments from readers. You can find her website and email address on her author bio page at www.ellorascave.com.

Tell Us What You Think

We appreciate hearing reader opinions about our books. You can email us at Comments@EllorasCave.com.

SILVER SHADOW

ፙ

UNCOVERING NAVARRO
~11~

&

SILVER BULLET
~135~

UNCOVERING NAVARRO

ဢ

Trademarks Acknowledgement

Chapter One

ℬ

"Sid, get that cute little tail of yours behind the yellow tape, now!" Moses Brown bit back a grin at the look of pure irritation that crossed Sidney P. Coffey's face.

"Hi there, Moses. Long time, no see." She ducked back under the crime scene tape and turned, taking a moment to pull the white cuffs of her shirt from below the edges of her leather jacket.

She was stalling. Moses could almost see the gears turning over in her head. The woman didn't know when to give up.

When she glanced his way, a smile was plastered on her face. "By the way, congratulations on the promotion, *detective*. The new suit makes your shoulders look even broader."

His gaze narrowed. The only time she wasted a second on small talk was when she wanted something—bad. "Sid, you're not gettin' inside that house."

Her blue eyes widened. "Do you think I was trying to—"

"Uh-huh. Don't give me that Miss Innocent look. I know you, sweetheart."

Her eyebrows rose, and her sexy mouth formed a pout. "Not even for an old buddy, like me?"

Moses folded his arms over his chest. "Old fuck buddy— let's keep that straight."

She huffed, and her eyebrows drew together in a disgruntled frown. "That sounds so crass."

"I'm just repeating what you told me, baby."

"Well, I was only being honest."

That was the thing he liked about her best—beyond her slim body and cute tush. She didn't mince her words. A man knew exactly where he stood.

She was also the only woman he knew who could keep a secret. Even though they often stood on opposite sides of the tape—him a cop, her a reporter—he could trust her. If he told her something couldn't make the evening news, she kept the tip close to her chest. *Her soft, curvy chest.*

She nodded toward the house, lights ablaze as the forensics team scoured it for clues. "How 'bout I promise to keep out of sight—"

He shook his head. "You know damn well the chief'd have my ass in a sling if I let you in there."

"But it's such a fine ass," she purred. Her glance gave him a once-over that left his skin burning.

He straightened and dropped his voice, "And don't you know it."

Her smile was genuine this time. "Maybe you need to refresh my memory." Her gaze slipped over his shoulder again. "What's going on in there?"

"You weren't listening to your police scanner?"

"You know I was." She wrinkled her nose. "Come on, give! A triple homicide? Who was it? More teenagers bite it?"

The little lady was too bright for her own good. He schooled his face into a mask. "I'm not at liberty to say."

"Not now anyway, huh? You know, the police aren't going to be able to keep this killing spree under wraps much longer. People are going to put two and two together. When they do, your chief's fanged friends won't be able to hide in the shadows." She sidled up close. "Later, maybe? We haven't *talked* in a long time."

Moses could feel his defenses crumble. Her fine blonde hair shone bright as sunshine under the streetlamp. Her flowery perfume tugged at his cock. He slipped his hand in his pocket and handed her his key. "I could be a while, sugar."

"Just wake me up." She walked past, deliberately rubbing her jeans-clad thigh against him.

He watched her hips sway as she walked away, until she turned the corner of the street. "Moses," he muttered to himself, "what the hell do you think you're doin'? That little woman's gonna wring you like a dishrag."

* * * * *

Sidney heard the creak of the apartment door as it opened. With a satisfied grin, she settled back against the satiny comforter.

Moses hadn't made her wait long after all. And soon she'd get her scoop—after a little play, of course.

Of all her recent *fuck buddies*, Moses was her favorite by far. His appetite for sex matched hers. Best of all, he didn't cling, didn't make more of her sharing his covers like some did. He knew the score—knew she liked her sex as most men did. *Dirty, nasty – and often.*

For her, sex was a purely physical release. An addiction she craved like some women craved chocolate. She ached with need. Already her nipples beaded, and her pussy oozed cream. Just the thought of his large cock sliding inside her had her blood humming in her veins.

To ease the ache between her legs, she slipped a hand between her thighs and stroked her cunt.

Moses pushed open the bedroom door. "Couldn't wait for me before you started the party?" His generous lips were stretched into a grin.

Glad she'd left the lamp atop the nightstand on, Sidney smiled and opened her legs so he could watch her play with herself. "I'm just priming the pump, honey."

He hadn't wasted any time himself. His dark chest was bare. His hands were already busy shoving his pants down muscled thighs. His cock sprang from confinement, huge and veined.

"Baby, you know I got a terrible thirst." His dark gaze smoldered as he watched her fingertips slide into her wet slit.

"I was counting on that." She dipped two fingers inside and swirled them in her juices, then she painted her nipples.

He strode to the end of the bed and crawled onto the mattress, his expression taut. His hands circled her ankles and jerked her legs wider apart.

Sidney yelped, but thrilled to his sheer physicality.

His face came down between her legs, and he made a growling sound as he sucked her lips into his mouth.

She hissed air between her teeth and lifted her hips, eager to accept his sensual kiss.

"Oh man, you know I missed the taste of you, girl," he said, rolling his face in her pussy. His large hands skimmed up her inner thighs, and his fingers spread her labia.

"Oh Christ," Sidney moaned. "Eat me, Moses." Her hands smoothed over the crown of his shaved head, and her fingers curved around his ears.

His tongue lashed out and rimmed her cunt, licking as deeply as he could reach along her channel walls, all the while the rough pads of his fingers tugged and massaged her pussy.

Sidney squeezed her eyes shut at the delicious sensations—his tongue caressing her sensitive flesh, his fingers now pinching the hood guarding her clitoris.

He sucked her lips into his mouth again and let them go. "If I wasn't hard as a rock, I'd spend hours here."

"Just like a man," she teased, breathless. "Full of regrets and blaming his cock."

"Rain check?" He kissed her inner thigh and looked up her body, his expression unrepentant.

"All right, lover. But you have to fuck me like you mean it."

"You're sassy when you're horny." He grinned. "Turn over—I promise to give you everything you got comin'."

14

Just as eager to get to the rough stuff, Sidney rolled to her belly and came up on her knees. She spread them wide on the slippery comforter and tilted her ass up to receive his cock.

Moses' hands curved around her waist, and he jerked her higher. "I'm gonna make you howl like a wolf."

"Promises, *promises*." Her words ended on a moan as the crown of his massive sex eased past her entrance.

Moses pressed forward, pulsing as he stretched her to accommodate his size. "Baby, you're tight. Ain't had a brother in a while, huh?"

"No one fills your...shoes," she gasped, wriggling backward to take him the rest of the way inside. Her arms trembled as she tried to hold herself up, but her vagina was already quivering and spasming around his cock.

Finally seated with his groin snug against hers, Moses leaned over her back and hugged her tight. "*Oh, damn!* You ready to be fucked to oblivion?"

She fisted her hands in the bedding. "Do the wild thing, baby!"

* * * * *

As Sidney drove to the estate nestled in the hills overlooking Seattle, she fought fatigue. After stopping at her apartment for a quick shower and change, she had precious few hours before the sun rose.

Her body was still warm, pliant and ached deliciously from Moses Brown's rough *play*.

Their conversation afterward had been brief. With his eyelids drooping and deep voice purring in her ear like a contented cat's, he'd finally given her the rundown on the latest homicides.

The dead men inside the nondescript house had been savaged, their necks laid open, their bodies drained of blood. Vampires. No doubt about it.

But something about the choice of victims niggled at Sidney's mind. Forty-something scientists meeting over dinner? Not an obvious target for creatures that tended to roam the streets seeking younger, tender morsels.

Not that she fully understood vampires' appetites and habits. Hell, she hadn't even known they existed until a few short months ago.

She'd been following a trail of missing teenagers taken out by gang violence — or so the police reports stated. Never satisfied with the official accounts, she'd done a little digging.

First, she'd found notices posted in the obits of the *Seattle Times* for rosaries, eulogies and remembrance ceremonies — but the bodies were never presented for viewing, and stranger still, she couldn't find a single instance of an actual burial. The few parents willing to speak to her had been told the kids' bodies were dumped in Elliott Bay and never recovered.

Next, her curiosity had led her to Moses Brown, a name that appeared again and again in the police reports. A uniformed cop at the time, he'd worked the areas where the teenagers tended to disappear. She'd hounded the man, stalked him to his hangouts and to his apartment door. She'd even joked with him that her middle initial "P" stood for "Persistence".

Then one night, following a tip from one of the victim's friends, she'd attended a Halloween party at a trendy nightclub called The Cavern, and she'd discovered the truth for herself.

The club was near the docks in West Seattle, situated among a shabby row of brick buildings. Its violet neon sign beckoned from the street, techno music pounded from the open door.

Once inside The Cavern, she'd tugged at the hem of her French Maid costume, feeling exposed and conspicuously older than the majority of the revelers. For a Halloween party, few of the young people in attendance actually wore costumes — if one discounted the dime-store fangs.

"Well, if it isn't Sidney Coffey — the 'News at Nine' girl."

She jumped at the sound of the masculine voice drawling so close to her ear and whirled.

The man in front of her was tall and lean, dressed in a black leather jacket and pants. With his pale skin, longish dark hair, and porcelain-smooth vamp dentures — he looked like Dracula gone biker.

"Do I know you?" she asked, raising her voice to be heard over the music.

"Not yet." His dark gaze swept down her body in a slow, sensual perusal.

No prude, Sidney could out-ogle most lounge lizards — but something about the predatory way this man loomed over her raised her hackles. She flashed him a small, tight smile. "Not ever."

His grin reminded her of a crocodile's toothy grimace. "We've started this conversation in the wrong place." He held out his hand. "Name's Nicky Powell."

Although he was handsome, Sidney had reluctantly laid her palm in his hand to shake it. "You already know my name." She lifted her chin in challenge and tried to pull away her hand.

He held her tight, the pressure just shy of cracking her knuckles. "You're a bit spiny. Delicious." He drew out the words like a man who meant to savor a treat. Then he bent over her hand and licked her skin.

Sidney blinked and tugged in earnest. "Okay, Vlad — enough with the tasting. Let me go!"

Instead of heeding her request, he followed her arm upward, licking and scraping his teeth along her skin, raising goose bumps and her heart rate. However repulsive he'd seemed at the start, her body started to quiver the higher his tongue caressed.

When he reached the cuff of her short sleeve, he looked up into her eyes.

Sidney swayed toward him, drawn to his bottomless gaze. She wet her lips, anticipating a kiss—

"Uh-huh, sugar. How many times I gotta tell you to leave off the rum 'til I get here?"

A strong arm circled her waist, and Sidney found herself looking up into Moses Brown's chocolate gaze.

Nicky released her arm and stepped back. "Officer Brown, how nice to see you."

Sidney shook her head, trying to rid herself of the muzzy, lustful feelings still ruling her body. When she looked up again, several young men stood behind Nicky, flexing their muscles and trying to look tough.

When she scanned the group, her body turned cold like she'd been doused with ice water. Their faces were familiar— she'd seen their pictures in the obituaries. "What the hell?"

Moses pulled her closer and leaned down to whisper in her ear. "Not now, baby. Wait 'til we get to the car." To Nicky, he said, "You won't mind if I dance with my girl, will you?"

Sidney shivered as the man's eyes narrowed, but he shrugged and tilted his head to his *posse* for them to follow him as he walked away.

"Moses," she hissed. "Those boys—"

"I bet you couldn't hold your piss for five seconds when you were a little girl." His hand slid from her hip to her arm, and he pulled her onto the dance floor. Once there, he tucked her body close to his, a thigh nudging between hers as he began a sexy dance that rubbed his body—chest to groin— against hers.

Her body still hummed from the other man's seductive lick-fest, but she trusted Moses wouldn't do her any harm, so she snuggled closer to his tall, hard-muscled frame, riding his thick thigh. Conversation was impossible the music was so loud, her questions would wait. She closed her eyes and just—felt.

Her body melted all over him as she ground her crotch on his leg, heat pooling between her legs.

"He's found himself another target. Let's get out of here," he whispered in her ear.

Sidney blinked dreamily and looked over her shoulder. Nicky Powell held a plump blonde woman in his arms who was struggling to free herself. "Looks like she needs help."

Moses nodded to two men moving in on the couple. "That's the owner—Dylan O'Hara—he'll take care of it. In the meantime, let's get out of here."

Sidney followed Moses' long strides as quickly as her heels and shaky legs would allow. For the first time, she noted a dark undercurrent of rising excitement stirring the crowd. Laughter had stopped, and all eyes turned to Nicky and the blonde.

"Keep walking!" Moses pulled her behind him, until once more she was outside the bar.

That night clouds had obscured the stars and a misting rain held the chill of coming winter. She'd raised her face to the mist, letting the cool clear the sensual fog from her brain. "You have a lot of explaining to do," Sidney said, casting Moses a sideways glance.

"I'll give you answers, but we need to get out of here quick."

She lifted her hand to point. "My car's over—"

He halted beside a black sedan. "Just get in."

Something about his expression got through to Sidney—his body was rigid, alert, his face hard, his eyes searching the shadows around them.

She opened the passenger door and slid into the seat. She'd hold her questions—for now.

As the engine growled to life, Sidney turned in her seat to stare at Moses. "Their parents think those boys are dead. Why haven't you told them the truth?"

"They are dead, sweetheart."

She hadn't believed him. Not at first. Moses took her back to his apartment that night, and while she found the release Nicky's seduction had inspired, she'd listened to Moses' story.

Straddling his hips, she lowered her pussy over his straining cock, relishing the unfamiliar bite of his super-sized sex as she sank on it. "Let me get this straight," she gasped. "You expect me to believe vampires really exist, and they're here in Seattle?"

Moses' large hands encouraged her to move forward and back, grinding his cock deeper into her channel. "I was there...when a couple of those boys were carried off to the morgue... They were stone-cold dead."

She admired his concentration. Her legs quivered, and she braced her weight against his broad chest.

"I almost feel guilty...taking advantage of the lust he built in you...like this." But his expression was anything but remorseful.

Sidney grinned, then bit her lower lip against a groan as she slid the rest of the way down his shaft. "You have a *long* way to go to convince me of your story, Moses Brown."

"Got all night, sister."

"Remember, I'm a reporter. I've heard some wild things in my time. Most of it turns out crap. I don't believe in anything I can't see, feel or smell for myself." She straightened and lifted, then sank, enjoying the long glide and the rippling orgasm building in her core. "I have to check all my sources."

"Plumb this source," he said, and pumped upwards, spearing her on his cock.

Oh, she'd checked out the plumbing all right—and his stories. But it had taken seeing Moses Brown dust a vamp before she'd believed him.

Now, she sat on the edge of the scoop of a lifetime. She just had a few more wispy threads to weave into her final story.

Outside the wrought iron gate of the private estate, Sid put her car into park and reached for the intercom button.

"How may I help you?" The voice was rasping like withered leaves, and the formal speech resounded with a hint of an Old-World accent.

"I'm here to see Mr. Navarro."

"I'm afraid he isn't in tonight, nor does he accept unannounced guests."

Sidney smiled into the camera lens beside the keypad. "If you'll tell him Sidney Coffey's here—I'm sure he's just forgotten about our appointment," she lied.

There was a pause—which meant her hunch was right. He was at home.

"I'm afraid, I must ask you to leave. As I said before, the Master is not at home."

She bit back a curse, hating to concede defeat, but there were other ways to skin a cat. "I'll try another time. Sorry for the inconvenience."

She backed out of the drive and circled the estate. The man must have buckets of money to afford a place like this. An intersection stretched before her and beyond it the lights of the city below flickered like stars on a smooth sea. She turned right for another pass around his property. She wasn't quite through.

A tall, brick wall surrounded the estate—not too tall, if one had a stepladder in the trunk.

Chapter Two

ʕʘ

Inigo cleared his throat politely. "Sir, I'm afraid we have an intruder."

"I suppose you should call the police, then," Master Navarro said, turning the next page of the ancient book he read without pausing.

Inigo shifted from one foot to the other, knowing he should do exactly as the Master had suggested, but their trespasser piqued Inigo's interest. Nothing ever disturbed the cadence of their days in the mansion. Master Navarro was a creature of habit. "Um...sir, perhaps you'd like to take a look for yourself."

The Master looked up from his text, no question in his expression—nothing to indicate whether he was annoyed or intrigued. His gaze held Inigo frozen like a butterfly pinned to a mounting board for a long nerve-racking moment. "Very well," he said, his voice evenly modulated. He rose slowly from his chair.

Inigo sighed his relief. While he wasn't exactly sure what the Master would do if he were ever annoyed, Inigo hoped never to incite that emotion in his employer. He knew instinctively, down to his toes, that he wouldn't survive such an occurrence.

However, life with this particular vampire was endlessly...predictable. Dealing with an intruder was at least a break in his routine.

Inigo followed close on the Master's heels, down the stairs to the basement, through the wine cellar, and into the security room. "She's coming over the north wall—and having a little difficulty by the look of it."

The woman's sweater had snagged on a tree branch as she straddled the brick wall. She jerked at the branch, but the tree wouldn't relinquish her garment. With a hasty glance about the yard, she wriggled out of the sweater, leaving it dangling like a dark flag.

Inigo blinked, for the woman wasn't wearing any undergarments, and her small breasts were the prettiest he'd seen in many a year.

The woman hugged herself, obviously freezing in the damp mist. Then she got her knees beneath her on the wall to give her greater height. She wobbled for a moment trying to gain her balance, and then reached out to the branch.

"Oh, my Lord," Inigo cried out as she pitched to the ground.

The Master turned from the monitor. "You may call the police now."

"Sir, did you not recognize her?"

"Should I know those pretty little breasts?"

Inigo flushed at Master Navarro's choice of words—that was precisely what he'd been thinking. "No, no. I mean, she's that reporter."

"Yes, I know." He fixed his narrowed gaze on Inigo. "Is there anything else?"

Disappointed with the Master's lack of interest, he straightened. "No, sir."

"I'll be in the library." Master Navarro left without looking at the monitor again.

Inigo's gaze returned to the screen. The woman hadn't stirred from the ground. First, he'd find a blanket. Then he'd call the police.

* * * * *

"Miss, are you all right?"

Sidney had already decided the evening couldn't get any worse. Now Lurch was leering at her tits.

Unfortunately, she'd fallen in the only patch of light cast by the streetlamp on the other side of the wall. She sat up and crossed her arms over her chest. "I think I'm all right—the grass is soft," she said, fighting to keep irritation out of her voice. She'd hoped to reach the front door *before* being escorted off the property.

"I brought you a blanket."

Sidney stared at the folded bundle he held out, then up at his face. It was really a rather kind face—if a little cadaverous. White, bristly hair stuck up around his head, and bushy eyebrows, looking like fluffy white beetles, shadowed his deep-set eyes. And he was alarmingly tall.

Sidney grabbed the blanket and wrapped it around her shoulders. Then she struggled to her feet, assisted by his dry, bony hand. "Just point me to the gate," she muttered, hoping he'd let her walk out with what was left of her dented pride. If a squad car showed up to take her to the station, she'd never hear the end of it.

"If you don't mind my saying so, climbing over the fence was a very foolish thing to do."

"It seemed like a plan at the time," she said under her breath. "Of course, my Plan Bs always suck."

His lips twitched. "Well, I'm glad you weren't seriously injured."

"Nope, I'm right as rain. I fell on my head—the hardest part of my body." A chill wind picked up, and she gathered the blanket closer around her. "I'll be on my way." With a grimace of a smile, she turned toward the gate. Best to make a quick getaway.

"Ah...miss!"

Sidney paused, knowing her escape couldn't be this easy—Murphy was running the show.

"You're shivering. How about I make you a hot cup of tea before you leave."

Sidney shot him a glance. What was he up to? She'd recognized his voice. He was the one who had turned her away at the gate. Was he planning to keep her here until the cops showed up? Or was he really offering her a kindness?

Her mama had never accused her of exercising an ounce of discretion. "I am cold. Tea would be lovely."

The old man led her around the side of the house, through a darkened fragrant garden, and into the kitchen. Warmth embraced her, and Sidney was sure steam rose from her damp hair and skin.

He pointed to an inviting alcove in the corner of the kitchen. "Have a seat at the table while I rummage for the pot."

As she sat at the cozy wooden table, Sidney couldn't help thinking how ironic it was—this domestic little scene playing out in a vampire's den.

"While the pot is boiling, I'll search for something you can wear," the elderly man said, then left through another door.

She counted to twenty before following.

The door led down a hallway, which opened into a large room with cream-colored walls and heavy, dark oak furnishings. She'd bet her paycheck the paintings gracing the pale walls were original, Old-World art. Despite numerous overhead electrical fixtures, candles were lit in wall sconces and on the mantel above a massive fireplace.

"A little old-fashioned, aren't you, Mr. Navarro?" Sidney muttered. Where was he? And did she really have the courage to seek a lion in his den? She hated to admit it, even to herself, but she was nervous.

Moses had said the master was a civilized vamp, but in the end, weren't they all ghouls?

She hitched the sagging blanket higher and chose another door, which led into a dark, paneled study. A fire crackled in a hearth, but the room appeared empty. Perhaps the master wasn't at home after all.

But his desk might reveal answers to some of her questions.

With a quick glance back at the living room, she quietly closed the door behind her.

"Miss Coffey, I think you've taken a wrong turn," a deep, lightly accented voice said.

Sidney whirled toward a leather armchair hidden in the shadows. Firelight flickered to reveal the outline of a man seated there. She didn't need two guesses to figure out who he was.

She drew a deep breath, racking her brain for a good excuse for her presence. "Um...Mr. Navarro. I was looking for you." She stepped deeper into the room—but the blanket didn't come with her.

She grasped frantically for the edges as it parted over her shoulders, but in her nervousness she stumbled forward. The blanket pulled away as she righted herself.

Her hands flew to her breasts. *Good lord, can this evening get any worse?* "M-mister Navarro," she stammered, hoping the dim lighting hid her burning cheeks and everything else. "Um...I seem to have caught my blanket in the door."

"Lovely though your breasts are, I think they should leave," he said, his tone lacking inflection.

The flatness of his voice, and the fact she couldn't read his expression in the shadows, left her unnerved. She hadn't thought through her plan past getting onto the property. Confronting the vamp himself, she realized just how precarious her situation was. He was a bloodsucker after all. Still, he'd asked her to leave—not become a dinner entrée.

Humiliated and more than a little scared, Sidney decided a hasty retreat was her best option. She turned back to the door and tugged at the knob, but the door didn't budge. She cursed under her breath and tugged again. Then her shoulders slumped in defeat. "I, uh...I've wedged the door closed. Could you help me?"

He sighed behind her, and leather creaked as he rose.

Sidney covered her breasts again and stepped aside.

As he approached, his features were revealed in candlelight.

Her breath left her lungs in a whoosh. She'd heard the master vampire was handsome—but not one of her sources had mentioned he was downright beautiful—or that his dark gaze could pierce like a skewer.

She fought the urge to step farther away, but then her fear aroused anger within herself. Sidney Coffey was no mouse. She lifted her chin.

One black, perfectly arched brow rose, mocking her show of courage. He reached past her and easily pulled open the door. "I trust you can find your way out."

The silky tone of his voice sent a shiver up her back, and her nipples drew tight and pointed beneath her palms.

From terror, she told herself. Certainly not from any sensual awareness. Never mind that this close, his height and lean, muscled frame made her feel very small and vulnerable. A sensation that never failed to stir her libido.

And the goose bumps lifting on her skin couldn't be caused by the midnight-colored hair that brushed the tops of his broad shoulders, or the olive complexion that contrasted darkly with his snowy cotton shirt.

Her gaze lifted. Black, fathomless eyes glittered back in a slightly narrow face, saved from appearing effeminate by his square jaw and the masculine shape of his mouth.

She lingered over that mouth. Perfectly symmetrical, not too wide, or too narrow—and firm.

Sidney swallowed and slowly returned to his unblinking stare. With her own mouth dry as a desert, she swallowed. It was now or never. She wouldn't get a second chance. She lowered her hands from her breasts and extended one sweaty palm. "Mr. Navarro, I'm Sidney Coffey, and I'd like to ask you a few questions."

Navarro stood still, bemused by the woman's audacity as she offered her slim, pale hand. He drew in the scents that warred with her tight, composed features. She had guts standing there, half-naked and shivering from a mixture of fear and arousal. "We have nothing to discuss. You may leave."

Two spots of color flared on her cheeks. She pulled back her hand and straightened her shoulders. "I know who—*what* you are. You're a master—one of the vampire council members."

For some reason, her temerity amused him. "Then why aren't you running for the door?"

Her chin rose while her upper chest gained a rosy glow. "I told you. I have questions."

Navarro let his glance sweep over her chest, and he smiled to himself at the telltale gasp that lifted her small, apple-shaped breasts. *Delicious.* "And this is how you usually conduct your interviews?"

"Of course not," she said, her voice clipped. "I seem to be having a...*wardrobe malfunction*, but I'm perfectly willing to conduct the interview now. Then I'll get out of your hair."

"This interview is so important?"

"A matter of life and death."

"Naturally. But whose?" He gave her neck a pointed stare, wondering what mischievous imp guided his actions. He didn't have time to toy with the woman.

How had this scrappy baggage invaded his home?

And where the hell was Inigo? Had his retainer acted on an impulse and allowed the woman to enter? Impossible...but, oh-so entertaining. He'd never have guessed Inigo would have the nerve to disobey one of his rules. Navarro couldn't remember the last time anyone had countered his command — with or without a little vampiric persuasion.

Nor could he remember the last time anyone had challenged him like this delicate little piece of femininity did now.

The woman nudged the blanket with her toes, trying to draw it closer without his notice.

Because the situation amused him, Navarro decided to goad the girl further. "I'll entertain questions under one condition." His gaze bored into hers.

Her gulp was audible. "What condition?"

He almost smiled, anticipating her flight. "That you remove all of your clothing."

Her eyes rounded, and her breath caught. "You'll answer my questions if I get naked?" her voice squeaked.

Navarro crossed his arms over his chest and narrowed his eyes. "I don't promise to answer anything, but I will let you ask your questions."

Her brows drew together. "You think I'll strip without any guarantee you'll give me what I came for?" Her heartbeat accelerated and her cheeks paled, but the smell of her musky arousal surpassed the slightly acrid aroma of her fear.

"Do you really know what you came for?" he asked, letting his voice drawl like a velvet caress.

She blinked, and her round, stubborn chin rose a notch higher. "There's no reason to be obnoxious. I trespassed, okay? If you'd let me in to begin with, I would have been long gone by now."

"It's my fault you're standing half-clothed in my study?" he asked, incredulous.

Her expression turned bullish. "Two minutes — that's all I need."

"I told you my condition."

Anger rose to obliterate her caution. She was a headstrong minx. He could hear her heartbeat thundering in her chest, see the pulse thudding at her temples. Navarro wouldn't have been the least surprised to see steam billow out her ears.

She reached for the waistband of her jeans. "I'm an investigative reporter," she bit out. "A professional!"

"Fascinating. Just what was the subject of your last report?" he asked, knowing full well, because he'd watched the news the previous night.

Her brows furrowed. "Passion Parties!"

Her scowl would have made a lesser man flinch. He gave a slight snort. "That's hard-hitting journalism?"

"It was an assignment," she said, with a disgusted twist of her lips. "The fluff I usually get stuck with—but *this* story is going to put me in the big leagues." She opened the buckle and slid down her zipper, all the while glaring daggers.

"What is a Passion Party?" he asked, baiting her and enjoying the anger that made her breath harsh and her actions jerky. Just how far would she really go for a story?

"Sexy parties." Her glare slid away. "Housewives hold them. They learn about using...sexual devices and model undergarments." She huffed and toed off her leather loafers, giving each one a kick that sent them flying against the wall.

The chit really was going to strip. He had no doubt if he looked inside her mind at this moment, he'd see himself with a red target circling his head.

Navarro turned to hide the smile that almost curved his lips. He walked to a side table and poured himself a drink. Once his expression was under control, he lifted the crystal decanter in her direction. "Care for a brandy? It will help keep you warm."

She muttered under her breath, pushed her jeans and underwear down her hips, and stepped out of her clothing.

With his superior hearing, he caught the words "Smart ass!" and bit back a grin. He shrugged, set down the decanter, and took his seat, letting his gaze slide over the creamy flesh of her rounded bottom.

Pretending indifference, he gave her pale limbs a dismissing glance and indicated the chair opposite his armchair.

She stomped over and flounced down on it. As soon as she was seated, she slid one leg on top of the other.

An action that effectively cut off his view of the triangle of curly hair at the apex of her thighs.

Situated before the fire, her body was illuminated by flickering firelight. The red-gold flame painted her pale flesh in golden tones. Lovely, he thought, though a little lacking in curves. If he had half a mind to seek a little refreshment, she'd offer only a light snack.

Navarro settled deeper into his chair and took a sip of his brandy. He glanced at her mutinous face over the top of his glass. "You have two minutes. You may begin."

Although he was sure she couldn't see his features clearly in the darkness, her gaze narrowed, accusing. "I'm following an interesting story," she said, her tone biting. "It involves teenagers who were pronounced dead, but are still walking around Seattle. A serial killer who was part of your organization—but mysteriously disappeared."

He stirred his glass with a negligent turn of his wrist, watching the firelight swirl in the amber liquid. "Sounds like old news."

Her fingers dug into the leather arms of her chair as she leaned forward. "How about a string of unsolved murders—" she blurted, "*also* teenagers, but in south Florida with MOs suspiciously similar to those here in Seattle? They started shortly after the pilot of your private jet filed a manifest. Wanna guess his destination?"

Navarro stilled. The murders weren't unsolved—the outcome just unpublicized—and the killer had paid the ultimate price. But the fact she'd made any kind of link between the killings and his actions disturbed him.

"You're kind of quiet," she said, her lips curving in triumph.

"Interesting facts," he said, keeping his voice even, although his amusement and patience had dried up. "But you haven't asked me a single question—and you only have one minute left."

The woman sat back in her chair, her expression benign.

She wasn't finished, yet. Navarro guessed she'd probably even forgotten she was entirely nude.

Her gaze was too focused, her smile almost feline—small and enigmatic. "Humor me," she said. "Just one more item of trivia. One of your *associates*, a fellow master on your council, was aboard that plane, but he didn't return. The murders resumed in Florida around the same time Dylan O'Hara arrived. Don't you think the authorities would find *that* interesting?"

Navarro relaxed. She had a few facts, but wasn't connecting all the dots. "No." He set aside his glass. "See how accommodating I've been? I answered your question."

A frown creased her forehead, and her shoulders slumped. "Okay, so maybe I haven't figured it all out yet—how he's connected and why the killings suddenly stopped—but I'm not through digging."

"Tell me, Miss Coffey. What do you think will happen if you approach your station with this information—and your creative spin? Do you think anyone will believe a shadow government comprised of vampires exists in Seattle?"

"It's the truth," she replied, indignation clear in her tone. "I just have to find proof."

"Why did you think it necessary to talk to me? Did you think I'd tell you anything, especially if your muddled theories were correct?"

"I didn't."

"Didn't what? Think?" His voice rose, and Navarro drew back. That last had felt like anger speaking. He hadn't lost his temper in years, but the girl was too headstrong. Had he been a different sort of vampire, she could have walked into a nightmare.

She shrugged one shoulder. "I just wanted you to know...that I know."

Navarro shook his head. No wonder she was relegated to reporting on how bored housewives spent their husbands' money. "I'm not understanding your logic. You think I'm a vampire and conspiring to hide a killer. If that were true, shouldn't you be worried I'll make a meal and be done with you?"

Her mouth opened and closed like a guppy's. "Well, you are a vampire—you've lived in this house for forty-five years, but you don't look a day over thirty."

That was the only part of what he'd said that she latched onto? The ridiculous woman obviously counted being right as more important than staying alive. "Again, *pardon my confusion*," he said, letting sarcasm season his voice, "but I hardly think my real-estate investments warrant the use of your venerable *investigative* skills."

"Don't you patronize me!" she said, her voice rising. "What is it with you men?"

"I think, Miss Coffey, you're a rather foolish woman. No doubt you've heard that before. You came here without a clue of what you hoped to achieve. You simply blundered your way in."

Her lips thinned. "Perhaps I am an idiot, but I have a nose for a good story. Maybe I'll turn my attention to a new development. Tell me, why would vampires seek out three fellows of the GenTech Institute and murder them? What interest would vamps have in a bunch of geneticists?"

Navarro drew in a sharp breath. What did she know?

She must have heard him. Her expression changed from indignant to thoughtful.

He waited, hoping she'd draw another irrational conclusion.

"Geneticists working on cloning," she murmured. Suddenly, her eyes widened, and her mouth clamped shut.

Damnation! "Yes, it's an interesting development. And something I'm already investigating myself, Miss Coffey."

She swallowed and lifted one finger. "I'll just be leaving. I've overstayed my two minutes."

"Come, Miss Coffey," Navarro said, with a deep inward sigh. He really didn't want to do this, but the chit had forced his hand. "We've only just become acquainted. I insist you extend your visit."

Chapter Three

"I can't stay here," Sidney sputtered, dismayed at his suggestion.

"But you will." Navarro took another lazy sip of brandy.

He sat so calm she wanted to kick him in the shins. "I will not!"

"As I said before, I am investigating this new…circumstance." However nonchalant his actions were, his expression remained watchful—his gaze piercing. "I want no interference from you."

Sidney shivered, and her nipples tightened. Nothing like a little threat of danger to remind her how vulnerable she really was—and just how much she liked that feeling. Especially in the presence of a drop-dead gorgeous man.

"Until I've satisfied my curiosity, you will remain my guest." His gaze dipped to her chest and his nostrils flared.

What had that look meant? Could he smell her arousal? She pushed off the chair, afraid she'd leave a puddle of evidence if she sat a moment longer. "We'll just see about that," she said, not trying to disguise her snarl. She bent to scoop up her jeans.

A booted foot stepped on a pant leg, and Sidney's heart lurched. When had he moved? How had he gotten to her side so fast? She dropped the denims and jerked upward. He stood so close her breasts dragged along his white shirt.

Sidney backed away a step, unnerved by his proximity and his dark stare. His expression gave away nothing about his thoughts. While she feared hers told him exactly what was on her mind. Half of her wanted to run screaming from the house — the other half wanted to test forbidden waters.

"Do you really think you'd like to know my bite?" he murmured, his gaze dropping to her lips.

Her eyes widened at the accuracy of his guess and the white-tipped incisors peeking from beneath his upper lip.

She shook her head even as her body released a trickle of creamy excitement. "I can't stay," she repeated. "I'll be missed. I have a job." She continued backing toward the door.

"It's Saturday morning. You won't be missed until Monday." He took a step closer — so slowly, she knew he was taunting her.

Sidney lifted her chin. "People know I'm here."

He gave her a long, intense stare. Then his eyes narrowed. "You're lying."

Damn him! She stomped her foot before she remembered he could see everything jiggle. "What if you don't find what you need by Monday?"

"Then we'll have to send out for clean underwear and a toothbrush."

"I'll need them before that!" Realization finally hit Sidney he was serious about her staying. How the hell was she supposed to investigate the story of a lifetime if he kept her prisoner? "I can't stay here indefinitely. People really will get concerned."

"I'll give your station manager a call — we're old friends."

"You wouldn't dare —"

"And I'll let our friend Moses know you're in good hands."

She stilled. "You know Moses?" She shook her head — here was a little fact Moses hadn't bothered to pass along. "How do you know Moses and I are friends?"

He leaned close and inhaled deeply. "I'd say you're considerably more than friends. I smell him all over you."

She jerked back her head and glared. "That was really crude."

He shrugged as though her opinion didn't matter one bit.

The action only managed to raise her ire another notch.

"You're safe—for now," he said, his glance raking over her. "I never take another man's leavings."

"Leavings? I don't belong to any man to be his leavings. And if anyone's *leaving*, it's me!"

With a wicked gleam in his eyes, he bent and picked up her clothing from the floor.

"Wait a second," she said, alarmed by the smirk quirking one side of his lips. "I need those."

Her jaw dropped open when he tossed them into the fireplace. When he folded his arms over his chest, she gave him the meanest look she had in her limited arsenal. "You hardly think that will stop me from leaving." She stalked to the door and reached down for the blanket.

His foot landed in the middle of the bundle. His hand settled on her bottom.

She didn't even wonder at how he'd managed to cross the room so quickly. "Fine! Keep the goddamn blanket." She straightened, but was unwilling to turn and look him in the eye. One glance and he'd know exactly what his broad hand was doing to her. "Don't think I won't walk out of here naked as the day I was born."

"It's cold outside—getting more so by the minute, my dear. You'll think twice before you head down the drive." He leaned close, his breath ruffling the curls next to her ear. "I'm really not that interested, my dear. I can wait until the smell of him no longer clings to your skin."

"Not interested? Then why are you squeezing my ass?"

"I'm testing to see whether there's even a meaty rump steak to be had. I'll have to get Inigo to fatten you up a bit— you're too scrawny."

Sidney gasped in outrage and pushed away his hand. "I'm not on the menu, you jerk."

"I agree." His other hand reached around and cupped her breast. "You're not even a late-night snack."

Her cheeks burning from his insults, Sidney flung open the door and stormed into the hallway, heedless of her nudity.

She came up hard against the servant's shoulder as he stood, straightening his tie. The man had been eavesdropping!

"Miss, may I show you to your room?" His gaze remained fixed on her forehead.

Sidney knew he'd already gotten an eyeful and flushed hotly. "Well, hell!" Soft laughter sounded behind her, and she rounded on the master vampire. "What the hell am I supposed to do with myself for the next couple of days?"

He gave her a rapacious smile—showing his lovely white fangs for the first time. "You're a resourceful girl. I'm sure you can find endless ways to entertain yourself."

"What makes you think I'll just sit here twiddling my thumbs all weekend long?"

"If thumbs give you pleasure…" he drawled.

Sidney felt warmth wash her chest and cheeks.

"Your curiosity will keep your active little mind occupied. I know you're dying to know what secrets my desk will give up. And can you really pass up the opportunity to learn more about a vampire's special kiss?"

Christ! Did he have to remind her hormones just how attractive his mouth was?

His eyes glittered, and his lips drew apart.

Her breath hitched, and she leaned toward him, feeling inexplicably drawn into his dark gaze.

His mouth curved mirthlessly.

Son of a bitch! Sidney straightened, realizing he was toying with her once again. She glared at him. "You have to sleep sometime."

He closed the door in her face.

Sidney wondered how difficult outrunning the old man waiting at her side would be.

"Beware the dogs in the yard," Master Navarro's voice sounded from the other side of the door. "Inigo let them out shortly after you entered my library."

* * * * *

"Who the fuck does he think he is? Keep me prisoner, will he?"

Navarro raised a brow at the loud mutterings of his houseguest as she paced the length of her room. Inigo had given her the guest bedroom with the hidden cameras and listening devices.

Although the sun would soon rise, Navarro felt no fatigue. The woman had invigorated his blood as no one else had in quite a long while — perhaps in the last century.

"*I don't take another man's leavings*," she mimicked, her mouth curling in disgust. "Well, I don't take cold leftovers — that's what you are, Navarro!" she shouted through the locked door of her bedroom.

Still naked, she flounced onto the bed, beating her heels and hands against the mattress.

Navarro studied her attributes. Alone, each was unremarkable. Her bottom was rounded, firm. Her breasts a scant mouthful, tipped with small cherry nipples. Her body was trim, athletic, but not overly so.

No, her curves and pretty face weren't what held his interest. It was her courage, the surprising twists her mind took, and the sensuality that plumped her lips and kept her nipples tight and hard, even now when only anger fired her passion.

No one had stirred his cock into any semblance of an erection in too many years to count. But here he was, his flesh pressing against the placket of his trousers while she threw endless insults at his head. *Delightful!*

Why this woman after so long? He'd had offers and opportunities too plentiful to count over the centuries. He'd never been a hedonist — never reveled in the sensual side of his vampire nature. It couldn't be that this slim girl reminded him of another slender waif with more guts than gray matter — the only woman to ever own his heart. His soul had learned a painful lesson when he'd lost his only love. One he'd never repeat.

But taking this woman would only be a delicious conquest. A long drink to savor. He would torture her with her own flagrant desire, withholding deeper pleasure to tease her curiosity about the nature of his true kiss. He'd draw out the pleasure-pain so long she'd scream — no, beg. He wanted her to beg for release, her body trembling with need, her eyes moist, her mouth swollen with his kisses.

That image gave him great satisfaction, even as he watched her strip the sheets from the bed and twist them into long ropes, tying them end-to-end. He'd denied himself passion for so long his body was rigid as a steel pole at the thought of sinking teeth and cock into her tender flesh. He would control their dance, set the pace. He was older, centuries-skilled. He could control his passion while he raised hers and subdued her reckless spirit with unfulfilled lust.

He would have her, but keep his heart distant. Not let her open that part of him that needed to stay hidden, secret. Never would he let the madness of emotions command him again. He was the master of the beast.

"Master, have you eaten?" Inigo asked quietly.

Navarro reduced the volume, but left the monitor open. "She's lovely, no?" He turned to Inigo, catching him as he glanced away quickly from the screen.

"A pretty little thing. Does she know the windows are barred?"

"Naturally she hasn't thought that far ahead." He gave his servant a hard-eyed glare. "You disobeyed me tonight."

Inigo drew in a sharp breath and straightened his shoulders. "Yes, sir, I did."

"May I ask why? You've worked for me for over fifty years. I can't recall your ever violating my command."

Inigo flushed and cleared his throat. "I did it for you actually, sir."

"For me?"

"You've been long without a companion. She seemed…durable."

Navarro glanced back at the slender girl who'd just demolished the delicate vanity bench. He must have missed her trying to raise the window. Ah well, that was what the rewind function was for—savoring the moment in privacy. "Durable," he murmured. "That's an interesting observation given that she appears no bigger than a child."

"I meant her soul, sir. She'll have no expectations."

"No expectations," he murmured. "Couldn't I get that from a paid companion?"

"But where would be the challenge?"

He acknowledged the point with a nod. "Indeed. Inigo?"

"Yes, sir."

"In the future, leave off the matchmaking," he said, never taking his eyes from the screen as the door closed quietly behind him.

Navarro picked up the phone on the console and hit the automatic dial.

"Master Navarro, what can I do for you?" came the deep, amused voice.

"Ah, Sergeant Brown, now why aren't you surprised to hear from me?"

"Sid giving you fits yet?"

41

"Did you send her my way?"

"Not directly, sir, but I know how her mind works. She couldn't keep her pretty nose out of our business."

"I'm afraid she'll be staying for the duration."

"What'd she do now? I warned her you'd be a hard nut to crack."

"Seems she took that as a challenge," Navarro murmured absently

"Sorry 'bout that." Moses Brown didn't sound the least bit apologetic. "Just as well you keep her out of trouble."

Preferring not to dwell on how well the sergeant knew his prisoner, Navarro changed the subject. "So do you have the morgue under surveillance?"

"Yeah. We'll see whether any of those techno-geeks rise from the dead tomorrow."

"Be careful. Their first hunger may rule their actions."

"Just make sure your people are in place to see who else might be interested in them."

"Sergeant Brown, about the girl…"

The man at the end of the line chuckled—a sound that didn't really spell amusement. "You wanna know if there's anything between us? Ask Sid—she'll tell you straight up. That lady doesn't mince words. Just make sure you spit her out all in one piece when you're done."

"You make her sound like an indigestible meal."

"Hard on the stomach? Nah? She's sweet all the way down." He chuckled again.

Navarro bristled. "Let me know about the morgue."

"If you decide to set foot outside that mansion…"

"We'll see. Let's solve this mystery first." Navarro replaced the receiver and turned up the volume on the monitor.

Sidney Coffey sat on the edge of the bed, her feet dangling toward the floor. Then she flopped back on the mattress. "What the hell am I supposed to do now?" She yawned and stretched her arms above her head. "Twiddle my thumbs, my ass. *Damn him!*"

One hand moved absently over her stomach and upward to her breast, gliding over a soft mound. The movement seemed to soothe her, and her eyelids drooped to half-mast. Her hand smoothed down and upward again, and she snuggled her shoulders into the tangled bedding, sighing. "Master Navarro," she murmured.

He stilled. Was she imagining his hands caressing her? Wishing the monitor had better resolution and was closer to the bed, he leaned forward. He wouldn't stretch his other sense to learn her true thoughts. Somehow that would feel like cheating. Besides, her thoughts would likely be very noisy.

His breath caught when her fingers pinched a nipple, and her eyes squeezed shut. She twisted the tip, and then touched it with one digit. It stood erect in the center of her small breast.

He imagined how his tongue would drag across it.

Her hand slid to the other breast, and she tugged the flowering nipple to full arousal.

His tongue touched his upper lip, and he envisioned closing his lips around a turgid peak and suckling while she writhed beneath him.

Her knees spread apart. The angle of the lens denied him a view of the tender flesh between her legs, but her expression enraptured him. Her eyelids fluttered, and her teeth worried her lower lip.

Then her other hand glided down, rubbing over the pale fur covering her sex.

Navarro spread his legs beneath the console trying to ease the ache building in his loins.

Her hand dipped between her legs and her shoulders lifted off the bed before she settled deeper into the covers.

Then she raised her knees until her heels dug into the edge of the mattress.

He could only imagine how open and accessible her sweet cunt would be if he were standing in front of her. Would she reach to guide his cock inside her?

Her hips pulsed upward, and her back arched as the pace of her hand's rhythmic movements increased. "Thumbs, toes, cocks..." she moaned as her breath grew faster, harsher.

Suddenly, she pulled her hand away and closed her legs. "Seriously, could a girl go to bed with a man who might take it literally if a girl said, 'Eat me'?" Her closed fist pounded the mattress beside her. "Navarro!" she howled.

Turning off the monitor, he was stunned to find his mouth stretched wide in a grin. His cock was fully erect and aching. His body and mind hummed with heat and...anticipation.

He, Navarro, who hadn't been excited by anything in more years than the woman could probably count.

Despite his body's readiness, he remained seated. It was too soon to approach her. Too soon to see to her release. She needed to learn who was master.

Let her stew for now—alone on her bed with only her...thumbs to appease her appetite. Let her desire grow until she'd drench at the mere sound of his voice. Then he might give her a taste of his kiss.

For now he'd wait and use the time to plan his seduction. Not that he didn't know the outcome—Sidney Coffey was a ripe plum ready to pick. Practically begging for his cock and bite. But she'd want to call the shots—be the seducer. So while the investigation continued without her interference, he'd amuse himself and teach her to follow his lead.

"Sir? What shall I do with the girl during the day?" Inigo asked.

Navarro started. He hadn't heard the old man return. That had never happened. "Give her food and drink, and make sure she sleeps most of the day. She'll need her rest."

Inigo nodded, pressing his lips together to suppress a smile until he'd let himself out the door. As he headed toward the kitchen, his step was light. The master had a look in his eyes he'd never seen. When he'd watched the woman on the screen his face and body had been motionless, enraptured. Who was the true captive here?

Inigo turned his thoughts to the late-night snack. Would Miss Coffey like a little wine with her sleeping draft?

Chapter Four

ॐ

"Master Navarro! You must awaken!"

Navarro opened his eyes, instantly alert at the distress in his retainer's voice.

Inigo stood beside the bed, wringing his hands.

Navarro huffed out a breath and stretched his arms above his head. "What has our guest demolished now?"

"She's gone, sir! I went to wake her so she could bathe before dinner. But she's gone."

"You locked the door?"

Inigo straightened, clearly affronted. "Of course. She used a nail behind a picture frame to pick the lock."

Navarro sat up and looked at the graying light, peeking around the edges of his curtains. Nightfall would be complete in minutes. "The dogs didn't deter her?"

"How was I to know those hounds from hell would appreciate a fine Burgundy?"

"She fed the dogs her potion!" Navarro laughed and climbed out of bed. "What about clothing?"

Inigo swept an arm in a wide arc. "She pilfered your closet while you slept!"

Sure enough, his closet door gaped wide and several items lay puddled on the floor. "She's not quite the dim-watted bulb I took her for." The knowledge pleased him.

"Where do you suppose she's gone? Home, perhaps?"

"Not that one." Navarro dressed quickly and shrugged into a leather jacket as he crossed the room. "She'll head to the last place I would want her."

"Naturally." Inigo nodded and followed him out of the bedroom and into the hallway. "And where would that be?"

"If she's intelligent enough to escape these grounds, she's clever enough to conclude our trio of scientists may awaken from the dead."

"Oh dear. She shouldn't be anywhere in their vicinity if they rise."

"My sentiments exactly. I'm heading there now," Navarro said, taking the steps two at a time. "Call Sergeant Brown and let him know she may be coming."

"Sir, will you need backup?" Inigo called after him.

Navarro paused at the front door. "You sound like a tired crime drama."

"I must fill my time during daylight somehow," he said, his expression growing prim. "*T.J. Hooker* reruns do quite nicely."

Navarro shook his head and closed the door behind him. "I would have been better off not knowing that."

* * * * *

Sidney stared from behind bushes, watching the entrance to the King County Medical Examiner's Office. As luck would have it, an ambulance had pulled into the circular drive moments before her arrival, and a body was being unloaded. She waited impatiently for the attendants to move away from the doors so that she could slip inside undetected.

"Sid, Sid, Sid."

A husky voice sounded next to her, nearly startling her into a scream.

"I do find you in the most interesting places."

Once her heart crept back from her throat, Sidney turned to give Moses a smug smile. "I must be on the right track, finding you here. You think those dead scientists are going to take a walk."

He nodded, not bothering to try to deny her assumption. "Tell me, Sid. How'd you plan on gettin' inside that building?"

"That door's open. I'm just going to walk right in."

"And what about the security cameras inside? You think they'll let anyone walk in off the street?"

Sidney huffed at the way he pooh-poohed her plan. "I have my press credentials with me."

"Those'll get you blown out the door faster than a sneeze."

"You're so negative, Moses. Don't you think I have any people skills?" she said, her cheeks heating with irritation. "I'll finesse my way into those second-floor coolers."

"You're as blunt as a mallet, lady. No one's lettin' you inside the morgue."

"But you're here now." She slid him a sideways glance from beneath her lashes. That look had never failed to gain his cooperation. "You have some pull."

"You think I'm going to take you up?" he said, shaking his head. "You're dreamin'. I'm going to keep you occupied long enough for backup to arrive."

"Backup? More police?"

Moses shook his head slowly.

"You're not talking about your *buddy*, Navarro, are you?" Even saying his name incited a physical reaction inside her body—pure rage, of course, at his highhanded tactics—*not* anger that he'd left her unfulfilled. She should thank the vamp—she still felt edgy, ready for action. "Hell, he couldn't keep me prisoner in his own house. How do you think he'll stop me now?"

"Have to admit, the man's slippin'. But I don't think he'll make the same mistake twice." Moses sounded like he admired the man.

Men—even dead ones—tended to bond over the subjugation of a woman.

48

"That reminds me," she said, dropping her voice with deadly intent. "I have a bone to pick with you, mister. You set me up! You knew damn well he'd try to stop my investigation."

"That I did." His smile was unrepentant. "But, sugar, it was for your own good."

"Don't 'sugar' me! I don't need a babysitter. I decide what's good for me. And that old-as-Methuselah bloodsucker ain't it."

Moses' grin grew into a lopsided smirk.

Her stomach plummeted. "He's right behind me, isn't he?"

"Uh-huh."

Sidney refused to turn and face the vampire, afraid he'd know just how frightened and excited she was with just a glance at her face. Instead, she turned on her heel and walked toward the sliding doors of the KCMEO.

A heavy hand landed on her shoulder, halting her progress. Sidney stiffened and fought her body's instant response. How she craved his touch! Then another thought arose to further push her sensual buttons—he'd left the compound for her!

He stood very close to her back, his clothing whispering against hers, then he leaned down. "I'm satisfied now that I'm not taking anything belonging to our policeman friend," he said, his breath ruffling the hair tucked behind her ear.

She bit back a moan. How did he do that? How had he taken her fear and irritation and turned it into molten desire in a single moment? He'd slipped right under her flimsy defenses, blindsiding her with that intimate—and insulting—comment. "I have a job to do here," she said, fighting to keep her voice even.

"And so do I, my dear. But seeing as our jobs bring us to the same place, would you like to accompany me?"

Not the invitation she would have preferred right this moment. His drawled request made her knees grow weak. Sidney almost couldn't stop herself from leaning back into his oh-so-sexy chest. "You'll take me up to the morgue?"

"We should hurry," he said, straightening, his voice brisk. "If the men were turned, they will be wakening now." He stepped around her and strode toward the entrance.

Like a puppet pulled on a string, Sidney followed his long-limbed frame, clothed in black tonight. He looked like one tall, dark shadow.

Steps crunched beside her. A finger lifted her lowered jaw. "When you can pick up your chin off the ground, follow close behind us," Moses said, stepping around her as well.

Sidney trailed after the men when they entered the receiving area, which looked unimpressive with its unpainted concrete floor and walls. They met no resistance. In fact, no one was in sight.

As they headed straight for the elevator, Sidney suddenly realized they were expected—that Medical Examiner personnel likely awaited them above, or were keeping out of their way. How large was this conspiracy of silence? Had she been the last person in Seattle to realize vampires walked among them?

Inside the elevator, Sidney found herself sandwiched, shoulder to shoulder, between the two men who acted as though she didn't exist. Two tall, well-built, and dangerous men...

Cursing her overactive libido, Sidney fought to keep her focus on the possible dangers they would face.

When the door slid open, Navarro shoved her behind him, and Moses closed the gap between them.

She shook her head over their macho show of protection and brought up the rear of their odd little formation, annoyed her view was entirely blocked by their broad shoulders.

She dropped back to clear her senses of the sensual fog their proximity had created and to get a better view of her surroundings. They passed through what could only be an autopsy room with its stainless steel sinks, surgical instruments and equipment whose purpose she'd just as soon never comprehend.

Finally, they reached the cooler with its huge steel door and keypad lock. Navarro stepped aside while Moses punched in the code and opened the door.

Navarro cast a glance over his shoulder. "You stay behind us at all times."

She nodded, her mouth clamped tight, almost overcome by the ripe, egg-like smell emanating from inside the cooler. While she might have felt on the verge of puking on her shoes, she didn't miss the sight of the stake clutched in Moses' meaty fist or the telltale broadening of the Master's shoulders. His back was turned to her, but she knew he had his game face on.

Sidney fished in her pocket for her ballpoint pen and raised it in front of her, clicking the end for extra sharpness. Then she followed the men, keeping so close to their familiar warmth and scents her pen poked Moses' back when he came to a sudden halt.

She peered around them, and her eyes widened. She'd expected nice shiny doors—bodies on sliding gurneys behind doors number one or three. Instead, there was a long row of bodies zipped into white nylon body bags, lying on metal trays. Overhead fans hummed and whirred noisily above, and Sidney started to feel like the floor was moving beneath her feet.

"Catch her," Navarro called out from far away.

Sidney opened her eyes and stared up at the two men— one's face was creased by a crooked, superior smile—the other scowled from a frighteningly ghoulish mask.

She jerked up from her makeshift bed. "You did not lay me on an autopsy tray!" she cried in dismay.

"You fell like a sack of hammers," Moses said, shrugging. At her narrow-eyed glare, his smile broadened. "Thought you were tougher than that."

She avoided Navarro's scowling, unholy face altogether and swung her legs over the edge when she saw a movement out of the corner of her eye.

"She's goin' south again," Moses muttered, grabbing for her shoulders.

"No," she gasped, pointing to the gurney behind the men. "It moved!"

Like a caterpillar trying to wriggle from its cocoon, the body inside the white bag writhed on the metal tray, muffled moans sounding from inside.

Navarro stepped close and used his stake to split open the bag.

A man emerged, blinking owlishly, visibly shaken—and very naked. Dried blood was caked on one side of his throat. He sat up with only his torso free of the bag.

With his graying hair spiked around his head, he stared up at Navarro's vampire face, and his expression turned to horror. "You monsters already killed me—did you have to follow me to hell?" he cried out.

Navarro stepped aside, and his face creaked like gristled meat, reforming into his handsome, human face.

Sidney couldn't decide which mask she'd prefer hovering over her in bed, but she'd forgotten about her upset tummy when the miracle of his transformation began.

"Doctor Deats," Moses interrupted, drawing the horrified man's gaze. "We're here to help you."

The man blinked again and stared down at the ripped bag. "I'm at the morgue?" he asked, sounding dazed.

"The Medical Examiner personnel waited to complete the autopsy to be sure you wouldn't rise."

"I'm not dead?"

"Yeah, you are. But I'll explain later. For now, we need to get you out of here." Moses began to pull apart the torn edges of the nylon bag.

Dr. Deats resisted his effort, tugging them closed again. He nodded toward Sidney and gripped the edges tighter.

"Like you got something she ain't seen a million times?" Moses glanced over his shoulder. "Sidney!"

"Yes, Moses," Sidney said, only mildly insulted by his comment.

"Go find the gentleman a sheet to wear out of here."

"Sure," she said, eager to quit the cooler that smelled more like spoiled potato salad the longer she stayed inside. She headed back to the autopsy room and opened a wall locker standing at one end, drawing out several sheets—the man did look overly modest.

As she started to shut the door, she noted the white tips of tennis shoes peeking beneath the door. "I wondered if anyone was working here tonight," she said, closing the cabinet.

But the face of the person wearing the shoes wasn't exactly one she expected to see. Instead, she found herself staring at one of the teenagers supposedly dumped into Elliot Bay. And he had friends with him—three equally young and toothy men. She tossed the stack of sheets at the head of the nearest one and spun on her heels. As she rushed for the cooler door, she dug into her pocket for her trusty pen.

"Our company has arrived," Navarro murmured, as he helped the third scientist from his body bag.

The three scientists held their shredded bags in front of them, blinking against the light and murmuring among themselves.

"Wondered when they'd get here," Moses muttered. "Showtime."

Navarro turned toward the entry of the cooler room and watched four young vampires approach. One pulled along a struggling Sidney. He had a passing thought for the guards that should have radioed their arrival, and then fought not to betray his rage at the rough treatment Sidney was receiving. He'd enjoy killing that particular cub.

"We'll be taking the old geeks with us," the young vampire holding Sidney said.

Her feet flailed several inches above the ground as she struggled against the arm that locked her against the vampire's side. "I would have thought you had this covered, Navarro," she said, her face reddened from her struggle. Her scowl looked as ferocious as a Pekingese.

"I did, my dear," Navarro said, keeping his voice calm. "But I'm flexible."

"We want the three old guys," the teen said, his gruesome smile widening. His glance raked over Navarro. "Who are you? Haven't seen you around."

"You wouldn't. You're weanlings — mosquitoes."

"Huh?"

"He's telling you you're insignificant navel fuzz, idiot," Sidney said, wiggling like an eel to escape her captor.

"Sidney…" Moses' voice rose in warning.

The vampire jerked her closer, causing her to gasp. "I could snap you like a twig, but these three are going to want fresh meat."

Irritation had Navarro clenching his hands at his sides. "Do you think I'll let you have them if you harm the girl?"

"You don't have to let us do anything. There are four of us and only one of you."

"I'm not navel fuzz," Moses gritted out.

"You're human—that makes you only as interesting as my next meal." The vampire glanced over his shoulder at the three hovering behind him. "Take 'em down."

The three teens roared and completed their transformations, their faces crackling as their vampire armor reformed their features into bony armored plates, pushing out their foreheads, elongating their teeth to form jagged, shark-like smiles.

Navarro tamped down his own monster. He needed all his wits about him, if he was going to safely rescue Sidney from the coward using her as a shield.

The first vampire stalked toward Moses, then suddenly leapt through the air, taking the big man down. Their scuffle overturned gurneys and dumped bodies to the floor.

Navarro didn't move as the other two approached him more cautiously, one breaking off to make a wide circle around him. Navarro closed his eyes.

"What the fuck are you closing your eyes for?" Sidney called to him. "You're not Bruce Lee!"

Navarro smiled at her inane comment and reached— stretching his other sense toward the two young men circling him now.

The one behind him lunged.

Navarro saw the arc of the stake coming at his back and leaned to one side. The air whooshed beside him as the man stumbled forward, out of balance from his powerful swing. *Fucking freak!* he heard the younger man scream in his mind.

The second vampire roared and flew through the air, a steel blade sliding from his coat sleeve, light glinting off the steel as it swung toward Navarro's' neck.

Navarro's arm came up under the sweep and shoved the younger man to the side, sending him crashing against the far wall.

Clearing his head with a shake, the younger vampire leapt once more to his feet and ran full-tilt for him.

Navarro drew a stake from the sheath at the side of his upper thigh and stabbed backward, impaling him. The young vampire's dust settled over him like a brown cloud.

Then Navarro opened his eyes to the vampire picking himself up off the floor in front of him. "I'll let you live so you can carry a message to your master."

"There are still three of us—and I have her!" the vampire holding Sidney screamed, wild-eyed.

Navarro knew he'd thought this would be an easy conquest and felt his panic. He'd finally realized he wasn't the one in control. Navarro ignored the agitated vampire and turned to his comrade. "Tell him, he'll never have the three scientists. They will be under my care."

The vampire nodded his head quickly and stumbled out the door.

"I've still got the girl," the young vampire repeated, pulling Sidney in front of him. He pushed her head to the side, exposing her slender neck. "You know it'd only take one deep bite. I'll make a trade."

Navarro shook his head. "No trade. No deals."

"Wait a second. Sounds fair to me," Sidney said, sounding more annoyed than scared. "It's not like he wants to kill those three guys."

Navarro ignored her comment, staring at the younger vampire—pushing through the psychic membrane that surrounded his mind.

He heard the pounding of the younger man's heart, the rush of blood squeezing through his arteries. He felt the sweat trickling between his shoulder blades beneath his coat and on his upper lip.

Then Navarro saw his thoughts as he imagined his next actions.

Navarro leapt toward him as he threw Sidney to the floor and launched himself toward Dr. Deats. They met in midair and crashed to the floor, rolling as they fought.

Navarro met each move with a countermove that soon had the younger vampire subdued beneath him. "A poor choice, going for the doctor. You think I care whether the scientist lives?"

Fear tightening his mask, the vampire growled, "Who are you?"

"The one who will send you to your judgment. Tell me who made you."

"My master will triumph, and when all are dead I'll serve at his right hand."

"You think him God?"

"I *know* he is the fallen angel, and he will rule over the earth."

Navarro snorted. "You believe that tired old fairy tale? He lied to you. He's not Satan. What name does he bear?"

"You can torture me, but I'll never tell."

"You don't have to. I see his face. Zachary. Zachary Powell."

The vamp blinked in surprise, then snarled, "He will avenge my death!"

Navarro cocked his head to the side. "Sorry, but this Zachary doesn't inspire so much as a shudder. Never heard of your archangel," he lied. "Where can I find him?"

"Find him yourself. I'll never tell."

No picture was forthcoming. Navarro sighed. "No matter." He plunged his hand into the younger vampire's chest, ignoring the man's screech, and squeezed his fingers around his heart. It burst, and Navarro slumped to the ground as the vampire disintegrated into dust.

"Holy shit!" Sidney breathed, her face ashen. She clung to the edge of a metal tray, swaying on her feet.

"We'd better get these three to safety before many more Moonies show up," Moses said, dusting his vampire off his jacket.

Dr. Deats raised his hand. "I don't suppose we can stop for a bite along the way? I'm ravenous."

The other two bewildered scientists' expressions brightened.

Navarro crossed to Sidney and swung her up into his arms.

She clung tightly to his neck.

He gave her quivering body a reassuring squeeze and turned to the others. "Let's return to my estate. O positive all around."

Chapter Five

ဢ

"So, would you have gone for him like that if he hadn't knocked me to the ground?" Sidney asked, plucking at a loose thread on her cuff to avoid looking him in the eye.

They sat in the library, facing each other once again. This time, she was fully clothed, but felt more naked than the last time. He held all the cards—all the power and the knowledge of what game was unfolding. He also held a royal flush so far as her emotions were concerned. Not that she could have verbalized exactly what those emotions were. All she'd admit now was, no one made her feel safer.

"Is that your way of asking if I cared whether you lived or died?" He swirled his brandy.

"I'm not asking if you love me," she groused. "Just whether you would have sacrificed me. A girl should know where she stands."

"I would have cared," he said quietly.

That was expansive—*not*! "But would you have done things differently?"

He didn't answer, but a little smile curved his delicious lips.

Sidney stared at his mouth. The man knew his appeal too well. She was his prisoner again, and he wouldn't let her slip from his control. While she despaired she'd never get back to her old life and finish her story, she was equally thrilled by being at his mercy. He could do whatever he pleased with her.

Unfortunately, he didn't seem inclined to take advantage of that fact. Here she was, a reasonably attractive woman—

single, squeaky clean, and fragrant after her shower—and he hadn't betrayed a single ounce of horniness.

"You said a name back there at the morgue," Sidney said, trying to derail her current train of thought. "Zachary Powell. Who is he?"

Navarro's gaze narrowed. "Someone you should hope to never meet."

"Well, that was enigmatic as hell," she muttered. "Is he any relation to Nicky Powell?"

"His brother. How do you know his name?"

"I met Nicky last Halloween at The Cavern. He's kind of cute in a creepy way. Moses seemed to think he was one nasty dude." She glanced directly into his eyes. "He's a vampire, right?"

"He was. So is his brother."

His economical choice of words chilled her.

Firelight and darkness painted Navarro as a dark demon. Shadows and red-gold flickers caressed his olive skin. His black clothing faded against the dark well of his chair, yet she knew how powerful and deadly his body was.

As she'd watched him battle the vamps inside the morgue, he'd looked like a dark champion with his Bruce Lee bursts of reined fire and Matrix-y Neo detachment. The leather coat had only made him appear all the more sinister...and sexy.

The way he'd quickly vanquished the two vampires at the morgue—with his eyes closed—told her he offered so much more than just a yummy-licious body. What would he be like as a lover? She prayed more Bruce Lee-ish.

She squirmed on her chair and wished she'd accepted a brandy when he'd offered it. At least, she'd have something to do with her hands. He'd been quiet since she entered his study, but he hadn't asked her to leave him alone. That was as good as an invitation to stay, so she plopped down opposite him. Only now, she felt awkward and totally transparent.

Her gaze fell to the hand resting on the curve of the armchair, and she imagined it curled around her breast. Then her glance darted to the hand cupping his brandy snifter as he swirled the amber liquid, and her insides knotted, imagining his fingers swirling on her intimate places. Lord, she had to get out of here. A little Moses might be just what she needed.

"Have you shared your bed often with our friend Moses?" he asked.

She jerked and felt heat rush to her cheeks. *He's so damn intuitive, it's scary.* "No. Not often. We're both busy people."

"So any port in the storm will do?" he asked, his voice devoid of any emotional inflection. "I can't imagine you would go for long without sexual release."

Her back stiffened as she tried to hold onto her temper. "If you're insinuating I'm easy—"

"Not exactly—just that your appetite is voracious."

She hissed out a breath. "It's all right for a man to seek sex when he wants it, but a woman shouldn't?"

"In my experience, a woman's sexuality is very different from a man's. More emotionally motivated than physical."

"Cut the crap, Navarro. I'm no whore." Her jaw tightened against a small pain that cramped her belly. She wished she had his detachment and couldn't be hurt by the insult she'd read in his words. If he'd been anybody else, she'd have flown at him. "I'm choosy about who I sleep with. I like sex—like the workout, the sweat. What's it to you?" She lifted her chin and narrowed her gaze. "Are you offering to help me out?"

He lifted one brow, but didn't reply.

She realized he'd orchestrated her anger, played her like a fiddle. Her irritation spiked higher.

"Since I'm keeping you from your usual pursuits, I feel an obligation to provide for your...comfort."

"I can see to my own *comfort*, thanks very much," she bit out. "After all, there are four other men under this roof."

"I warn you about approaching the scientists for sex. They're still new to this life. Their sexuality and bloodlust are too raw for them to be entirely trustworthy. Their souls survived the transformation intact, but they could get carried away. Especially, since I'm sure they never had as tasty a treat as you in their previous lives."

"Thanks for the advice. I'm not likely to expire from lack of sex—besides I can take care of my own needs."

"Yes, you do like thumbs," he murmured, the corners of his lips twitching.

She glared. "Are you steering our conversation down this road for any particular purpose?"

"I'm afraid I'm rusty at small talk. I was attempting to extend an invitation."

"You want me to sleep with you?"

He shook his head. "No euphemisms between us. I want to fuck you."

Her mouth opened around a gasp. "Since I'm the only woman on this estate at the moment? Am I just any old port?"

"Not at all. I need to keep closer rein on your actions. To do so, you will need to share my quarters when you sleep. I thought you might be more comfortable with that idea if we fucked beforehand."

She shot up from her chair. "That's about the coldest proposition I've ever received. Thanks, but no thanks." She stalked toward the door.

As she reached for the knob, she felt the air rush against her back a moment before his tall frame pressed into her.

"There would be benefits for both of us," he drawled into her ear.

Sidney suppressed a shudder at the feel of that wall of muscle blanketing her back. "Maybe, I'm just not that interested," she said, her voice betraying a telltale quiver of awareness.

"Tell me you haven't been curious." His breath trailed the side of her face and down her neck, and he sniffed. "Your body flowers whenever I'm near."

"Maybe I'm thinking about Moses," she gritted out.

His hands slid down her sides and gripped her waist hard. "I will tell you I haven't had another woman in my bed in years—decades, actually. I haven't had any interest in sharing sex until you arrived on my doorstep. Is that warmer?"

Her body flooded at the slight violence of his grip. She closed her eyes and leaned into him. "Getting there," she whispered. "We're both adults. Both have needs."

"We can help each other and satisfy our appetites—a mutually agreeable arrangement."

"An arrangement…" she said faintly. This is what she'd imagined. What she'd known with other men—something wild and physical—no commitments. How come her heart hurt a little at the thought it didn't mean anything more to him?

"I'll share the ultimate kiss with you," he said, then trailed his lips down her neck. "Share a rapture you've never experienced." He nipped her earlobe.

A shiver racked her body. "Is it so special? I've wondered."

"The women I've known were willing to risk death for the experience."

That sounded so conceited! But she knew he was probably right. "Just because I'll share your bed doesn't mean I won't try to escape again."

"I'd be disappointed if you didn't make the attempt," he murmured. "But do you think you'll even have the strength when I'm through?"

That did it. She was ready now. She turned in his arms, and her fingers loosened the laces at her neckline. While she stared at him, her heart hammering in her chest, she tugged the sweater over her head and dropped it on the floor.

His arms remained at his sides. Did he intend to watch? She tossed back her hair and slipped off her shoes.

"So eager?" he asked.

"Why wait?"

He tilted his head and gave her a look that was half-amused and half-daring. "Aren't you afraid we'll be interrupted here?"

"The three stooges are playing bridge with Lurch in the kitchen. Besides, I don't really care if they walk in or not."

"You stopped removing your clothes. Can't you talk and strip at the same time?"

She liked that little hint of eagerness and opened her jeans, quickly pushing them down her legs. She'd deliberately left off underwear when she'd changed at home after her escape earlier, hoping she'd have an opportunity to shock Navarro. Even while she'd gloated over besting him, she'd known her freedom would be brief. She'd hoped it would come to this moment.

Stepping out of her pants, she stood naked in front of him, wondering what he was thinking and why he hadn't moved. "Well?" she asked, hating that she felt uncertain and self-conscious of her nudity.

His gaze smoldered, but he returned to his chair and sat. "Come here," he murmured.

She sauntered toward him on legs that suddenly felt like Jell-O. The closer she came, the more clearly his features were revealed in the firelight. His eyes glittered hot, his mouth was a thin tense line, and his jaw was tight.

He extended his hand, and she laid her palm in his. His fingers closed around hers and pulled her closer still until she stood between his knees. "Climb onto me, Sidney."

The hint of command in his voice tightened her belly. She slid a naked knee along the outside of his left thigh and leaned forward, a breast near enough to his mouth she felt a breath brush her nipple. Then she slid the other along the outside of his right thigh.

Perched now on the chair, straddling his legs, she felt a trembling begin that weakened her and she sat on his lap, gasping at the rasp of fabric against her pussy. Her hands settled on his shoulders to steady her.

Her face was even now with his, and she waited for his response. She'd taken the first step. What would be her reward?

A hand rose from the arm of his chair, and he slipped his fingers between her legs to delve into her cleft.

Although she wanted more than anything to squeeze herself around his fingers, she held still, wondering at his slow pace—chafing because she was naked again, and she had yet to see his body.

He pulled out his fingers and rubbed them with his thumb, and then brought them to his nose and inhaled.

"It wouldn't take a vamp or a bloodhound to tell I'm horny as hell, vampire," she said, impatience making her irritable. "Why are you playing with me?"

He licked his fingertips. "I'm not testing whether you're ready. I'm learning your scents and taste. You've been aroused since your interview last night."

Sidney couldn't halt the flooding excitement that wet the crotch of his pants. "Again, I'm not shocked you know that. What I want to know is whether you're going to do something about it."

The corners of his mouth lifted in a mirthless smile. "Do you know anything about a vampire's lovemaking?"

"I know you like to drink blood when you fuck, and that the women enjoy it—a lot."

"And that's all?"

His stall tactics were only making her more desperate for his touch. She nodded and leaned toward him, rubbing her tightening nipples on his shirt. "Why don't you dispense with the anthropology lecture and get straight to the lab? I learn best by doing."

His hand rose and slipped behind her head. He threaded his fingers in her hair and tugged back her head. "Sex with a vampire is a risky thing. Aren't you the least bit afraid of the drinking part?"

Her breath caught at the small pain. "I give to the Red Cross every couple of months." She swallowed hard. "Will it hurt?" she asked, licking her lips.

His gaze dropped to her mouth. "A little—at first. I'll go easy with you."

"And if I don't want easy?" She shifted on his lap, letting her open cunt drag over his clothed cock.

He pulled her hair. "Be careful what you wish for."

Sidney had had enough of waiting. Ignoring the bite of his hand fisted in her hair, she leaned forward and kissed his mouth.

His lips remained closed, so she caressed them, opening her mouth to suck on his lips, then licking along the seam to tempt him. All the while, her eyes remained open, staring into his.

He didn't blink, didn't breathe. His expression betrayed no hint of passion. Even the cock beneath her remained furled against his leg.

Confused, she leaned away. "Don't you want this?"

"I want you to obey me in all things."

Sidney raised her eyebrows. "Say again?"

His hands moved, closing around her waist. He lifted her off his cock—only an inch.

She could still feel his heat rising to her open pussy.

"I will have your obedience."

Her hands shoved against his chest, but he held her fast. "I don't follow any man's lead. This is a mutual thing—what we do."

"Not with me, my dear," he said, his voice almost hard. "You will follow me. You've already made a nice start undressing when I commanded."

"I got naked first, because I wanted it. Not because you commanded it."

He shrugged. "However you want to paint this. You will obey me because it pleases you."

She shoved again and tried to slide her knees from the chair. "I've changed my mind. Let me go."

"Don't you want to know my kiss?"

"Not anymore—especially if you think you're going to fuck my mind."

"I'll do that too." He lifted her higher. "First, a little hint of the pleasure to come, hmmm?"

Before she could utter a protest, he grasped her nipple with his mouth and sucked.

Sidney pressed against his shoulders, wriggling in his arms, truly afraid now. The sensations he stirred inside her were too strong, too sharp.

His tongue rasped over the tip, and he mouthed her, suckling harder.

Her breath caught on a ragged sob. She knew what was coming next, and she didn't want it—not like this—not with him fully clothed and her helpless in his arms. "Stop it!" She grabbed his hair in her fists and tried to pull his mouth away.

His teeth bit into her flesh—stinging, sharp. Pain pierced the sensual haze for a moment, shocking her into stillness. Then he drew, bringing her blood from all points to her breast in a rush of pure heat.

Sidney's head fell back, and she whimpered while her body went limp. She never wanted the sensation to end. Her belly clenched and trembled. Deep inside, her vagina spasmed—clasping, releasing. Her hips pulsed in the air, her whole body spiraling tighter while his mouth drew her closer and closer to explosion.

Suddenly, a cry broke from her throat, and she was shuddering inside his arms. Darkness closed around her for a long moment as she orgasmed.

He let go of her breast and nuzzled the twin wounds with his tongue, closing them. Then he tucked her head close against his shoulder and held her while the trembling eased.

Sidney sniffed and blinked away unexpected tears. "Why must it be this way? Why do you want me weak?"

"To protect you."

"You think you'll hurt me if you let loose?"

"I'm afraid I'll kill you."

Sidney's first thought was that might be the sexiest thing a man had ever said to her. Her second was she must be one sick puppy to feel that way. She lifted her head and stared into his eyes. "What if I'm willing to take the chance?"

His expression remained shuttered. "I'm not."

She lifted her chin to show him she wasn't cowed. "I'm no scared little virgin. You think I'll lose every skirmish?"

"It's inevitable." His eyes stared into hers, frightening her with their directness and dispassion. "I'm more experienced, and I offer something you've never had."

She snorted. "I thought I just did—have it, that is."

His hand smoothed back her hair from her face. "That was just an appetizer, my dear."

Her body flushed hotly, already ripening in anticipation of his next "lesson". "You have too many clothes on," she said, sounding sulky to her own ears.

His lips curved. "I'll decide when I take you."

She tossed back her hair. "Maybe it's been so long you've forgotten how."

"You won't dare me into rushing things."

She shifted on his lap, rubbing her pussy over his groin. "If I didn't know you plan to take me, I'd think you might be gay."

"Because I can control my own response?"

"Because you can resist me."

"You think you're so irresistible?"

She leaned toward him and licked her lips. "Ask Moses," she whispered against his mouth.

His eyes narrowed. He could be needled. But was that jealousy or just irritation? "Don't mention him when you're with me," he said, his tone biting.

"Give me a reason not to think about him. He has *enormous* appeal to a woman," she drawled.

"Size matters to you?"

She slid him a glance from beneath her eyelashes. "Don't worry, I won't throw you back if you don't measure up."

Suddenly, Navarro rose, moving so fast Sidney's vision blurred. She was left gasping as he laid her over his desk.

Navarro leaned over her, his mouth an inch above hers.

"Another vamp talent?" she asked, her voice thin and trembling, not daring to raise her legs to grasp his waist the way she wanted.

"Some of us are more skilled than others." His breath gusted on her face, and his loins pressed against her naked pussy, turning her insides to mush. "Our talents increase over time."

She swallowed. "You must be one helluva fuck."

"You'll never know if you keep testing my resolve," he said, his gaze dropping to her lips.

She licked them. "Who's testing anything? Can't you tell I'm dying for it?"

"Not yet."

Chapter Six

☙

Her pussy gushed at the hard tone of his voice. Sidney couldn't hold back the faint moan that broke from her throat. "Navarro, please."

"I will. Eventually." His mouth took hers then, lips sliding in a drugging kiss.

Spearing her fingers into his thick hair, she tugged to extend the kiss. She thrust her tongue inside his mouth, and he nipped it, but that didn't deter her. She laved his tongue, tasting copper — knowing he tasted it too. Fire licked her pussy, heat curling deep inside her belly. Slowly, she lifted her legs to clasp his hips, and she rubbed her sex against him while her mouth suctioned his.

Navarro broke the kiss and leaned back, shaking his head until she released his hair.

Panting beneath him, she begged him silently with her gaze to take her.

He closed his eyes, and his chest rose and fell quickly. His cock slowly filled as she pumped her hips upward, teasing him, caressing him through his clothing. "You will follow me," he said, gritting his teeth.

Satisfied at last she could arouse him, Sidney unwound her legs from his hips and lay back against the desk. If surrender would get her what she needed faster, she'd let him think he'd won. "Okay," she said, "I'm yours to command."

His eyes opened, and his expression was just shy of incredulous. "Do you really think that's all it will take?"

Sidney's heart stuttered, then began to thud dully in her chest. She'd underestimated him—he'd been playing her again. "What do you want?"

"Complete submission—nothing less." Navarro's hands slipped between their bodies, and he fondled her breasts, tweaking the nipples until she moaned again. "I won't give you what you crave until you're mindless with need."

"You don't think I'm there already?" She gasped as he twisted hard. Her eyes drifted closed for a moment, lost in the pleasure-pain. When she opened them, his intense stare made her breath catch.

"That's what it will be like—you won't be able to help yourself. You won't be thinking 'what does he want to hear?'—you won't be able to form a single coherent thought. Then, when you beg me, I may come to you."

She wanted to deny him—wanted to tell him to let her get up. She didn't want this.

But she'd be lying.

Instead, her belly quivered, and her breath grew choppy. *Christ!* Just the description of what he wanted from her excited her more than she thought she could bear. She waited while he watched her—his expression carved in stone.

He pushed up from her body and trailed his fingers lower—just the tips scraping her trembling stomach, lightly circling her navel, halting at the hair curling on her mons. His fingers threaded through the short curls and tugged. His thumb dipped into her cleft and circled her swollen clitoris.

Her whole body clenched. Tears leaked from Sidney's eyes because she knew he would easily wrest the reaction he wanted from her body, and she was helpless to prevent it. Physically, she couldn't overpower him. And much to her chagrin, emotionally she was even weaker. He'd make her beg endlessly then gift her with release—when it pleased him. She'd thought this would be another gymnastic rumble between the sheets—but he was going to steal her soul.

"I'll take you with my fingers and tongue, and when you're ready to burst, I'll bite your clitoris. Do you want it fast or slow?" he asked, still staring.

She shook her head, tears spilling faster. She'd never been one for waterworks, but he scared her. If she said fast, he'd take her slow. If she tried reverse psychology on him and asked for slow—his *taking* would grind to a crawl. Her body already ached for release. She bit her lip, refusing to answer.

"You're beginning to understand," he murmured, moving down her body. "Put your hands behind your head, love."

Swallowing a lump of confusion, she did as he asked, slipping her clasped fingers behind her head. She was stretched on the desk, her meager breasts flattened except for their erect points, her back arched, her legs dangling toward the floor.

He knelt between her legs, and all she could see was the top of his dark head. Then she felt his fingers stroking her moist folds. Her toes curled, but she didn't dare raise her legs to invite him to delve deeper.

Slowly, languorously, he traced the petals of her sex, plucking the outer lips, gliding into her moisture, spreading her honey with his fingertips.

"Such a pretty pussy you have—and so wet." The point of his tongue licked along the edges of her inner lips.

Sidney's breath hissed between her clenched teeth. *I won't beg. I won't beg.*

"You will," he whispered. Fingers dipped inside, pumping in and out—shallow thrusts that had her pussy swelling, and her channel gushing around him.

He can read me like a fucking book. She fought to keep her hips from countering the action and squeezed her eyes shut.

Another finger pushed inside, stretching her, and his tongue dug between her inner labia, licking upward, finding the hood guarding her clit. He rubbed it, circling on it, until the knot of nerves beneath the hood swelled painfully hard.

Sidney's breath grew jagged and loud to her own ears. Still, she fought against crying out, and her body quivered in rhythmic spasms.

His thumb joined his fingers and he twisted his fist, pushing to gain entrance to her body, aided by her inner juices that slurped with his gentle thrusts. His mouth closed around her clit and suckled hard.

Sidney groaned, her head shaking side to side. *No, no, no!* When his teeth scraped her sensitized nub, her legs jerked and widened.

"Put your heels on my shoulders," he said, his voice even, betraying no sign of strain or excitement.

She resisted, while her belly tightened—a curl of need winding around her core. She gasped, feeling her pussy melt in a fresh wash of liquid need.

He pushed his fist past her opening, and Sidney's groan came unrestrained, deep and guttural. Her legs lifted, falling wider apart. Her cunt was so full—so stretched—ripples clasped his fist, rolling, pulling him deeper.

Her heels settled on his shoulders and she sighed, for now she could open her legs as wide as they could splay. Her tender flesh was open to the air, to his roaming mouth and fingers. Her hips lifted, pumping against his mouth and hand.

His tongue lapped, seemingly greedy for her taste. Low murmurs of approval rumbled on her flesh like blessings.

Sidney was a mindless wanton now—her moans stretching longer, louder. "Please, Navarro. Pleeease!"

Teeth sank into her clit, and she screamed, her back arching sharply, her hands outflung, her body shuddering, spasming—while he twisted his hand in and out and his mouth drew on her clit, causing blood to rush to her cunt in an electric, molten stream of passion.

When the trembling subsided, he dragged his hand from her vagina and licked the punctures closed.

Sidney watched him as he stood, feeling dazed, boneless.

His expression was still watchful, his jaw tight now. When he leaned over her, her eyelids drifted shut. The last part of her she could hide behind.

He lifted her into his arms and strode toward the door. "Now you understand what I want from you — how it will be between us."

Sidney laid her cheek on his shoulder, knowing he'd won but not caring. She was helpless to resist him.

* * * * *

Navarro knew the moment she awoke. Her breath gasped softly and a tiny frown formed between her eyebrows. The chit kept her eyes closed, waiting until she knew whether she was alone.

Smiling at her doomed tactic, he reached and stroked her breast, answering her unasked question. He put the exclamation mark on his response by settling his body close to her side, resting on one elbow so that his head was higher than hers. The better to watch her.

Her breathing grew louder, punctuated with soft snores.

He leaned down and kissed her shoulder, hitching the blankets more securely around their waists. "I know you're awake," he drawled.

She held herself perfectly still for a long moment, then whispered back, "You're naked."

"A little hard to miss, hmmm?" Beneath the covers, he brushed his erection against her thigh.

Her eyes scrunched more tightly closed. "That's not fair," she said, a frown creasing her forehead. "I didn't get to watch you take them off."

"I thought it might be a little too much for your overwrought nerves."

Her eyes flew open, her gaze clashing with his. "Overwrought?"

"You passed out," he said, his tone smug.

"I was sleepy."

He gave her a sly smile. "Now, you're awake."

Her gaze dropped to his chest. "You're bigger than you look in clothes. Not that you didn't look…big, that is. I just didn't expect so much…" She swallowed and her gaze returned to his. "Are you going to take me now?"

"Yes."

Finally! He didn't need to stretch his extra sense to hear her internal thought. Her cheeks grew rosy, and her mouth softened.

Lazily, he cupped her breast and squeezed the small mound.

She thrust into his hand, encouraging him to play.

He traced the velvet-soft areola and scraped his fingernail over the center.

She shivered, and her heart beat faster. Her nipple beaded instantly.

Her body's quick obedience deserved reward. He clasped the tip between his thumb and finger and twisted it until she squirmed beside him. Then he gave the other nipple a tender tweaking.

Sidney's teeth sank into her lower lip, and her eyelids drooped.

Navarro leaned in for a kiss, intending a quick buss before he got down to the business of taking.

But Sidney opened her mouth beneath his and thrust her tongue inside, her soft sigh mingling with his breath.

With that slight encouragement, Navarro ravaged her mouth, sliding his lips over hers, darting his tongue inside to duel. When he pulled away, he struggled against the urge to roll her body beneath his and stab into her depths.

His hand wandered lower, gliding over her tummy and downward to slip between her legs.

She didn't make a sound, but she opened her legs wider to accommodate his exploration, rolling her hips softly as he traced her slit.

Finding her drenched, Navarro suppressed a growl. She'd napped only half an hour, but each minute that ticked past had him wrestling the beast inside that wanted to pounce on her and be done with it. His cock ached with need.

As she'd slept, oblivious to the lust tightening every muscle of his body, he'd pulled back the covers to look at every succulent part of her. He'd breathed in her scents, sniffing along her skin as he'd made that journey, his mouth watering as he'd hovered over her pungent sex. He'd even dared to lap the pulse that beat steadily at the side of her throat, anticipating the meal he'd make of her tangy blood.

Impatient to complete his exploration, Navarro rolled over her, ignoring her gasp, blanketing her from breast to toe. His sex settled in the space between her thighs.

He was glad he'd left on the light. Not that he needed it to see her. He wanted to overwhelm her, fill her sight, every sense, along with her pretty cunt. He rolled his hips and nudged her pussy with the crown of his cock.

Her eyes widened. "Is that you?"

"Afraid?" he asked, dragging out the word.

She shivered deliciously, her belly quivering beneath him. Even her next inhalation trembled. "There may be a problem," she said, her voice thin.

"You took my fist earlier," he said, gritting his teeth as he pushed past her entrance. "You'll take my girth, if not my length."

"I had no idea. Perhaps, we should go really, really slow?"

He pushed deeper, stretching her opening, and closed his eyes, fighting the need to thrust. She was right. He might tear her flesh if he didn't ease into her.

She gasped. "You're just full of surprises," she said, sounding more nervous by the second.

"Not chickening out, are you, love?" He flexed his buttocks and drove a little deeper, relieved when more of her inner juices flooded her channel. He pulled back and shoved inside. This time the going was easier, wetter, and her hips rose to meet his thrust. "You have to tell me later whether I measure up."

She choked on a laugh. "I can't believe I said that to you." Her knees came up either side of him, her thighs clamping around his hips. She rocked her hips against him, encouraging him to move a little faster, fractionally deeper.

His forehead sank onto her shoulder as he pumped, tunneling farther with each stroke. "Are you all right? Can you take more?" God, he hoped so. His balls drew high and felt hard as stone, his cock felt ready to burst. Still, he controlled his pace and the depth of his thrusts.

"I don't...I can't..." The hands clenching his shoulders released and glided into his hair. She rubbed her face against his, her body rocking faster, pulling hard on his hair.

Navarro gritted his teeth and held himself away from her, forcing his hips not to close the gap between their bodies — she was too small, too tight. She was perfect.

"Please, please," she said, winding her legs around his back, trying to bring him down on top of her. "I'm close. So close. Faster. Oh God!" Her hands slid over his back, stroking, massaging, and gliding lower.

When her fingers trailed the crease between his buttocks, Navarro groaned. "Careful what you do there."

"Afraid," she drawled.

He snorted. "No, but you should be."

A finger grazed his opening and a shudder racked his body. He retaliated, thrusting deeply, grinding the base of his cock against her clit.

"I could use more of that punishment," she said, her words coming fast and strained.

"Think you're ready to take all of me, love? Be sure." He tunneled again, feeling the first ripple of an impending orgasm clasp his cock.

"Yes," she hissed. "Please."

Navarro withdrew, ignoring her moan of dismay and helped her turn and come to her knees.

Her bottom quivered when he laid his palms on her cheeks. Pressing her stance wider with his knees, he nudged her once, unerringly finding her wet slit, and then drove deep into her body.

Sidney issued a muffled scream.

Navarro pulled back and held himself still, his jaw clenched. Then he shook his head. "No, I can't stop. Too late." He draped her back, planting his hands on the bed beside hers. "Give me your neck," he gritted out.

The woman shuddering beneath him didn't question what he wanted. Her back arched, her head falling to the side.

Navarro nuzzled her neck, then licked, letting the moisture from the glands deep inside his mouth numb her skin. Then he opened his jaws, putting his teeth against her neck and sank fangs into her—slamming his cock deep at the same time.

Sidney howled long and loud, not moving as he unleashed his monster, his face crackling as he morphed, his muscles growing thicker, harder, his cock expanding to stretch her so tight her cunt clenched him like a vise.

Coppery blood filled his mouth, pumping with each quick beat of her heart, coating his tongue, sliding down his throat. He drank while his body hammered at her pussy, faster, sharper.

Transformed, his conscious receded, and his body and mouth acted on instinct.

The woman under him, gloving his sex, fed his appetites. He kept her locked to his body, subduing his host with his mouth and cock.

She screamed, a thin ragged cry that pierced his mind, reminding him of the need to take just so much blood, and he released her, licking the wounds to enjoy a final taste, closing them. Then he noted the deep spasms clutching his shaft, pulsing as she mewled like a small animal.

He leaned back and wrapped his arms around her belly, pulling her upright with him. Then he lifted and lowered her, hard and fast, their thighs slapping together, until he felt her jerk and shudder, and his own sex erupted, spewing inside her.

When their release ended, he rocked with her dangling limp in his arms and slowly, the red haze cleared from his brain. The monster retreated.

Navarro shuddered, clasping Sidney close to his body — thankful his beast had reined his appetite. Now replete, he turned his attention from his own selfish gratification to Sidney, to protect and comfort her as she roused slowly.

Her head fell back against his shoulder, and she drew a deep, ragged breath. "Will we do this often?"

"Afraid?" he whispered, closing his eyes, hoping for the answer he needed.

"Yes. Sex with you just might be the death of me."

He sighed, dispirited. He'd asked too much.

"Those orgasms are killer." Her arm came up, and she reached behind to cup the back of his head. "Next time, I get to be on top. I think I missed quite a sight."

* * * * *

Sidney woke before daybreak and stretched. Her body ached. Especially, her pussy — the tender tissue still felt swollen and hot. All in all, a delicious sensation to wake up to.

She opened her eyes and turned her head to find Navarro resting beside her. He lay on his back, two pillows stacked beneath his head. The covers were pulled to his waist again. The pale gray light filtering beneath the curtains was just enough to illuminate his face. His dark perfection, like some ancient prince in a gilded painting, took her breath away.

His gaze found hers. "Will you remain in my home today?"

Sidney forced her fanciful thoughts aside. If he had an inkling how easily she could be ensnared... "Do I have a choice?" she replied, keeping her tone tart.

His lips twitched. "Not really. But I'd like to know your preference anyway."

Rolling to her side, she tucked her hands beneath her cheek. Her mind racing to shore up her defenses. "I don't see why it matters."

"It matters — to me." His expression, always so watchful and controlled, held a hint of pathos that touched her.

Damn him, for confusing me! "I won't poison your dogs," she said softly. That was as close to a surrender as she would give him. "I'm whacked anyway. Need my beauty sleep." A millennium of sleep wouldn't help her match his!

He settled back on his pillows and smiled. "That would only take a nap."

She cocked an eyebrow. "Was that a compliment?"

His penetrating gaze held hers. "Do you need one?"

Thanks for making me feel like a needy twit! "Every woman needs one once in a while," she replied grumpily.

"But appearances are so unimportant, and sometimes beyond your control. Wouldn't it mean more for me to praise your resourcefulness?"

She snorted and rolled her eyes. "How many centuries have you lived? Praise a woman's mind, and she knows she looks like a hag."

He gave a dramatic sigh. "Perhaps men aren't intended to fathom a woman's mind."

"Can't you guess what's on mine?" she asked, letting her fingers walk down his stomach to nudge the covers.

"Curious?"

"I want to see that pole you call a dick."

He coughed, clearing his throat. "You have such a way with words. I can tell why your news segment is so popular."

"I don't write fiction, and I only get a few minutes to make my point. I like to think I'm economical. So how about it?" She plucked the hairs that formed an arrow pointing down his muscled abdomen. "Do I get to see?"

"Woman!" His fingers closed around hers, and he pulled her hand toward his mouth. "Is my sex all you have an interest in?"

Sidney waggled her brows. "It looms large in my mind."

He kissed the back of her hand and then returned it to his stomach, still clutching her to prevent further wandering. "Shouldn't we save the mystery for another time? I fear once you've seen all of me you'll lose interest."

"Do you think that's possible?" she murmured, pulling her hand from beneath his. She teased his navel with a fingertip.

The blanket covering him tented over his loins.

"Looks like someone has something to say about it, too."

Navarro took a deep breath and grabbed the edge of the blanket. "Very well. I will let you look, but only because I'm afraid you're becoming the dog after my bone."

Sidney grinned wickedly. "And you were accusing me of being blunt. I have to warn you, my middle name starts with a 'P' — for 'persistence'."

His gaze rose to the ceiling. "And I thought it must have been for 'Pain-in-the-a —'"

Sidney wagged her finger, delighted at his teasing. "Nuh-uhn. No cursing. Or Inigo will declare me a bad influence." She glanced down the covers. "I'm still waiting."

Navarro folded his arms over his chest. "I think I would rather give you the privilege."

"Think I'm shy?"

"Not a bit."

Taking a deep breath, Sidney was surprised to find she was a little nervous about "unmasking" his cock. She knew it would be gi-normous, larger than even Moses' fine organ. But such a stellar attribute hammered home the fact she was ordinary. Her appeal only transitory.

She swallowed and gripped the blanket, and then slowly dragged it down.

Chapter Seven

ಐ

Navarro made a note to ask Inigo later who "Mr. Ed" was.

He'd received a confusing image of a whinnying, white horse with his head hanging over a kitchen half-door. That image, and Sidney's breathy, "Helllooo, Mr. Ed", quickly faded as her fingers wrapped around his shaft.

"Wait a second," she said, releasing his cock. She turned to glance at his face. "Are you going to call all the shots again? I don't want to get punished for my *enthusiasm*."

Navarro shook his head, words being impossible to form at the moment. His cock was fully in charge.

"Just checking," she said, and returned her avid gaze to his "pole". "How do you walk with this thing dangling between your legs?"

"He rarely dangles," he said, gritting his teeth when she gripped his shaft again and pulled it perpendicular to his body.

"I get it now!" she said excitedly. "John Holmes must have been a vamp! That donkey cock of his couldn't have been human."

Not having a clue who John Holmes was, but making another mental note to find out who his competition was, Navarro forced himself to remain lying on his pillows as Sidney pushed his cock around, staring at it from all angles.

As her slim fingers fluttered on his shaft, Navarro felt his control begin to slip. "Do you think you can stare him into an orgasm?"

She blinked and glanced back at him. "Are you by chance telling me to hurry it up?"

"Yes," he hissed between his teeth.

A siren's smile curved the corners of her mouth. "Poor baby," she said pursing her lips.

Witch! She knew he imagined those lips closing around the head of his penis.

"Sidney," he said, his voice rising in warning.

She snorted. "It's not fair. If I don't *hurry it up*, you'll just take over. Won't you?"

He pointed at his cock. "Do I have to command you?"

Her chin came up immediately, but then her head tilted. Her expression was pensive and curious at the same time. "I think...yes."

Navarro understood intuitively he'd been given a rare gift. Sidney P. Coffey liked being in control of every situation. Now, she'd surrendered herself. Her trust made him feel all-powerful. "Climb between my legs, little sex slave."

"Hrmph!" she snorted again, but stepped on her knees into the narrow space between his legs.

"Now, take the head of my cock into your sweet mouth."

Immediately, her nipples dimpled. With excitement glowing on her cheeks, she leaned forward and grasped his shaft. Her mouth opened wide to swallow him.

Navarro suppressed a groan as her wet mouth surrounded him in lush heat. "*Suck it.*" His nostrils flared as he caught the scent of her steaming arousal.

Her lips suctioned, her head moving left to right, and back, her gaze holding his all the while. Then she took a little initiative and chewed the soft bulb gently.

His hips lifted off the bed, pressing his cock deeper into the moist cavern of her mouth.

She pulled away and leaned down to trail her tongue along his shaft, licking down and up, lapping him in thick strokes with the flat of her tongue like a tasty ice-cream cone.

All his muscles, belly to thigh, tightened with sensual tension. Sweat beaded on his upper lip.

Her hands slid down to the base of his cock. One cupped his balls, now hard stones in their tight sac. The other tightly gripped the base of his shaft. She licked downward and opened her mouth to take his balls into her mouth.

Navarro sucked in a deep breath as she mouthed his scrotum, her tongue stroking his balls inside her mouth, rolling them, tugging them. His hands fisted in the bedding.

Sidney's breath grew shorter, gasping. The scent of her arousal grew stronger. Sweat broke on her forehead and wispy strands of pale hair stuck there.

Navarro reached down and threaded his fingers through her hair and tugged, using his grip on her hair to guide her movements and bring her up his cock.

When she reached the crown, he nudged her lips, and she opened wide, sinking down his cock, her hands closing around his shaft to twist and pull while she bobbed now, taking him as deep as her throat would allow.

Wet heat, suctioning lips, and circling hands had Navarro groaning, his buttocks tensing to deliver shallow thrusts.

Sidney grunted softly each time he stroked deep. Her teeth lightly strafed his straining flesh.

Suddenly, she reared up and straddled his hips. Her expression was tight, desperate. "I can't wait. I have to—"

"Mount me."

She nodded and took a deep breath, rising high above his cock. Her fingers crept between her legs, spreading her labia. She tunneled her fingers inside herself, and her eyes closed. Moist, slippery sounds accompanied her exploration as she drew the wet to the petals framing her sex

Then she centered her hot pussy over his crown, sliding him around her entrance to coat the head with her juices. Her legs trembled and she sank, taking him inside. She moaned.

Her cunt felt hotter than it should around his cock. "You're sore, still swollen. Can you do this?" he gritted out.

She nodded again, whimpering, and sank deeper, and then came up. Down, up, down—going deeper with each stroke, rotating her hips to twist and ease him deeper still. Sweat trickled between her breasts.

Navarro slid his fingers over it to massage the moisture into her breasts, kneading the flesh, plumping it as he curved his body upward to take a nipple into his mouth.

Sidney's head fell back, and she stilled as he laved the tight points, first one then the other, not resuming her rocking motions until he released her nipple and fell back against the pillow.

Her hands landed on his chest as she levered her bottom up and down, her face flushing a fiery red. Rosy, swollen lips trembled around her gasps. Her gaze held his, her expression determined, yet vulnerable.

He loved the way her plump lips trembled, and he was determined to make her moan.

Navarro cupped her breasts and massaged the soft mounds, then glided lower to grip her hips. When her trembling increased, he aided her movements, lifting her up, sliding her down, faster now—deeper.

Sidney widened the stance of her knees and sank lower, leaning forward so that their groins ground together, crisp hairs scratching.

Navarro slid his fingers between them and dug between her legs to find the hard kernel at the top of her cunt. He fluttered a fingertip against it, enjoying the jerk of her hips. Because he wanted to experience more than just her physical reactions to their escalating passion, he stared into her eyes, opening himself to her thoughts, climbing inside to feel what she felt, hear her thoughts.

Sidney was a very noisy girl.

Ohmigod, Oh God! Christ! I've never been so full. His cock's incredible. He's not a donkey—he's a freaking Clydesdale! Ah! My clit! Yes, yes! Like that. Jeez, rub harder. I'm gonna blow!

Navarro felt the burning heat of her vagina, raw, swollen, liquid, molten. His cock caressed her to her womb, gliding, stretching, *cramming* deep. *How does she take me?*

Why is he staring at me like that? came Sidney's thought. *Like he can see right into me? Can't let him know how special… How much I need this…him. Ohmigod—I'm coooomiiiing!*

Navarro felt a sensation like a tightly coiled spring explode deep inside her womb, followed quickly by rolling contractions that clasped his cock, pulsing around him to draw him deeper, squeezing him toward orgasm. Her thoughts, coherent thoughts, were obliterated by a blinding rush of sensation that sucked the air from her lungs, squeezing a long, keening cry from her dry as dust mouth.

Her body rocked, and she delivered jerky, uncoordinated movements, her knees trembling while her body was racked with shuddering waves of darkness.

A moment before she fainted, Navarro pulled away from her mind, his cock clamored for his attention. He'd been so deep into her experience, he hadn't realized his own body was close to exploding.

His hips bucked wildly, pumping upward, impaling her with sharp, rapid thrusts as he climbed. He felt the tightening of his facial armor, plates of bone that thickened with his passion, pushing outward. His gums itched, and then stung, as his fangs slid down. But he held the leash this time on his monster, roughly, containing him. He'd taken too much blood the last time. He wouldn't let him feed. Instead, he channeled the wildness to his hips and pumped faster, harder.

Sidney came around, still held upright against his loins, and her expression, drowsy and aroused, revealed a resurgence of passion. She regained her knees, leaned closer to his body, and countered his movements, slamming down to meet his upward thrusts, until the air snapped with their sweaty, violent pounding.

Her face grew taut, her lips thinned. "I can't believe it — it's happening again," she gasped. "More, Navarro, give me more!" She slid her breasts against his chest, tangling the points in his hair. Then she scraped his nipples with her fingernails, plucked, and tormented them.

He resisted, grinding his teeth. His body stretched tight as he pounded into her.

Sidney, however, was relentless. She nipped his chin, his chest, and then clawed his shoulders.

"Stop it!" he growled. "You don't want him to come out and play."

"Don't tell me what I want," she said, curling to take a flat nipple in her mouth. She bit and held it between her teeth while he continued to buck violently against her pussy.

He pushed her head away and held her back from his body, only letting her open thighs and cunt touch him as he pushed higher toward release. But release was harder to attain in this body, it took longer — and by the narrowing of the chit's eyes — time was running out.

Sidney held his gaze and brought her hands to her breasts, cupping them high, and then tugged the points hard until she moaned against the pain. Her pussy tightened, gripping his dick like a wet, shrinking glove.

But still he resisted, keeping his focus on his cock, rocking in and out, spearing high to punish her with sharper thrusts.

But Sidney only smiled, grunting softly as his hard strokes forced air from her lungs. "Think you can resist?" she taunted, and then she drew her lower lip between her teeth.

Navarro shook his head, reading her intention, pounding harder to try to reach the precipice before she succeeded. "*Don't do it, Sidney,*" he roared.

She bit and pressed her lips together, smearing blood on her mouth. Then she reached behind her and gripped his balls, rolling them in her palm, squeezing, tugging.

Navarro clutched the bedding, clamping his jaws tight, straining with every muscle in his body to resist the temptation teasing his nostrils.

When her fingers plucked at one stony orb, and her bloody lips stretched into a feline grin, he knew he was about to lose. She pinched his ball—hard.

He roared upward, feeling the rest of the transformation take him, morphing in one exquisite second.

Sidney's eyes widened, and her mouth dropped open.

Too late now, love! With that last sentient thought, he pushed her off his cock and drove her onto her back, mounting her, flexing his buttocks backward, then thrusting, cramming himself inside her, forcing her to take all of him in one long, endless glide.

Anger tinged this claiming, he hooked his arms beneath her legs and forced her limbs higher, so he could tunnel deeper still. He wanted to punish, show her who was master.

She squealed, air hissing between her teeth.

He'd hurt her, but her pain only incited the beast. Territorial, possessive, he intended to leave his mark upon her soul. He growled from deep inside his chest and hammered at her writhing hips, drinking her cries with his mouth latched to hers.

When finally the beast reached the precipice, he drank the trickling blood from her lips and slammed his hips one last time to drive deep into her core. Circling, he ground against her as his seed pulsed into her, claiming her womb. He continued to grind and pump until the last spurt was drained from his sex, and slowly relaxing, the red curtain lifted from his mind.

Navarro roused himself, wrenching from Sidney's body. He sat back on his haunches, horrified that he'd given his inner monster free rein.

She lay still beneath him, her chest shuddering with soft sobs.

He backed away from her and slid off the bed, recoiling from the memory of his violent, unleashed taking of her small body.

She didn't move. Her legs splayed wide, her thighs glistening with pearlescent cum. Then she sniffed, and turned her head toward him, a question in her eyes. "Where are you going?"

"I thought you might want to be alone."

"Just like a man," she said, her voice sounded tired, weak. "First sign of tears, and he's hot-footin' it for the door."

Navarro hung his head. He'd thought he could control the beast—control Sidney—and have his cake too. "I apologize. I'll send Inigo to you with clothing. He'll have a driver take you home."

She sat up slowly on the bed, her expression wary. "You're kidding, right?"

"No. I release you," he said, his voice rough as gravel as he forced words past a tight throat.

Sidney climbed off the bed and stomped toward him, a scowl darkening her face. "You are a Grade-A asshole!"

"I know. I've apologized. If you wish to seek medical treatment—"

She pointed a finger at his chest and poked him. "What is it? You got what you wanted from me? Now, you're showing me the door?" She drew her hand back and slapped hard against his cheek. "Well, congratulations! I never felt like a whore before, but right now I don't think a whole bar of Dove would make me feel clean again." Tears glittered in her eyes, and she shoved him, walking past him to the bathroom.

Navarro hooked an arm around her waist and pulled her close until her back pressed against his chest. She wasn't angry with him for the reason he had first thought. "Did I hurt you?" he murmured into her ear, needing to know.

She strained against his arm. "You sure as fuck did, bastard." Her harsh words lost power when she sniffed again.

Her voice was filled with a woman's hurt—from scorn, not injury. "I meant, physically, did I hurt you?"

She drew in a long breath, her head falling back against his shoulder in surrender. "Yes. But I wanted it that way. I wanted all the wildness."

He'd been dying for it too. "That was a dangerous game you played. It might not have ended well. I wasn't in control."

"That's probably why I dug it so much." She sighed. "I thought I'd died when I came."

Navarro turned her in his arms, bracketing her face so that her gaze couldn't slide away. "You're very small. When I transform, and that other part of me surfaces, he can hurt you."

A little smile twisted her lips. "I think he likes me," she whispered, and touched her tongue to her swollen lower lip.

With a slight shake of his head, he asked, "Who's the monster here?"

"You made me." Her fingers walked across his chest and she tweaked a flat nipple. "Are you still letting me go?"

"Do you want me to?" he asked, holding his breath for her answer, knowing he'd keep her even if she denied him.

"Not yet." She rose on her toes and pressed a kiss to his mouth. "Ouch!" She drew back and touched her lip.

"Let me." Cupping her face, he tilted her head back and sucked her lips between his. He laved her lip, healing and numbing her broken skin. When he was done, he swept his tongue inside her mouth and kissed her.

When he drew slightly away, she looked dazed. "You taste like blood—and me."

"Ambrosia," he moaned and slid his lips over hers again. Already, his loins felt a tingling, heated stirring. Sighing, he set her away from him.

Sinking back to the ground, Sidney gave him a wry little smile. "I think I'm done for the day—so far as..." Her cheeks reddened, and she made a little gesture toward his cock.

"Is this shyness?" he asked, tracing the blush on her cheek.

"Course not! Just didn't want to burn your ears."

"We don't have to fuck, Sidney. There are a few places on your body I'm not yet acquainted with."

"But I want to fuck!" she said, her lips pouting. "I'm just really sore."

"Let's improvise. We still have some time to while away before dawn. I'll let you have your way with me—any way you please."

Her expression brightened. "Will you follow my suggestions?"

He narrowed his gaze. "Only if you don't tempt the beast."

"Darn." She blew out a breath, and looked up at him from beneath her lashes. "I don't think I want to know what's coming. Surprise me?"

Twice now, she'd given herself into his hands. If he'd had any doubts he'd frightened or really harmed her, they melted away in the glowing blush that spread over her cheeks and chest.

He grabbed her hand and tugged her toward the bed. "We'll go slowly this time—savor our journey. All you have to do is lay back and let me work."

Her feet dragged. "Wait. If you're going anywhere down there—I need to wash. I'm pretty sticky."

Glancing over his shoulder he tugged harder, until she fell against his chest. "I'll enjoy licking you clean, love."

* * * * *

Sidney lay limp as a noodle, her arms and legs spread wide on the bed. Navarro had made good on his promise, although he'd had to repeat the process again when he'd made her cream once more with his wicked, questing tongue.

"Are you sleeping again?" he murmured, his face nuzzling her inner thigh.

"Me sleep? I have an itch that won't quit."

"Shall I scratch it for you?"

She gave a snort of laughter. "Please, I can't seem to move at the moment."

His mouth trailed kisses down her thigh. "I think I've learned everything I need to know about this side of you, dear. Roll over?"

Sidney groaned, and he helped her turn onto her stomach. She was glad she could bury her hot face in a pillow. "You're not going to let me keep any secrets, are you?"

"No—and give me that pillow."

She tossed it backward, swinging at his head.

His soft laughter raised goose bumps along her spine. "I have to tell you, I'm not too comfortable showing you this *side* of me."

Navarro laughed again and lifted her hips, sliding the pillow beneath her. "I promise to be gentle."

"So long as Trigger doesn't go whinnying around down there."

Chapter Eight

෨

"You seem preoccupied with horses," Navarro said, his voice teasing.

"Huh?" *How does he know that?* Sidney had kept her earlier comparisons silent earlier. *Has to be just a coincidence!* She relaxed. "Just saying."

"I get your point. I'll have to ease you into that particular act."

"Given your *point* — I think you could *ease* me until Christmas, and I still wouldn't be ready," she muttered, nervous now that his hands were massaging her bottom.

"Such a pessimist." His lips grazed each cheek.

Sidney shivered. Navarro teasing her made her jumpy as hell. Condescending, brooding, commanding — that she'd already had. Was the excitement already wearing thin for him? Or was her ass really that funny?

"You have a spectacular ass, Sidney. Relax." He dragged out his words in a slow, teasing drawl.

She jerked. *Damn!* She wished she wasn't so transparent. Burying her head in her arms, she hoped he was over being patient. The stress of not knowing what he was up to had her whole body tingling with anticipation.

When his body stretched over hers, covering her back with warmth, she sighed.

His nose nuzzled her ear while his hands slipped up and down her sides.

He can't be tiring of me, if his dick is already prodding unexplored territory. Oh no, he is not going there!

Then his lips close on her earlobe and nipped it.

"Ouch!"

"Stop thinking so much."

"Can't help it. I didn't know I could come like a roller coaster. You've barely let me catch my breath."

"Are you complaining?"

"No…course not. Just…" She wished he'd stop talking, asking questions that drummed up feelings she was too uncomfortable to acknowledge.

"Afraid?"

"A little," she admitted, cringing inside.

"Of me?"

Of how much I feel. "No," she snapped. *You keep kicking the door open on my heart every time I think I can close it.* "Shouldn't you be scared?"

"Of what? That I might discover you've a woman's heart after all?" He kissed her shoulder, and then rubbed his cheek against her.

She nodded, her throat thickening. "I might want to cling. I don't do it very well. I get whiny."

"You've done it a lot?" he asked, his caresses growing still.

"Once. It was pretty ugly." She tried for humor to mask her pain. "I got all splotchy-faced and soggy-nosed. I think I might have broken a dish or two over his head, too. Sixteen stitches — or so the emergency room bill stated."

"Were you badly hurt?"

His voice so soft and deep, she felt another kind of caress — one that had her wishing she were a different kind of girl. Softer, needier — the kind a man wanted to protect. "No. I sucker-punched him — he never had a chance."

"Such a little warrior," he murmured. "But I meant, did he hurt your heart?"

"Just my pride. I caught him screwing my best friend. I didn't love him. I just wanted to know I was loveable, I guess. But I found out I didn't need him or his loving after all."

"Are you sure about that?"

She stayed silent, not wanting to lie.

Navarro kissed the side of her face.

Sidney turned to meet his lips. For the first time, their kiss was soft and exploring.

His lips released hers. "I can't promise you forever, Sidney, but for however long we need each other—I won't share you. And I won't bring another to my bed."

He looked so serious, her heart nearly broke. *I can't do this.* "No more Moses?" she asked, lifting an eyebrow, telling him silently all she wanted was the sex. *Please don't let him see the lie!*

He stared for a long moment, then his lips quirked. "Threaten me with Moses one more time, and I'll spank you."

Glad that at last he was relenting in his pursuit of her inner feelings, Sidney relaxed. "Since I'm in a vulnerable position at the moment, I'll refrain."

"See how easy it is to do my bidding?" He abruptly slid down her body. "Now, no more whining."

Sidney relaxed until his hands plumped the pillow beneath her, adding height to her ass.

Navarro took his time arranging her for his pleasure, spreading her legs wide, tilting her bottom to give him greater access.

Her breath hissed out when his tongue rimmed her pussy. It was all she could do not to squirm with delight. When he settled in to lick and stroke her sex, paying special attention to her clitoris, Sidney sighed and arched higher.

"Like that, do you?"

"Mmm-hmm," she moaned, clutching at the bedding. Already her vagina melted, oozing cream, which he lapped and spread over her swollen lips.

"Can you take my fingers, love?"

"Please, I'm so wet…it won't hurt."

Two fingers penetrated her vagina, gliding past her entrance. Sidney squeezed her inner muscles to keep them there, causing a soft slurping sound. She widened her legs a little more, and raised her bottom higher still, all embarrassment over her exposure to his wicked gaze gone as he pumped his fingers and sucked on her clit.

Navarro murmured, a rough unintelligible sound, and withdrew his fingers. His hands parted her buttocks, and Sidney froze. She was past protesting—whatever he did at this point had to be pleasurable. He hadn't disappointed yet. She yielded for several heart stopping moments while his tongue traced her crease, skipping over her the little hole.

Sidney didn't know whether to be relieved or disappointed. This was a new experience. Her bottom seemed to have its own ideas and quivered.

"Nervous?"

"Just get on with it—the wait's killing me."

His laughter, deep and deliciously masculine, muffled as he licked a fine line back down until he grazed her anus.

Sidney gasped and held herself rigid for a moment. Then pressed her face into the bedding. "Please, Navarro," she whispered, sure he wouldn't hear her muffled plea.

A wet point targeted the center of her asshole and flickered.

Sidney jerked, and before she thought about her reaction, she reared back, demanding more. *More* of his slippery kisses, *more*…penetration!

The flat of his tongue laved her asshole, again and again, until she rocked to the rhythm of his strokes—delight and heady trepidation, mixing with an excitement so lush she thought she'd come from just the wicked stroke of his tongue—*there.*

Wicked, nasty sex. That's what she'd wanted, and she was getting it in spades! This was the ultimate pleasure...*almost.* "Navarro, I need more," she moaned.

"I thought you might." The rascal sounded amused, even smug.

Sidney smiled, not caring, just wanting more of the exquisite sensations.

"I'll numb you a bit, love," he murmured, and his tongue lapped over her again. "That ought to do it." Then a finger was sliding past the tightly furled nether lips, stroking into her ass.

"*Ohmigod!*" she cried out. She felt discomfort, but no real pain, and a burning that only excited her more.

He pumped his fingers, twisting to ease the muscles clamping around him. Sidney tried to relax. She wanted more. Her bottom pulsed, encouraging him, dragging on his fingers to increase the sensation.

More moisture fell and another finger slid inside. *So tight! Jeez, I'm gonna pop!* Sidney's breath grew harsher the longer the deliciously painful, lava-hot probing went on. "Navarro, I need something more. I wanna come. Pleeease!"

His mouth and chin ground into her pussy, while his fingers continued their wicked stroking above. Just when she started shooting over the edge, he clamped his lips around her clitoris and sucked hard.

Sidney gave a startled, strangled scream and lurched back, rocking on her knees, almost dislodging his mouth. But he continued to draw, continued to twist his fingers inside her ass, until her whole body shuddered into orgasm.

Boneless, she collapsed against the bed, enjoying the drugging throb of her last inner convulsions.

Navarro tugged the pillow from beneath her and pulled the blanket up to cover her. He kissed her mouth, his breath scented with her pleasure.

Sidney sighed and slept.

* * * * *

Deep beneath the house in the security room, Navarro awaited the arrival of the team he'd assembled to address the new menace. Although in the past, he'd preferred his privacy and kept a finger on the pulse of council interests from afar, this time he'd decided to direct efforts himself.

Zachary Powell and his disturbing interest in the GenTech fellows left him feeling as though a dark, ominous cloud obscured an imminent evil. That he couldn't yet give it a name increased his unease.

He glanced at the monitor with the view into the guest bedroom.

Sidney still lay beneath the blankets where he'd left her.

Navarro would have preferred climbing back into bed beside her to wake her slowly and drink of her passion again. He'd been surprised when she'd continued sleeping, snoring softly as he showered and dressed. But it did make things easier — she'd have tried following him down here. Now, she'd never make it past the basement door without the key code.

"Well, that answers one of my questions."

He glanced back at Moses Brown as he stepped into the room, eyeing the monitor.

"She's still in one piece," Moses said. He lifted one dark brow. "Although I've never known Sid to sleep so soundly."

Navarro felt a smug grin stretch his lips. "The lady's exhausted."

Moses' mouth twitched before breaking into an answering smile. "I guess I should feel a little insulted, like my manhood's been called into question. But the thought of the hoops that woman must have put you through kinda blunts the blow."

Navarro nodded and turned off the monitor. Then he straightened when the rest of the team poured into the room.

Moses perched on the edge of the console, eyeing the vampires with a guarded expression. "Now, why am I feeling like the buffet?"

Joe Garcia, newly arrived from southern Florida, slumped against a wall, hands in his pockets. "You don't have to worry about me. I stick strictly to the blood banks."

"Nice to know," Moses muttered. He lifted his chin toward Dr. Deats and his associates. "But Larry, Curly, and Moe still haven't gotten past the 'look at me, Dad' stage."

The scientists stood in a half-circle as they morphed their faces back and forth, exchanging muffled laughs.

Navarro's gaze slid to Dylan O'Hara, also fresh off the private jet. "Is Emmy keeping an eye on business above stairs?"

The Irishman grinned. "She's ordering pizza. She has penchant for delivery boys, says the smell of pepperoni adds spice to her meal. But she won't let your yummy-snack sneak past her."

"Yummy-snack?" Navarro's eyes narrowed. "Emmy's a bad influence."

"Yes, Emmy's a very bad," Dylan agreed, but his smile was pure satisfied male.

The last man to enter the room had Dylan stiffening like a hound scenting prey.

"Viper," Navarro said, nodding to the vampire. "So glad you could join us." To Dylan, he said, "Viper, here, is one of our undercover operatives."

Dylan stepped in front of the new arrival, his fists clenched at his sides. "Was that before or after he lent Nicky his den to try to lay a trap to murder Quentin, Emmy and myself?"

Viper tossed back his long dark hair. His Latin features remained shuttered. "How was I to know he intended to drain her? Rotten luck." He shrugged. "Although, by the look of her upstairs, things didn't end too badly."

Dylan leaned forward like he might take a swing. "I predict they'll end badly for you, you bastard!"

Navarro rose from his seat and stepped between the two vampires. "Dylan, you can't kill him now. Viper is here because he's needed."

Dylan took a deep breath and stepped back. "Later," he said, lifting his chin to Viper.

Viper's gaze narrowed, but he didn't respond.

"Let's begin," Navarro said, casting his glance around the room. "You have to be wondering about this summons and the presence of our new brethren." He tilted his head toward the scientists. "We have a mystery to solve, and an old enemy appears to be at the center of it." He turned to Dylan. "Did you ever discover what drew Nicky Powell to Vero Beach?"

Dylan shrugged, his smoldering gaze still glued to Viper. "Other than drug trafficking, no. We had heard a rumor he was joining his brother there, but we haven't found a trace of Zachary."

Navarro nodded. "It appears Zachary never left Seattle. I think he has larger plans than creating a new drug cartel. Dr. Deats," he said, leveling his stare on the man who appeared oblivious to the somber mood inside the room. "The vampires who attacked you—they made no mention of their intentions?"

The doctor's shoulders shuddered. "None. It was over so quickly, I may have missed any conversation."

"Your research—explain briefly to the group what you were working on."

Dr. Deats straightened his shoulders. "We're just one of several research facilities around the world working on cloning—not humans, naturally, but mammals."

"I would think it's pretty safe to say that the drugs in Vero were just the means to an end," Navarro said. "Zachary sent Nicky to set up the operation and funnel money back. If Zachary is interested in setting up his own laboratory, he would need a lot of money."

"Nicky wasn't in business long enough to fund an operation like that," Dylan said.

"I doubt seriously that Nicky's efforts were the only illicit activities Zachary had an interest in. And if he was ready to put Dr. Deats and his associates to work, I'd say he's got a very sophisticated network." Navarro turned next to Joe Garcia.

The Cuban cop straightened, his chin jutting in defiance. "Don't know what the hell I'm doing here."

"I think you have an inkling," Navarro murmured. "The operative I sent last to Florida didn't complete her mission. Pia was to report on rumors that a breeder is inside your compound. I believe that breeder is your wife."

Joe's body went rigid. "My wife doesn't enter into this conversation. The subject is strictly none of your damn business."

"You think I don't already know?" Navarro asked silkily. "She's pregnant. Carrying your get."

Dylan and Joe exchanged a charged glance. Dylan turned to Navarro. "Why is she important to this discussion?"

"If there's a possibility Joe's bred a litter of born vampires, I think Zachary is already aware. He may make an attempt to clone the children."

Joe Garcia's olive skin blanched pale. "Then what the hell am I doing here?"

"Relax," Navarro said. "I sent a security team to augment your SU force. Your woman is safe. I thought you might like to be part of the trap I'm setting."

"You're going after Zachary Powell, then?" Dylan asked.

"No. I'm waiting for him to come here. I have everything he wants," he said, staring at the three bemused geneticists.

Dr. Deats cleared his throat. "Are we the bait?"

"I'm afraid so."

"Well," he said, straightening his stooped shoulders, "life certainly takes odd twists. Just days ago, I complained to Brad here that I needed a little excitement in my life. What do you want us to do?"

"For now, play bridge," Navarro said with a small smile. "We have to wait for Zachary and his children to make their move."

"If we've got trouble headin' our way," Moses said, "then why are you keepin' Sidney?"

Although irritated by the man's continued interest in his houseguest, Navarro nodded his agreement. "You're right. She isn't safe here. I want you to take her, keep her hidden. Zachary already knows of my interest in her."

Moses nodded. "You mean, the punk at the morgue."

"Yes."

"Sure you trust me with her?" Moses asked, his mouth curving in a sly smile.

"Of course not." Navarro gave him a withering glance. "But I'm willing to take the chance of losing her…affections. I would rather she live. Wait until daylight to take her out of here."

"That's a long time to wait," Moses said.

"I guess you'll have to ask Dr. Deats to switch his game to poker."

"What makes you think they won't strike tonight?" Dylan asked.

"I don't know that they won't. I'd like the three of you," Navarro said, nodding to Dylan, Joe and Viper, "to keep watch on the grounds."

Dylan's lips drew into a snarl as he stared at Viper. "Sure you can trust me not to dust this asshole?"

Navarro's eyes narrowed. "You won't touch him because I'm asking you to set aside your animosity until this is over."

"You still haven't explained what Viper's role will be in all this," Dylan said, his tone still surly.

"His work is mostly done. He told Zachary Powell how to get inside this place."

Chapter Nine

ဆာ

Sidney's stomach gurgled loudly, waking her up. She sniffed the air. *What is that smell?*

"'Bout time," came a cheerful feminine voice. "It's way past sunset, and I've already eaten half the pizza by myself."

Sidney stared at the woman sitting cross-legged on her bed through the one eye not mashed against the pillow. "Who the hell are you?" she asked, rolling onto her back.

Strangely, she wasn't alarmed to find a complete stranger sitting beside her. It must have had something to do with the woman's beatific smile as she chomped happily on her gooey slice.

The woman wiped her mouth with a napkin. "Emmy O'Hara. I'd shake your hand, but I've got bits of mozzarella stuck to my fingers. You gonna tell me why I'm supposed to keep you out of trouble?"

Sidney blinked, trying to gather her scattered wits. So, the beautiful, plump, blonde-haired woman was supposed to keep her out of trouble? *Navarro!*

"He's got some kind of hush-hush meeting going on downstairs. Probably doesn't want me to hear what's going on anyway — everyone thinks I can't keep a secret. So, I decided to come up and see who the troublemaker is."

"He?"

"Master Navarro. Your new honey."

"How'd you know he's my…honey?" she asked, just now realizing the covers were around her waist. She hitched up the blanket to cover her breasts.

"I can smell him—even over the pepperoni and anchovies. Want a piece?"

That was the odor. Sidney sighed, relieved she'd discovered the source of the fishy smell. She had initially worried she might be in really bad need of a bath. Then she realized what the woman just said. "You can smell him? You're a vampire!"

Emmy O'Hara nodded. "Yup. Don't worry. I won't try to bite. I already had Jeff."

"Jeff?" Sidney asked feeling faintly sick.

"The pizza delivery boy. Nice kid. Lovely Type B."

Sidney shivered and pulled the covers up around her neck.

"Oh!" Emmy's eyes rounded, and she held out a hand. "I just drank a little. He was quite happy to share. The young ones take less than a minute to come."

"Come?" Sidney asked, her words feeling strangled.

Emmy's head canted. "You're kinda new to this vampire thing, aren't you? It's not like I had sex with the guy, although he thinks I did." She wrinkled her nose. "I kinda gave him that idea before he left. It's the trade I make. They give me dinner, I give them an orgasm. Now, Dylan doesn't much like it, but he knows it's harmless. My meals never really touch me. This body is all his," she said, running a hand over her generous hips. She waggled her eyebrows and grinned. "Pizza's just dessert."

"Dylan *O'Hara*?" Sidney asked weakly.

Emmy's eyebrows shot upward. "You know him?"

"I saw him once…" Sidney felt her heart lurch. "You're the blonde at The Cavern!"

"You saw me at Dylan's old nightclub? I was only there once. That was the night we met." Her eyes grew dreamy. "He rescued me from Nicky Powell and made love to me up there in his office afterward. I have to tell you—once you've had vamp there's no goin' back! You know what I mean?"

Sidney found herself nodding her head. The woman's nonstop chatter left her feeling winded and a little dazed.

"So, tell me, I'm doing a kind of unofficial poll. Is Navarro really hung? I mean, I've wondered if it's just a vamp thing— the bigger than possibly human cocks—or if maybe they just get bigger the older they get. Which would make Navarro's like—Donkey Kong!"

The woman's stare was so innocent and expectant, Sidney found herself nodding again.

"Lily, that's Joe's wife, you'll meet him later. He's downstairs. Anyway, she's writing a book about vampires, and she's gathering statistics. Only none of the vamps at The Compound will let her get their measurements. So, do you think Navarro would let you?"

Sidney smothered a laugh. "I don't think so. We don't really know each other that well."

"That's okay. I had to ask, or Lily would be disappointed in me." She closed the pizza box and wiped her sticky fingers. Then she lay down on her side, her head resting on her hand. "So, is Navarro like the most incredible lover you've ever had?" she asked, her eyes alight with curiosity and mirth. "My Dylan's got like almost two hundred years of experience— kinda blows my mind to think about all the women he had to pleasure to get that good."

Sidney's cheeks felt flushed, and she couldn't hold back a smile. "Navarro's..." She, Sidney Coffey, who made her money with words was stuck for just the right one. "...he's incredible," she whispered. "And it's not like I haven't had really, really great sex. But he's the only man who makes me want to give up control."

Emmy shivered with seeming delight. "They do get all master-y, don't they? Gives me goose bumps."

* * * * *

"Better go break up the gabfest," Moses muttered. "Guess I ought to be grateful Sid's into vamps, right now."

Navarro sat in front of the monitor, stunned, wishing he hadn't turned it on to check on his prisoner.

Dylan clamped a hand on his shoulder and laughed. "Now, you know what Joe and I have to put up with back home. Be glad you've got a continent between you and Emmy."

"She's a very bad influence." Navarro toggled off the monitor and rose. "I'd best get up there before—"

"—Emmy gets your girl to spill the beans about your 'measurements'?" Joe laughed. "Lily will be disappointed. By the way, your girl has lovely tits."

Navarro gritted his teeth as Dylan and Moses choked back laughter. He was thankful that at least the rest of the men had departed the room before he'd thought to check in on his houseguest. It was bad enough Dylan, Moses and Joe Garcia had heard the women's nonsensical conversation and spied on Sidney's sweet attributes.

"Odd how these twenty-first-century women manage to nail our old hides to the wedding bed," Dylan said, clapping his shoulder again.

Navarro opened his mouth to deny his comment, but decided not to add to the other men's amusement. He rose from his chair and aimed a deadly glare at the smirking men. "I believe you have work to do."

"Sure thing, *stud*," Moses said, his shoulders shaking.

Navarro stalked out of the security room and up the stairs.

* * * * *

Sidney popped the last corner of the pizza crust into her mouth and moaned. "I'm stuffed!"

Emmy giggled. "Don't say that around my Dylan. It doesn't have quite the same connotation for the Irish. He'll think you're preggers!"

"Fat chance of that! I've been on the pill for ten years. Besides, vamps can't reproduce, can they?"

Emmy's usually open expression shuttered instantly.

Sidney's acute olfactory sense smelled a story. "They can?"

Emmy shook her head. "Only in the rarest circumstances."

Sidney wasn't letting loose of this bone. "But they can, right?"

"Unless you're from a long line of breeders," Emmy said in a rush, "you can't get pregnant by Navarro." When she was finished, she looked a little green.

"Good thing, too," Sidney said, to lighten the conversation. "Can you imagine living with two broody vampires?"

"Try four!" Emmy said, with a wide grin.

"You live with four vampires?"

"And all guys! All that testosterone in the air can get pretty stinky!"

When Emmy laughed, Sidney realized her mouth must have been agape.

"It's not what you think!" Emmy chortled. "We have like this huge mansion and four couples are sharing it at the moment. It's safer for everyone that we all stick together."

Sidney shook her head, trying to follow the woman's new tangent. "Why safer?"

Emmy clapped a hand over her mouth. "Oh lord, the guys are right. I can't keep a secret to save my life. It's not even as though you're holding me down and shoving bamboo under my nails, but my mouth opens and it just comes rushing out."

"So you have four couples living together? You and Dylan—"

Emmy shrugged. "Jeez, you must have been Gestapo in a previous incarnation—you could coax a secret out of a priest!"

Since Sidney knew she hadn't really been prying in the first place, she just kept quiet and let the woman ramble.

"Let's see, there's me and Dylan, Lily and Joe, Darcy and Quentin, and Max and Pia. Only Max is still kinda the odd man out on account he's of the furry persuasion."

"Furry persuasion?"

Emmy leaned toward her and whispered, "A werewolf."

"A werewolf?" Sidney straightened. This was something new! "They really exist?"

"Sure! I was floored too, when I first saw him morph. Hell, I didn't even know vampires existed until Dylan went all fangy on me! But Max is cuddly as a Rottweiler around Pia, so we tolerate him. He has special skills—that's why he's still part of the Special Unit."

"You'd discriminate against werewolves? I mean, aren't you all kind of ghouly?"

"They're our mortal enemies—except for Max. He's kind of going through an identity crisis."

"So Max is a werewolf?" came the silky voice from the doorway.

Sidney's gaze swung to the open door. Navarro filled the space with his smoldering presence. She hadn't realized she'd missed waking up next to him, until now. Just how fast could he clear the room so they could give each other improper greetings?

"Emmy..." Dylan's voice rose in warning from behind Navarro as they crossed the room.

Navarro glared over his shoulder at Dylan, then turned back to Emmy, pasting on a feral smile. "Emmy, any more secrets abounding in your home?"

"I think that about sums it up," she said, her eyes wide.

"A werewolf in your SU?" Navarro's glinting stare drilled Dylan, whose shuttered expression revealed nothing. "A breeder impregnated with the first vampires to be born of a woman's womb in a millennium? I think I need to pay a visit once our current problem is laid to rest."

"Of course. You'd be very welcome," Dylan said stiffly. "Emmy?" He held out his hand to assist her from the bed.

"I'll just leave the pizza in case you're hungry, Navarro," Emmy said softly, her face downcast.

Navarro stopped her with a hand on her arm. "I don't blame you. But there can be no secrets among us. We're entering dangerous territory and must trust each other." He glared over her head at Dylan.

Dylan nodded, and tucking Emmy's hand in the crook of his elbow, he led her from the room. The door closed shut behind them.

The silence following their departure was palpable. Just how much of her conversation with Emmy had he heard?

Navarro's hooded gaze made her nervous. Sidney cleaned her fingers with her napkin and just resisted blowing breath into her cupped hand. She knew she stank of anchovies and pepperoni.

His hands made quick work of the buttons on his cotton shirt. "Did you find out enough about our little subculture to hold your curiosity at bay for a while?" he asked, his voice deadly and low. He dropped the shirt to the floor.

A nod seemed an appropriate response. She couldn't have pushed a word past her dry mouth. So, she nodded, her eyes eating up that broad plane of olive skin and lean muscle. Navarro's reined anger had her pulse thumping.

"Emmy's a trusting creature. Never seems to meet a stranger." He opened his belt and slid down his zipper, shoving his pants down his muscled thighs.

His cock was already engorged—Sidney couldn't help noticing that fact. She cleared her throat. "She's nice."

"And informative."

"It was just...girl talk." When one of his brows rose, she searched for something else to say, he had her so rattled. "Pizza?"

He shook his head. "Put it on the floor, then get on your knees."

Sidney's vagina flooded with excitement at his taut face and strained voice. *Lord, I'm gonna get it now!* She shoved the closed box to the floor with her toes and came up on her knees, clenching the bedding in her hands.

The bed dipped behind her, and her buttocks tensed.

His hands curved over her bottom. "Are you too sore to take me?"

"I'm aching," she murmured, pressing into his hand, "but for another reason entirely." She bit back a moan when his fingers dipped into her pussy.

"You're already aroused. Was it all that talk about a male vampire's *attributes*?" he bit out.

Sidney frowned and glanced over her shoulder. "Were you eavesdropping at the door?"

Again, he lifted one mocking brow. "My hearing is quite superior."

She turned back around and groused, "Remind me to run the water the next time I go to the bathroom."

His fingers pressed into her. "If it was just 'girl talk', what has you primed for sex already?"

Sidney huffed. It just wasn't fair. He wouldn't allow her even the smallest measure of privacy—not even her own thoughts. "It was that look on your face, when you came into the room."

"What look?" he asked, while his fingers swirled, encouraging her body to gush more liquid arousal.

Sidney lowered her head and shut her eyes, fighting to hold her train of thought. He wanted to talk. She didn't want him to know how quickly she was losing her mind. "All angry...with your fists clenched...and your jaw tight as a pit bull's."

"Why weren't you afraid?" He pushed deeper and squeezed her ass.

"I was," she moaned. "But I love that...intensity. I imagined all your anger letting loose on me...on my body...when you're inside me."

"You shouldn't tempt me."

His cock brushed her bottom, and Sidney trembled. *Soon, he'd slide inside...* "Why, Navarro? Why shouldn't I tempt your beast?"

"*Damn you.* Leave it alone." His fingers withdrew. Then his body came closer, his thighs sliding against the back of hers, his cock gliding along her moist cunt.

Sidney tilted her hips back, tempting him to press inside. "How am I supposed to understand, if you won't explain why I can't have all of you?"

Navarro pressed his lips to her shoulder and shuddered. "Once, a long time ago. I hurt someone I loved." His cock nudged her portal gently and pushed inside. As he drove forward, crowding into her, he leaned over her back and whispered into her ear. "I killed her."

He'd said it so softly, at first she wasn't sure she'd heard right.

Then her eyes filled with unshed tears. No wonder he held himself aloof, afraid to connect with a woman. She cried for him, even as he thrust into her, stroking her passion higher. She'd heard the pain in his voice and the guilt. "How long...after you were made a vampire...did that happen?" She let the tears fall, but let her body soar.

"One day," he said, his voice hoarse. "She was my wife." He thrust into her harder this time, deeper.

So matter-of-fact, those four words. But she could imagine how long he'd striven for dispassion to say it just like that. She knew he was considered ancient, even for a vampire. How many centuries had he suffered with the knowledge?

Tears dropped to the sheet beneath her, shaken free with each hard stroke. But as sorrowful as her heart felt for the strong, lonely man behind her, her body craved the joining, welcomed his sweet violence. "Fuck me, Navarro! Make it hard...I can take it!"

"*Damn you!*" he said again, only this time, there was an edge of emotion she hadn't heard before.

It was enough to tell Sidney now was the time to push. If she wanted him—and she knew now, she did—she had to punch through his reserve. "Stop!" She reached back and pressed on his thighs. "Stop!"

He halted his thrusts, his breath harsh behind her.

Sidney pulled away and rolled to her back, lifting one leg, then the other, from between his. Then she opened her arms. "Please."

Navarro's expression was stony, but his eyes glittered like hot, dark coals. His hands clenched on his knees.

She knew he debated leaving her now. Reaching deep inside herself, Sidney let her mask of bravado slip, exposing her heart to his gaze. She, who had never expected to love or be loved, offered this man, *this vampire*, everything she was.

How do I tell him I love him? How can I make him believe he can love me? "I'm not fragile, Navarro," she whispered, letting her arms fall to her sides, feeling cold, hoping she hadn't misread his longing.

His stare, so penetrating, so frightening in its intensity, bore into her. He shook his head, and then his jaw tensed. "I won't make promises, Sidney."

She crushed down a stab of disappointment, and said, "I'm not asking for forever."

"But you will."

"I promise you I won't." And she meant it. If tonight was all she had, she wanted to know that for at least these few hours his heart belonged to her.

He closed his eyes and took a deep breath. When he opened them again, his expression softened, and he leaned over her, his thumbs brushing forgotten tears from her cheeks. "Then just for tonight."

She lifted her hands and bracketed his face. "I'd kiss you, but I have pizza breath," she said, gifting him with a watery smile.

The corners of his mouth quirked upward. "I've survived worse." He came down then, stretching over her like a warm blanket.

"I always thought vampires were cold creatures," she murmured, rubbing her cheek into his palm.

"The blood drinking keeps us warm, but we don't retain heat very well."

Sidney knew their conversation wasn't really the important thing happening here. She smiled. "Seems like you'd want a warmer climate."

"A warm partner does just as well."

"Then you're in luck." She wrapped her arms around his back and undulated her hips. "I'm on fire, Navarro. For you," she said, hoping he'd see the love in her eyes.

He kissed her then, his lips caressing hers, his tongue lapping at her closed mouth. "Mmmm. Anchovies. My favorite."

She felt a smile firm his lips against hers, and she opened her eyes and grinned. "I'm awfully glad you didn't assume that was me."

"I have a discerning palate." His expression grew solemn, and his hand threaded through her hair. "Have I mentioned how lovely you are?"

She blinked away more tears at the tenderness in his voice. "Never."

"Then I've been remiss."

"Yes, you have." She smiled. "But you still haven't said it."

"You're lovely." He kissed her lips again. "Forgive me?"

"Make love to me," she whispered.

He nodded and reached for her legs, urging her to wrap herself around him. Then he surged inside, filling her as no other had before or ever would again.

As he stroked inside her, building their passion higher, Sidney pressed kisses to his shoulders and neck and clung tightly to his body. She had a lifetime of loving to squeeze into the remains of this night.

Chapter Ten

ഉ

At the urgent knock on the bedroom door, Navarro pressed a kiss to Sidney's forehead and slipped from the bed. He padded on bare feet to the door and flung it open.

Inigo and Moses crowded through the doorway.

"Master, they're here!" Inigo said, his face lined with worry.

Navarro shared a charged glance with Moses who was armed with a crossbow. He tossed a robe at Sidney. "Get dressed!"

"What's happening?" Sidney asked, rising from the bed to shrug into the robe.

"We have visitors." Navarro stepped into his trousers and strode barefoot to the door. "Moses," he barked over his shoulder, "Get her to the basement!"

"Moses?" He heard the question in Sidney's quavering voice, and regretted he hadn't told her. Now, he didn't have time. He crossed to the doorway and out the door without looking back.

At the bottom of the stairway, Dylan met him and tossed him a stake. "They've disabled the gate and are surrounding the house," he said, his voice clipped as he led the way through the darkened kitchen and out the garden door.

"Viper and Joe?" Navarro asked, keeping his voice pitched low as they crept softly through the grass, staying close to the bricked side of the mansion.

"Circling behind them. I sent Emmy for takeout half an hour ago. It's just the four of us."

"How many did you count?"

"Twelve, and they're loaded for bear — AK-47s and Kevlar."

"Dr. Deats and his friends?"

"Already below."

Navarro hoped Inigo and Moses wasted no time getting Sidney there as well.

He reached the corner and peered around at the front of the house. He made out the shadowy silhouettes of three intruders and signaled to Dylan behind him before darting to the cover of a tree.

When the men passed within feet of him, Navarro rushed out and aimed a kick at the man nearest him, knocking away his weapon. When the vampire swung his fist, Navarro pushed up his arm and shoved one stake deep into the man's armpit, straight into his chest cavity.

While dust and clothing fell to the ground, Navarro was already flying at the next intruder.

A pitched battle, punctuated by bright, staccato bursts of machine gun fire and the enraged howls from the young soldiers, erupted on the grounds. The vampires, encumbered by their flak jackets and heavy armaments, and handicapped further by their full transformations, were quickly picked off by Navarro's much smaller and cunning force.

Already, Navarro could tell the detachment of Zachary's soldiers had been halted from breaching the front door of the house.

As he tackled his next adversary, it niggled the back of his mind that this attack had been too easy to quell. With his knee pressed into the center of the vampire's back, Navarro grasped the webbed harness of his machine gun and yanked it free from the weapon. Then he wound it around the vampire's neck and snapped it, pulling off his head.

Navarro bounded from the sooty pile of clothing, and shouted, "To the house. They've breached the house!"

* * * * *

With the sounds of muffled gunfire in the distance, Sidney chewed a fingernail as Moses turned on the monitors lining the long console, one by one. Moses had given her the Cliffs Notes version of what was going down. Sidney was too scared at the moment to be furious with Navarro—but later, she'd have a bone to chew!

"Damn, he's got some fine equipment!" Moses said, as the yard surrounding the mansion came into view. "He's got infrared cameras pointed at the grounds."

It took a moment for Sidney to understand what she was seeing—thermographic imaged heads suspended above arms and legs, engaged in pockets of fighting with four more recognizably human shapes. "Why can't we see their torsos?"

"Oh my. They must be wearing body armor," Dr. Deats said from behind her.

"Flak jackets, sugar," Moses agreed.

"Why aren't our guys wearing them?"

"Looks like they're doin' fine without 'em," he murmured as one after another of the torso-less figures disappeared from the screens.

Sidney began to breathe easier, and then she noticed monitors with interior views of the house, the living room, entryway, her bedroom—

"Superior hearing, my ass!" she muttered.

The last was a view into the darkened kitchen. Shadows streaked through the room, approaching the basement door, moving so fast their actions blurred.

"Inigo, the cellar door's locked, right?" she asked, horror tightening her throat as one figure paused at the door and pressed something over the keypad lock.

"We got company?" Moses asked, his glance whipping toward her monitor. "Holy shit! Everyone take cover!"

Just as Moses knocked her to the ground and covered her, head to toe, a loud explosion rocked the room.

* * * * *

"Dammit! A fucking diversion!" Dylan shouted from behind him.

Navarro didn't voice his horror. Sidney was standing right in Zachary Powell's path. His heart thudded like a slow drumbeat. He charged through the entry, not bothering with the knob. He knocked the door off its hinges.

When the blast hit, it tossed him backward, into Viper and Dylan who'd been close on his heels.

"The bastard's in the basement!" He scrambled to his feet and ran toward the back of the house.

Viper tackled him in the hallway and held him pinned to the ground. "Thank, man! He's already inside. If you charge into that room, there won't be anybody left."

Navarro rolled with him, fighting to get free, also fighting the monster screaming inside his head for release.

"Think! We can't take him inside that room. We have to wait!"

"But Sidney—"

"From what I've seen, she's a smart girl," Viper said, his voice low and urgent, "but she doesn't stand a chance if we go barreling in there."

"Son of a bitch, get off me!"

"Dammit, Navarro!"

Navarro grew still beneath him. "I understand. We wait. But get the fuck off me."

Viper rose and stepped to the side.

Navarro rolled to his knees, his head low to the floor. This was his fault. His arrogance had placed her in danger.

Goddamn, it couldn't be happening again. He wouldn't lose her! He jumped to his bare feet and ran out the entryway.

They'd meet Zachary in the garden.

* * * * *

Zachary Powell was scarier than his brother. He had the look of a stone-cold killer—movie-star perfect features, empty ice-blue eyes, and a smile filled with jagged, white teeth. His mahogany hair fell to his shoulders—his bare shoulders. Unlike the rest of his team of murderers, he was shirtless.

Sidney, clutching Navarro's silky robe closed, took a precious moment to ponder that anomaly. It wasn't likely *he'd* been woken in the middle of the night.

He tugged open her robe from her clenched fingers, and his gaze raked over her. Then he leaned close and inhaled. "Sidney Coffey, the 'News at Nine' girl. So, you're Navarro's woman. How delicious!"

The way he drawled the last two words had Sidney's stomach lurching.

He nodded to one of the younger vamps with him. "She comes with us."

The young vampire grinned and motioned for her to precede him.

Fighting panic, Sidney closed her robe and cast a desperate glance behind her as she was forced through the wine cellar. There'd be no rescue forthcoming from there—Moses lay in a bloody heap on the floor. The blast had knocked him unconscious.

The three scientists, prodded with machine guns at their backs, followed behind.

With the monitors laying in pieces on the floor, she didn't know whether rescue awaited them above. At the moment, she only hoped that Navarro had survived.

Once up the stairs, Sidney slipped on the tiled kitchen floor. Moisture beneath her feet had her steps sliding. Had Inigo mopped earlier?

No, even in the dark she could see her dark, smeared footprints. She'd cut her feet.

Her captor shoved her from behind, "Keep moving!"

She stumbled into the garden, feeling no relief from the fact the gunfire had ceased, and the sound of distant sirens meant the police were on the way. Her life could be ended by the time they made it to Navarro's estate. She shivered as a gust of cool wind whipped at the edges of her robe.

Ahead, Zachary and his young vampires moved faster, exiting the garden, spreading out as they headed to the far wall — ironically, toward the very place she'd begun her wild adventure.

Sidney placed one leaden foot in front of the other, wishing she could stall, hoping for a glimpse among the trees of one particular tall, dark, shadow.

A blur from the corner of her eye bled from one tree to the next. Sidney's heart beat faster.

Suddenly, rapid movements, panicked shouts, the crack of fists on flesh — so many wonderful occurrences, her mind couldn't fathom what was happening. Only her heart knew it meant — *Navarro*!

He leapt past her and swept her escort away — a groan, a cloud of dark dust, powdering her as it caught by the wind.

Navarro shoved her roughly to the ground, and Sidney stayed, her hands clutching the grass to anchor her there. She closed her eyes tight and prayed, promising a month of Sunday confessions, a hefty tithe — true contrition — if only God would spare Navarro.

And she shut out the sounds of more gunfire, violent curses and blows — and a sharp flap, like a sheet hanging from a clothesline on a windy day.

Huh?

Sidney stared upward as Zachary Powell extended his arms from his sides. The streetlamp from the opposite side of the wall cast him in silhouette as he transformed into his frightful vampire persona—bony facial armor, expanding muscle and sinew—*and wings that sprouted from his back and shoulders and elongated as they unfurled.*

With a roar that sent a chill down her spine colder than any Arctic wind, he flapped his enormous wings and rose in the air. He cast one malevolent glance down to someone behind her, then turned sharply in midair, and flew out of sight of those left gaping from behind the estate's wall.

Hands grasped her waist and pulled her up to stand. She wavered, and an arm slipped around her. She glanced up to meet Navarro's dark gaze. "I'm okay," she said. "The others?"

"Fine." The word was terse, biting. Then he dipped down and swung her up into his arms. "You're bleeding. I smell blood."

"My feet. It's only my feet." She realized her lips trembled, and her jaws chattered together. She'd forgotten it was cold outside.

Dylan O'Hara halted in front of Navarro. "What the fuck was that?"

"Let's get inside. The police are pulling through the gates now."

Sidney lay her head on his shoulder, suddenly so exhausted she hadn't the energy to demand her own explanation for the creature she'd watched ascend into the sky.

When she'd rested, Navarro had a lot of explaining to do.

* * * * *

After Navarro deposited Sidney in her bedroom, leaving a shaken Inigo to care for her cut feet, he gathered with the members of his team in his study—less Viper, whose reputation with the law was just shy of reprehensible. Moses Brown, bruised and bandaged, ran roughshod over the forensics team gathering evidence for their home invasion investigation from the grounds and the basement.

For the moment, disaster had been averted.

"So, are you going to explain to us what we saw?" Dylan asked, his hands cupping a snifter of brandy, sitting in the chair opposite Navarro.

Emmy perched on the arm of his chair beside him, unusually subdued. She still pouted she'd missed all the excitement.

The three scientists, their faces alight with giddy excitement sat on the sofa. Joe Garcia stood before the fire, his back to the room.

Navarro's jaw tightened. "What you saw was a born vampire."

Joe's back stiffened.

Dylan cursed. "Nicky Powell sired his brother—they were both originally human. What you're saying is impossible."

"So it would seem." Navarro steepled his fingers together, and stared at Joe Garcia's back. "I think we've grossly underestimated Zachary's progress on the genetic engineering front. I think he's already tried gene splicing. I believe what we witnessed was a successful test."

"Excuse me," Dr. Deats held up his hand. "As I do have some expertise in this area, may I speak?"

Navarro nodded, giving the man the floor.

"There are many problems with that theory. First, I don't believe anyone currently working in the field has reached the degree of sophistication it would require to accomplish such a feat. While we've spliced genes to create larger, faster-growing salmon and crossed flounder genes with tomatoes so that the tomato can grow at lower temperatures—we've done this at the conception of an organism, not to a fully developed one."

"Vampires are nearly immortal because all our cells regenerate while we sleep," Dylan murmured. "But for there to be any splicing between a born and a sired vampire, doesn't there have to be a DNA donor? Who among us has even met a born vampire?"

Joe Garcia whipped around to face the room. "Fuck! What this means is someone has already breached our security in Vero Beach. Lily had fluids drawn from the sac surrounding our babies in her womb for testing—"

"An amniocentesis test," Emmy said, her eyes growing wide. "It could have been lifted from the doctor's office or the lab. But, dammit, the doctor's one of us. A vampire!"

"For the right price…" Dylan murmured.

"We have to get back," Joe said, his fists clenched, his face a mask of dawning horror. "How fast can your plane be ready?"

Navarro rose. "I'll have Inigo notify the hangar. I have to pack."

* * * * *

Sidney awoke in the darkness, more rested than she had felt in days. She lay in Navarro's guest room, in the bed where she'd discovered a passion she'd never known, where she'd surrendered her heart. At last.

But where was the master vampire who'd accomplished the impossible? She rose, stepping gingerly to the floor, but found her feet weren't the least bit sore. Was that Navarro's doing? Sweet man. She'd been so out of it the night before, she had only hazy memories of his hands stroking over her body while she lay in the warm circle of his arms, her cheek resting on his broad chest as she'd drifted into dreamless sleep.

She found the clothing she'd removed the previous evening folded neatly over a chair and dressed. Then she went in search of the others.

Inigo was in the kitchen, pouring hot water into a teapot. At the sounds of her approach, he slowly raised his head and gave her a kind smile. "It took nearly the whole day to clean up the dust and broken pottery. I was just making tea for you."

"Thanks, Inigo, but I need to find Navarro."

His smile faded, and his eyes softened with concern. "My dear, he's gone."

She stilled. *Gone?* "But, he didn't even say goodbye." As Sidney's heart plummeted, the kitchen door opened.

Moses stepped inside. His mouth stretched into a lopsided smile. "Your vampire's at his hangar, gettin' ready to leave your ass here. Whatcha gonna do about it?"

* * * * *

The tires of Moses' police vehicle squealed as he came to a stop outside Navarro's private airplane hangar. The doors of the hangar stood open, but the bright lighting inside revealed it was empty.

Sidney released her death grip on the dashboard and fumbled for her seat belt.

Moses shoved her hands away and unclipped it. "Now, go!"

"But he's already gone," she said, trying to curb the wail building inside her.

He shook his head. "Man, you got it bad. The plane's over there," he said, gripping the top of her head to turn her gaze.

A small jet sat on the tarmac as a crew with clipboards checked off the preflight list.

Her breath rushed out.

"I'd bet anything he's still in the hangar," Moses said softly.

Sidney swung her gaze back to him. How could she tell a dear friend and lover thank you for helping her throw herself at another man?

Moses' eyes were moist. "All I can say is he better be worth it."

Sidney cupped the side of his face with her palm. "Thanks, Moses, for being my friend."

His smile didn't hide his wince. "Just be happy, sugar."

Sidney dropped her hand and stared at the hangar. "He might just throw me back. He made no promises. And he's never said he loves me." There, she'd voiced her worse fears aloud.

"You'll never know, unless you get your ass inside there, now."

She swung her gaze back to him. "Will you wait for me, just in case?"

"He won't throw you back." His eyes were soft as melted chocolate. "But I'll wait." He reached across her and opened her door. "Now, go!"

She smiled and stepped out of the sedan, and walked on shaking legs to the hangar. Once she passed the door, she blinked at the brightness, but followed the low murmur of masculine voices to an office at the side of the building.

Emmy O'Hara saw her first, and a pleased smile curved her lips. "Knew he was forgetting something," she murmured.

The room went silent as all gazes turned to Sidney.

Her cheeks warmed under their stares. How embarrassing! Would everyone be there to witness his brush-off? Sidney struggled for a moment, fighting the panic fluttering in her belly.

Then Dylan and Joe stepped to the side, and Navarro appeared in her line of vision. Tall, dark and dead — dressed in that killer leather trench coat. She remembered how he'd left her inside his big old house without so much as a goodbye and lifted her chin. "Mister, you still owe me a story."

"It's time to board the plane," he said, his gaze never leaving hers.

The room emptied around them in moments, and the office door shut quietly behind them.

Sidney wished she had an ounce of Navarro's eerily accurate intuition. Then she'd know whether that dark, broody stare meant he was irritated with her being there, or if he was struggling for just the right words—just like she was. "Why didn't you tell me you were leaving?" she asked, knowing the question revealed her hurt.

"I wanted you safe. I thought it best."

"Did you think I'd make a scene? Beg you to take me with you? If you recall, I told you I had no expectations—and we didn't promise each other anything." But she'd had hopes. Hopes that were crumbling into dust the longer she stood there, feeling foolish and knowing she wore her disappointment on her face. "It just wasn't very polite."

"I'm sorry."

Sidney turned from his piercing gaze and stared out the glassed window on the office door. "So that's your polite? Apology accepted," she whispered and reached for the doorknob.

The air whooshed behind her, and Navarro's body pressed her to the door. "I wanted you safe," he said, his voice a ragged whisper in her ear. "My arrogance almost got you killed."

"Navarro," she moaned and leaned into him. "I'm not fragile, and there are never any guarantees in this life." She turned in his arms and looked up, letting him see the love and tears filling her eyes. "I'm not asking for forever—I just don't want to miss '*Now*' with you." *Just tell me you love me!*

His arms encircled her, and he leaned down to rest his forehead against hers. "I do love you."

Sidney brought her head back, smacking it against the door. She stared at him for a long moment, and then narrowed her eyes. "You know what I'm thinking!"

Navarro's lips quirked. "It's a talent I have. Part of why I secluded myself for so many years. People have very noisy minds. I've been learning to shut out their voices."

"But not mine?"

"I wanted to hear your thoughts."

She pushed at his chest until he stepped back. "So you already knew I was falling in love with you, and you still left me like that?"

"I wanted you sa —"

She waved her hand. "I already heard that part." Sidney raked her hair with her hand. "I bet you've been inside my head from the start."

"Not from the start — I wasn't that interested at first."

She leveled a killing glare his way, and didn't miss the mirth twitching his lips. "What? I'm not pretty enough?"

"That's not it. My attraction grew slowly. It wasn't until I decided to have you —"

"You decided?" Sidney felt like screaming. "You conceited assho —"

Navarro grabbed her and cupped her chin, forcing her face up. "I am that. But I love you, Sidney P. Coffey. But right now, I have a plane to catch." His mouth crashed down on hers.

Sidney leaned into his body, wrapping her arms around him, drowning in his kiss. *No way are you getting on that plane without me!* She rubbed against him, chest to mons. *I'm on fire for you, Navarro.*

He broke the kiss. "The flight's five hours."

She reached for his belt and unbuckled it, all the while pressing kisses to his neck. *Too long, gotta have you now!*

Navarro backed up to the desk dragging her with him. When he sat on the edge, he hauled her into his arms. "They'll see us through the glass."

Sidney straddled his hips and shoved his coat off his shoulders, sealing his mouth with hers. *Won't take a minute. Promise! They won't even have time to wonder what we're doing.*

When he tried to break the kiss to reply, her mouth smiled against his. *Look who's got the advantage now!*

Laughter shook his chest, and he gripped her hair to pull her back. "I've changed my mind. You're going with me."

Sidney smiled, and a warmth she could only attribute to a happy heart filled her chest. "Too late—I already made up my mind to go. It's my decision."

"You're a stubborn woman."

"My middle name doesn't start with a 'P' for nothing."

"What is your middle name?"

Sidney wrinkled her nose. "Promise not to laugh?"

"No."

"Persephone."

Navarro's wicked grin told her he hadn't missed the irony that she'd been named for the woman Hades had held a prisoner in his dark realm until she agreed to be his wife.

Sidney pushed up his shirt, but his hand closed over hers. "We really do have to leave now."

She raised an eyebrow. *You're really gonna make me wait?*

"The loo is quite spacious, love."

Mile High Club, here I come!

As Sidney trotted beside Navarro across the tarmac to the waiting plane, she said, "That was one helluva weekend you gave me. But I'm reminded I don't know a thing about your past."

"We have forever to learn each other's dark secrets."

"My life will take a minute."

"Mine won't. I was a Crusader…"

Headlights blinked, and Sidney glanced over her shoulder. She gave Moses a wave, and said a little prayer that he'd find the same happiness she had now with Navarro.

Navarro tucked her hand in the crook of his elbow. "Any regrets?"

As she met his dark, glittering gaze, Sidney shook her head and smiled. "I'm gonna cover the story of the millennium. What more could a girl ask for?" *Bet that made you nervous, huh?*

Navarro sighed. "You're really going to enjoy torturing me with my gift, aren't you?"

As she climbed the steps, she couldn't resist a little more teasing. "How long do you think it will take for the captain turn off the seat belt sign?" *How many ways can I torture you until then? Shall I tell you what I plan to do to you with my mouth?*

"We might have to share a seat," he murmured, a wicked hand caressing her bottom.

"A vampire with an imagination," she replied, breathless.

"A vampire with a raging—"

Navarro!

SILVER BULLET

୬

Trademarks Acknowledgement

ଞ

The author acknowledges the trademarked status and trademark owners of the following wordmarks mentioned in this work of fiction:

Lamaze: Lamaze International, Inc.

Taser: Taser International, Inc.

Chapter One

ॐ

He met her at the water's edge as she returned from her solitary walk, her bare feet sand-encrusted and her steps slow and measured. One hand pressed the small of her back—a disquieting gesture that caused him no small amount of alarm. The purple of dusk was reflected in the circles beneath her beautiful brown eyes.

"Darcy-love, why didn't you wait?" Quentin Albermarle slipped his arm around his wife's slender back, not surprised when she leaned into him to share her burden.

"You wouldn't have enjoyed yourself." She lifted her head to stare into his eyes, one brow arching in amusement. "I wanted to watch the sunset."

Her teasing smile warmed his soul. How had he lived before knowing her? Now, he couldn't remember a night that didn't begin and end with her. "Well, you have me there," he said softly. "Sunset's not something I'd find the least bit pleasant." He turned her in his arms and settled his chin on the top of her head as his hands circled her stretched-taut belly. "Still, I'd prefer it if someone accompanied you when I can't be here. It isn't safe," he admonished her lazily, enjoying the breeze that lifted her dark hair to float against his chest and the pleasure of her warm body aligned with his. "It's not like we haven't enough hirelings to spare one for your walks."

"I wanted a little alone time and it was light when I started." She shrugged. "I guess I'm walking a little slow these days."

Quentin's jaw clenched at the familiar fear that struck him. Her ordeal wouldn't be something he could conquer for her. And he suspected the Lamaze classes he'd endured at her insistence were as much for his benefit as hers.

Taking a deep breath, he let the air hiss between his teeth and watched the slim gold line that rimmed the navy sea blink out. "More reason to stay inside The Compound, don't you think?"

"The walk was nice. I can't get too flabby or I'll have hell getting back in shape for work."

Quentin had his own thoughts about how she looked— her features were a little less lean, but softer and more feminine. He also had rather strong thoughts about whether she should ever return to the police force. But there was time for that discussion later. "You're beautiful and wearing my favorite shade of blue."

Darcy looked down at her sky-blue sundress and snorted. "You know darn well it's the color of your eyes."

"I know. Seeing you in it makes me feel like my ownership's stamped all over you."

"I'm wearing your colors, hmmm? You are a primitive man at heart. I like that."

"And feeling downright primal at the moment. I didn't like not finding you beside me when I woke," he let his words rumble, then admitted the truth, "I was worried."

"I'm sorry. I was restless waiting for you to wake from your beauty rest. Besides, I only have to worry about the things that go bump in the night, right?"

He nuzzled her neck, breathing in her fragrance—her mother's raspberry soap and her own feminine musk. "Were-bastards don't fry in the sunshine," he growled, knowing his comment would get a rise out of her.

"Hush!" she said, smacking his hand. "No name-calling. Remember, Max is my friend."

He smiled into her hair and lightly squeezed her belly. The child within complained and delivered a solid kick just beneath his hand. "I was thinking of dear old Max when I said it."

"You really need to learn to get along with him. I know he's a little intense, what with him hating vamps in general, but Pia has him leashed."

"That's what has me worried. That walking disaster paired with a werewolf—it's a wonder she's not hacking up hairballs."

"Wrong species." She giggled. A lovely tinkling sound, all the more precious because she didn't do it often.

He snorted. "Just plain wrong, if you ask me."

Darcy cleared her throat. "Speaking of which, when's the plane coming in?"

"It'll touch down in about fifteen minutes. Then wait until Navarro gets a look at our new pet. Don't be surprised if we see fur flying."

She tilted back her head to look into his eyes, her expression a little pinched. "This Navarro…is he a good guy?"

Quentin shrugged. "He's one of us."

Her eyebrows rose. "Oh, and that's supposed to be reassuring?"

"I'm a good guy," Quentin said softly. "Trust me to make sure introductions are handled appropriately."

"The way you say that—all British and proper…" She shivered. "…does things to me." Then her expression grew serious. "All right, Quentin, I'll trust you so long as you make sure he gives Max a fair chance to prove he's part of the team."

Quentin snorted again.

"Now you have to admit the guy's been a big help tracking the remnants of that rabid wolf pack."

Quentin wasn't ready to give the were any credit. "Takes a dog to sniff another out," he mumbled.

Her nose wrinkled. "You're so prejudiced."

"I have reason to be." Then wishing to end a conversation that caused her distress, he kissed her lips.

With a sigh, she surrendered her body, leaning more heavily against him. Her mouth opened beneath his, and his tongue lapped inside. She returned soft loving strokes that had him hard as a doorknob in seconds.

He dragged away his mouth, glad the breeze off the ocean was whipping up enough to cool his overheated skin. "Witch," he whispered.

"What did I do?" she asked, wide-eyed.

The curve of her lips told him she felt his frustration. He narrowed his gaze. "Just you wait…"

"Won't be long now." She rubbed her bottom against his arousal.

What could a vampire do to stop the woman he loves from teasing him into full-fanged arousal? He dragged his teeth along the side of her throat in a silent warning to behave.

"And that's supposed to scare me?" Soft laughter shook her body. "You shouldn't use the same tactic to make me horny."

His breath gusted in a short laugh. "Bugger, is that the problem?"

"Someday you're going to tell me what it is you have against weres." She turned in his arms and stared up, moonlight reflecting in her eyes. "And I should be a little angry about the way you always use sex·to change the conversation."

With her large belly between them, Quentin's lips twitched. "This from the woman who's discovered the ultimate distraction method of digital manipulation—"

Darcy pressed her finger against his lips to halt his words. "You're not doing it again."

Quentin raised his eyebrows in question.

"Changing the subject." She huffed a long sigh. "I'm worried about Max meeting Navarro. We're only just getting used to the fact he's Lycan, and now Navarro's coming from the Northwest council because of this problem with another Powell brother. Things are happening too fast."

Quentin glared. He opened his mouth to give her a glib answer, but her finger mashed his lips.

"What, you have something to say?" Her finger swirled on his lips then lingered a moment until he dutifully kissed the tip.

When she withdrew it, he said, "Is the problem that you think Navarro won't listen, or that Max is going to misbehave?"

Darcy's brows drew together. "Both."

He gave an exaggerated sigh. "You're going to make me intervene on his behalf, aren't you?" *Damn!* He wished she didn't care so much about the wolf.

"Maybe. Is Navarro really going to give him a fair shake, or will he do what's expedient? I mean, I know vamps and weres have this long history of warfare between the species."

"Navarro isn't one to make 'expedient' decisions. Hell, I'd second him if he did in this case. But Navarro's...deep, likes to consider things before he acts. Now if it were up to me..."

"I know, you'd have poor Max's were-head mounted on the wall."

"Poor Max?" Quentin grinned. He couldn't help it. The thought of Max's head glowering above the mantel cheered him considerably. But Darcy's darkening expression had him saying, "You think I'd want that ugly mug of his preserved?"

"Quentin! This isn't funny. I'm scared." The frown still marring her brow, Darcy played with a button on the front of his shirt. "I don't get why you're so set against him."

"I have my reasons," he said, folding her upper body closer to his chest.

139

"Well, that certainly fills in the blanks." Her nose nuzzled his neck, and she sighed. "You know, it's not fair that you have this long past I don't know anything about."

"Ask me anything," he said, his voice gruff. "I'll tell you what I can."

She leaned away. "Really?"

Quentin hadn't realized how important the issue was until her expression softened and her eyes grew moist. He cupped her face between his palms. "I'm yours, Darcy," he whispered fiercely, "body, soul and endless history. I'll bore you to tears with the retelling of all the mundane facts of my misspent youth."

Despite the moisture welling in her eyes, Darcy's lips curved in a wry smile. "I know I won't be bored. Just finding out how you first met Dylan will likely be enough to satisfy my curiosity for weeks." A shadow crossed her face. "But not now. I'm a little tired."

Downplaying his worry, he smiled. "Come rest a while with me?"

"You just got out of bed."

He waggled his eyebrows. "I'll hold you."

"You know what that usually leads to," Darcy said, arching a brow.

"Have I been too demanding?" he asked, his tone mild, knowing she'd rise once again to the bait.

"Not at all, as you damn well know." She swatted his chest with her open palm. "I'm frustrated as hell!"

He leaned toward her and nuzzled her ear. "Haven't I pleased you?" he growled.

Her breath hitched, and she groaned. "You know you have. Your mouth makes me crazy—the fact my belly's so big I can't watch you drives me even crazier. But I want to please you, too."

"Soon enough, love," he said, wishing he had her turned so he could rub his aching cock against her bottom for relief. As it was, her belly prevented any contact. "This never-ending erection is my penance."

"Why do you owe a penance?"

He shuttered his expression from her knowing glance.

But she was too attuned to his moods. Her head tilted and she smoothed a hand over his cheek. "I know it's hard for you. This isn't your child. I don't blame you a bit for being resentful."

He closed his eyes. "This child will be ours in every way except its conception." He meant it. He really did.

"I know that." She touched his forehead. "You know that." Then she placed her hand on his chest. "But your heart doesn't. Don't feel guilty about the way you feel." Her eyes shone with love and acceptance.

Funny, sometimes he thought he could see his whole world in her eyes.

"Everything will be all right," she said softly. "You'll see."

He turned his head and placed a kiss in her palm, too overcome for the moment to reply.

Another movement in her belly distracted him. This time it felt like the baby rolled inside her.

Darcy grimaced and moaned softly.

"Is something wrong?"

"My back aches, and I've been having...twinges."

His heart stilled. "Is it the baby? Is it coming?"

"I think so."

"You think so?" he asked, panic rising to constrict his throat. "How long have you known?"

"Since mid-afternoon—I thought a walk might help quicken this whole thing."

141

"You knew you were in labor and you went for a walk *alone*?" This time he shouted.

"Uh-huh," Darcy admitted, a smug little smile tilting one side of her mouth. That expression looked familiar.

"Fucking hell!" *I'm in a panic — and she's smirking at me!* "Quick," he said, turning her to walk back to The Compound, "we need to get you to the hospital."

Darcy laughed and grabbed for his hand. "There's no rush. I've been timing the contractions."

"Timing the…contractions?" he parroted, his voice rising. "That's what I've been feeling? I thought the baby was kicking wobblers."

Another grimace crossed Darcy's face.

Quentin cursed beneath his breath. Through letting her call the shots, he lifted her into his arms and strode toward The Compound. "Not another word, ridiculous woman."

As he approached the gate, the floodlights that were set to detect motion failed to light. He slowed his steps, the hair lifting on the back of his neck.

Darcy stiffened in his arms.

"I know," he whispered, noting the lack of human guards around the perimeter. "Something's wrong."

"Put me down."

He did and quickly shoved her toward deep foliage next to the wall. "Wait here."

"Like hell!" she hissed. "What if the trouble's out here? Vamps and weres both have a great sense of smell."

"All right," he said in a clipped tone, damning himself for his carelessness. With the wind coming off the ocean, he'd found no scent to give him warning. He punched the security code on the touch pad. The lock on the gate released with a soft snick. He slipped through and held it open for Darcy.

Once inside the wall, he noted the stillness — no hint of the guards' movements, no distant murmurs of conversation. He sniffed the air and froze, finding the scent he feared most.

Wolves!

"Damn him to hell!" he gritted out, rage already hardening his body.

"Who?" Darcy said, clutching his arm.

"Our pet!" he spat. "He's brought friends."

With Darcy matching his steps behind him, Quentin crept into the courtyard, past the flowering bougainvillea and palms, past the edge of the tiled patio to peer inside the darkened living room.

Darcy shouldered her way into position beside him. "We have wolves — plural — in The Compound?"

"Stay behind me."

"But Lily," she said, a note of fear entering her voice, "they're here for Lily. We have to get to her."

"Once in the house, you will run straight for the panic room. Today, you're not a cop, Darcy. I'll take care of Lily."

"All right, but Quentin," she said, tugging at his sleeve, "this isn't Max's doing."

"Then why didn't he sound the alarm? He and Pia are supposed to be the watch tonight."

"I don't know. But I do know he couldn't do this. He wouldn't betray us."

"Be quiet now, love. Remember what I said. Get to the panic room." He opened the door and let Darcy slip past him to make an awkward dash for the stairway. The panic room was along the upper corridor. He followed behind her, facing the opposite direction, waiting for a foe to charge up the stairs and cursing the fact he hadn't brought a weapon other than the silver-bladed knife strapped to his ankle.

What had he been thinking? The weres in the area appeared to be conquered. The few stragglers of the pack that

143

had wreaked havoc in Vero Beach had been easy to find — they'd left bloody trails in their wake.

In retrospect, they'd been too easy to find.

As Quentin braced himself for the fight of his life, his mind raced. Where were the human guards? He detected no scent of death in the air. And what of Pia and Max? If Max wasn't responsible for the breach in security, then who was?

A gasp erupted behind him, and he whirled to see three weres in varying forms of transformation creeping down the hallway toward them.

As he faced them, deep-throated snarls erupted from the wolves.

The newly installed panic room lay just beyond the three. Quentin guessed they had been about to enter, so at least he knew where Lily was.

He pushed past Darcy and shoved her against the wall, bending at the last moment to slide his knife from beneath his pant leg. "Watch for your break," he shouted.

Still crouched low, he summoned the beast inside, letting his body bulk out with just enough of the monster to even up the odds. When his shirt strained across his shoulders, he lunged at the closest of the wolves — a brindle bastard, fully transformed and nearly foaming at the mouth.

They met in midair. Quentin rolled with him, coming up on his feet after slashing deep into the wolf's neck. The next, a dark-furred cur, caught him from behind and knocked him to the ground.

Darcy shouted and a shot rang out.

Quentin couldn't look back. He kicked backward and grabbed for the muzzle locked around the top of his right shoulder. Adrenaline and rage numbed him to the pain of teeth sinking deep into muscle.

The knife traded hands, and Quentin stabbed over his shoulder, hoping to spear eyes. When the wolf broke his hold with a screeching whine, Quentin came to his knees and slammed the wolf clinging to his back against the wall, at the same time digging his right elbow into a vulnerable belly. With the stunned creature wriggling to come to its paws, Quentin slammed the blood-slick knife in its chest.

With the red haze of rage threatening to steal his intellect, Quentin pitched through the bedroom door, ready to take the next foe.

The sight that met his eyes brought a howl of pain and denial. Before the closed panic room door, Darcy lay beneath the bloody claws of a man-wolf, a gaping maw in her belly, her arms and hands nearly shredded. A gun lay on the ground beyond her feet. Darcy hadn't gone on her walk without backup after all.

Quentin's heart screamed and he crouched, ready to spring at the wolf to tear its head from its shoulders, when he saw the slightest movement of Darcy's lips.

Thank God! She still lived.

The monster's lips pulled back in an unholy grin and he held up a red, wriggling baby, its placental cord dangling from its round belly.

Quentin had only a moment to note Darcy's child was a boy with a thick cap of dark curls.

Then the creature placed the child in his mouth and completed his transformation to wolf, dropping on all fours to the floor.

The dark wolf approached him and brushed boldly past.

Quentin clenched his fists and let him pass, fighting the encroaching haze—Darcy lived. The baby was likely already infected by the bite Darcy had received, and if not, it soon would be from the saliva of the wolf using it as a hostage for safe passage out of The Compound. The baby was lost whether the beast ate it or not.

But Darcy wasn't—yet. And while she had breath, there was still a chance to save her.

He crossed the room and knelt beside her, taking her head into his lap, cupping her face between shaking palms.

Darcy's eyes fluttered open. "Quentin....the baby," she whispered, her voice thin, her breath labored. "Save the baby."

"I will, love," he lied and bent to end her life.

Chapter Two

∽

Dylan O'Hara contemplated the many ways he intended to make his wife pay for her interminable teasing throughout the long flight from Seattle. Her lush body, encased in a red pantsuit that hugged every sweet curve, was a flag to his snorting bull. The woman had squandered their one opportunity for a quickie when their companions had sequestered themselves in other parts of the plane. She wasn't near enough for him to give her the spanking she deserved.

At the moment, Emmy's lush mouth curved in wicked delight as she pressed her ear to the plane's bathroom door.

"For fuck's sake, Em, give them some privacy," Dylan said, knowing there wasn't a snowball's chance in hell she'd obey, and wishing he had the lack of decorum to join her. Curiosity about the old Master's new amour was nearly eating him alive. He'd always thought Navarro was strictly asexual.

"Shhh!" his wife whispered, a finger to her lips. "There's a whole lot of moaning goin' on in there." Emmy cupped her ear and bent closer. "Wait, she's doing the please-oh-please thing. Oh! Sidney just told him to bang her like a drum!"

Dylan pressed his lips together to prevent a grin—he shouldn't give the minx any further encouragement, but he couldn't resist. "And what was his reply?" he asked, his voice strained with suppressed amusement.

"He said he'll give her the whole damn percussion section if she'll just be quiet." She pressed her ear close again and snickered. "God, I wonder if I'm ever that needy-sounding when we're doing it. It's kinda embarrassing. Oh! Now she's doing the praying thing. Must be getting close."

Dylan grinned. Emmy was a howler, and her eavesdropping was arousing her—her cheeks flushed a lovely rose, her breaths coming faster.

Her eyes widened like saucers.

"What?"

"He told her to shut up or he'd give her mouth something to chew on for a while."

Dylan snorted. "Good man! Only thing that works."

Emmy giggled again, and then leapt back when the door beneath her cheek rattled with an insistent pounding from the other side.

Dylan chuckled and held out his hand. "Em, time to leave them be."

His wife wrinkled her nose. "Spoilsport."

"You know, Navarro probably knows exactly what you were doing."

"Impossible. I was quiet as a mouse."

Dylan rolled his eyes and didn't bother to remind her that she'd just given him a blow-by-blow commentary that grew louder the more excited she'd gotten. So loud a vamp's superior hearing wasn't needed. "Be that as it may, Navarro doesn't need to hear you with his ears, love."

Emmy's gaze landed on him, startlement causing her to pout her lips. "What do you mean?"

"He's got a little something more than the average vamp in the way of powers."

"Oh? You mean something besides harnessing an inner demon with superhuman strength, like me?"

He patted his knee, knowing her curiosity was stronger than her sense of self-preservation. When she perched on his lap, he said, "Yeah, he can enter another person's mind and see what they see and *hear* their thoughts."

"Really? How come he's so special?" she asked, her voice breathy as he lifted the blonde hair from her neck for him to nibble.

"He's old as Methuselah, sweetheart. The older we vamps get, the more any latent talents we possessed as humans emerge and strengthen." He shifted her closer and slipped a hand between her thighs.

"So, you're like *ancient*. What superpower do you have?"

Dylan waggled his eyebrows. "I was counted as a right whore when I was a youngster."

"Oh, so your forte is sex?" She grinned and encircled his shoulders with her arms.

"Didn't you get lucky?"

"Not yet," she said, as she snuggled on his lap, squirming on his aching cock. "What do you suppose I'll get?" she asked, walking her fingers up his chest.

He pulsed his hips. "One guess."

She pouted her lips again, knowing it drove him crazy. "No, I mean in the way of special powers."

He grimaced. "Lord, with your talent for gab, I'll have to keep that mouth of yours occupied twenty-four-seven." He cupped the back of her head, bringing her closer for a kiss.

Her resistance was only for show — to remind him who was really doing the seducing here.

Dylan recognized the glint in Emmy's eyes and wondered whether the aft coat closet had enough room to play her favorite game — "Hide the Sausage".

Just as his mouth closed on hers, the door to the captain's cabin slammed.

Emmy drew back, and they both turned toward Joe Garcia as he barreled out — his jaw straining, his hands clenched at his side, his eyes wild and hard as obsidian.

Dylan set Emmy on the seat beside him and stood. "What's happened?"

Joe's chest heaved and his dark eyes lightened to gold as he attempted to curb his inner demon.

Dylan grabbed his arm. "Joe!"

The younger vamp's lips thinned. "The hangar team just called to give us a heads-up—we've got trouble at The Compound."

* * * * *

Navarro crept toward the outer wall of The Compound with Joe Garcia and Emmy and Dylan O'Hara at his back. They'd followed the musty scent of wolf from a point beyond the highway where the wolves had been dropped, down the long drive to the wall that surrounded The Compound, and right up to the front gate.

"How the hell did they get through this gate?" Dylan whispered, his hands gripping the iron spokes. "Not only is it supposed to be guarded, you need electronic key access."

"Which isn't working at the moment," Joe snarled.

"I'm worried about the security force," Emmy said, wringing her hands.

Navarro searched the air for scent, ignoring the overpowering lupine stench. "I don't smell blood."

Dylan's expression hardened. "An inside job?"

Joe's jaw tightened. "Fuck Max! I'll kill him myself."

A ragged howl—vampire, not lycan—erupted from within.

"Inside now," Navarro said. Gathering tension in his muscles, he crouched low before leaping to the top of the thick curtain wall and down to the ground on the other side.

The others landed beside him, bodies and faces honing with vampiric bloodlust, teeth bared.

Navarro pointed to his eyes then at Emmy and Dylan, indicating they should circle the house to search. Joe, he kept behind him, determined to rein in the young vampire's rage.

Joe would be no help to his wife Lily, still inside The Compound, if he let his inner beast surface now.

Navarro was glad his woman, Sidney, was still with the limousine parked farther down the road along with the three geneticists they'd brought from Seattle. That he'd had to give the limo driver orders to sit on her if she tried to follow filled him with grim amusement. Sidney might try to beg, cajole, threaten or lie to get her way, but the driver wouldn't risk displeasing a Master, no matter how tempting the sexy little baggage could be.

He could well imagine how Joe felt at the moment, wondering whether his woman still lived. Only last night, Sidney had been in Zachary Powell's grasp, with the winged vamp ready to make a meal of her. Navarro drew in a deep steadying breath and focused on the task before them, stretching out his mind to search the grounds for an animal's intellect...but finding nothing.

Along the outer walkway encircling the house, one door stood ajar. Navarro and Joe slipped through it, following the scent-trail of wolf through the room, the foyer, and up the long curved staircase.

At the top of the stairs, Navarro found the remains of two men sprawled on the landing, wolf-stink clinging to their naked skin, stab wounds leaking blood sluggishly into the carpet.

Joe shoved him from behind. "Lily!" His whisper was harsh.

Navarro pushed him back and entered the bedroom first, finding at last the tangy musk of human blood—a lot of it.

On the floor lay a woman, her stomach opened, gray entrails visible inside a gaping wound. Blood seeped steadily, darkening her blue dress. Her face was ashen, her features pale and lifeless. Quentin Albermarle crouched over her, draining what was left of her life, his harsh breaths punctuating each long draw.

So this was Quentin's new wife. Navarro shuddered. The agony etched on the other vampire's face and the destruction of a young, vital human, who minutes ago had been filled with the promise of new life, produced a heavy ache in the center of his chest.

Pushing back feelings that threatened to overwhelm him, Navarro's gaze fell on the woman's wounds, the ragged tears made by claws and the deeper gouges that could only indicate a wolf's bite. "Quentin, you must let her go."

The golden-haired vampire lifted his face, a look of pure hatred twisting his features. "Try to stop me and I'll kill you! Get out!" he snarled, lisping a bit around his elongated fangs. He raised his wrist to his mouth and slashed it open with his teeth. Then he held it above the dying woman's slackened mouth and let his blood drip onto her tongue.

"Sweet Jesus!" Joe jostled past Navarro and stared down at the couple, his body trembling. "Darcy," he said, his cry anguished.

Quentin's face hardened, and his shoulders bunched. His jaws opened wide around a roar as his gaze narrowed on Joe.

Navarro found the tension between the two vamps telling. So despite their seeming truce, not all issues were resolved between the two vampires regarding Quentin's wife. Understanding Joe's grief for the loss of his child and soon his former lover, nevertheless Navarro grasped Joe's shoulder to hold him back.

Joe tried to shrug off his hand and fisted his own at his sides. He closed his eyes and turned. "Lily," he whispered. "I have to go to Lily."

Navarro released him and took a step back.

Joe skirted Quentin and his woman and ran to the metal door beyond, pounding on it. "Lily, are you in there?" he shouted, his voice thickening with the need to fully transform.

With emotions running thick and thoughts whirling and clashing like Hell's demons, Navarro fought the urge to release his own inner beast. He could commiserate with their pain, but he couldn't permit it to suffocate him. *Focus!* He fought the bloodlust and the red haze receded.

"Joe?" a woman's voice, broken and thick with emotion, sounded from the speaker next to the door.

Joe slumped against the metal. "Baby, are you okay?"

"I'm fine. What about Darcy? I can't see her on the monitor. Joe, what's happened to Darcy?"

Joe's gaze fell on the dying woman, and his eyes filled. "Stay inside until it's safe. Don't open the door until I tell you."

"Joe!" she cried out.

Navarro grabbed his arm. "Sweep the house. Make sure there aren't any more cur-dogs inside." Best to keep him busy venting his rage in a productive way—and keep him away from Quentin.

Joe's shoulders bunched, a refusal on his lips, and his gaze fell on Darcy one last time. Then he nodded and left the room.

Alone with Quentin and his dying wife, Navarro hesitated. Since he'd opened his heart's door to Sidney, sentiment flooded in, bringing overpowering surges of anger and grief. He felt awkward, even inadequate, but needed to offer comfort, while at the same time issuing a command that would devastate one of only two men on the planet he considered friends.

He knelt beside Quentin and placed his hand on the other vampire's shoulder. "Quentin, you have to let her go. She was bitten by a wolf."

Quentin reared back his head and roared, his face crackling as his vampire mask presented fully. He snarled, but kept his hand poised above the woman's unmoving lips.

Navarro understood his pain, but he also understood the woman's soul was already gone—stolen by a wolf's bite. If she were turned to a vampire now, her bloodlust would be uncontrollable. If she lived.

Blood pooled in her mouth and she had yet to swallow.

Navarro's jaw clenched at the gruesome evidence of her suffering. For so long he'd kept himself apart from others, building a wall around his heart. Their thoughts, their pain, even their joys had made him writhe inside. Over time, his heart had grown cold—and blissfully inured. Until Sidney. She had changed all that in just a few days. What would he do if he were faced with the same gut-wrenching decision?

Perhaps he had only to bide his time and let Quentin come to the realization his woman was lost to him. Her body was likely too damaged to withstand the transformation anyway.

He rose and backed away, then closed the door behind him to shut out the sounds of Quentin's anguished breaths as he sobbed, his lifeblood seeping away as surely as Darcy Albermarle's humanity.

* * * * *

The wolf rushed through the open door, into the darkened room beyond, its claws clattering on the tiled floor.

Woman! Mate! It had to find her.

Following wolf scent and the musty odor of blood, it sped through the room and up the curved staircase toward the light beckoning at the top.

Heedless of any danger, the wolf charged upward, stretching its limbs to leap several steps at a time in its desperation to find her—the slim, dark-haired one.

At the top of the stairs, the wolf came to a halt, hackles rising on shoulders and back at the smell of blood—wolf blood. Bodies stretched on the floor before it, blood soaking the carpet beneath its paws. But what gave the animal pause were the looming, growling figures that faced it, standing above the corpses.

Enemy! Danger breathed in their combined rage.

The wolf started forward, first left then right, retreat being impossible because the dark-haired woman was nearby and sobbing. The sounds of her harsh cries brought up a howl that echoed in the narrow hallway.

The wolf heard the sounds the men made, harsh and loud, echoing in the hallway, but didn't comprehend, only recognized the hatred tightening the voice of the nearest manlike creature.

Another sob drew its attention, just as the nearest foe leapt, wrapping powerful arms around the wolf's throat—so tight it couldn't breathe. It wriggled and jerked, gnashing teeth, but the man held fast to the wolf while another drew a shining rope over its muzzle.

Another spate of harsh sounds and a moment later, a jolt knocked the breath from its body and brought the wolf to its haunches, leaving it quivering in the aftermath. Still, it fought to stand.

Another jolt, this time searing in its ferocity left the wolf powerless, its tongue lolling from between its jaws. Blackness encroached, and in the moment before it surrendered, the wolf knew itself trapped.

* * * * *

Max Weir awoke slowly, every muscle in his body aching. He rolled from his back onto his knees, and rested his forehead on the floor for a moment to recover from the change of equilibrium, shocked his whole body trembled from the effort.

Something had kicked the shit out of him.

When he lifted his head to see, he felt a sharp tug and the bite of metal around his neck.

Instinct kicked in and he roared, tucking in his head to lunge against the chain. When he failed to budge it, he reached deep inside for the strength to transform.

"Turn, and we'll kill you where you sit." The voice, soft and deadly with slight European inflections, was one he didn't recognize. But Max did recognize the steel beneath the words and resisted the primal urge to let loose his inner beast on his captors.

Still woozy and struggling to regain his full intellect, Max shook his head experimentally and realized it wasn't one leash, but two, pulling in opposite directions to keep him lowered to the floor.

Again, Max raised his head, slowly this time, and blinked against the bright light, bringing focus to his eyes. He was in the living room of The Compound, in the very center where they'd cleared away the furniture. He knelt on the beige carpet, still naked after his latest chase.

A sideways glance revealed Dylan and Joe held the ends of his chains wrapped around their fists, their expressions set and lethal. His gut twisted, betrayal tasting bitter after all he'd done to keep his spot on the Special Unit following the revelation of his true, *were* nature.

Max's lips curled, baring his teeth. *Show the bastards the feral beast.*

"I've no patience for posturing."

Again that damnable voice. Max slowly lifted his head to stare at the vamp who could only be Navarro, the Master from the Northwest Council.

He sat in a chair facing Max. His dark sloe eyes narrowed as he stared.

"Why am I chained?" Max asked, not surprised to find his voice hoarse, his throat raw. He recalled a struggle and choking.

"The more appropriate question would be why are you still living?" Navarro asked, no hint of his thoughts in his even tone.

Unable to glance around, Max sniffed to determine if others watched, but found no more nearby scents. Only the odor of death, overlaid with the musk of several wolves. Somewhere distant in the house. "They got inside The Compound?"

"Don't give me a ration of shit, *were*," Joe shouted, jerking on his chain.

"You knew they were close?" Dylan asked from the end of his chain, his voice soft, but menacing.

Max gritted his teeth, fighting for breath as the metal constricted around his throat. "I caught their scent and followed them — *outside* the gate."

"Why didn't you radio to the others and sound the alert?" Joe jerked the chain again.

"Bastard!" Max spat. "Commo was out."

"What did you do with the guards?" Joe asked, with another tug.

Max gasped. If he ever got free, he'd tear his *buddy* a new asshole. "Not a fucking thing... Didn't encounter any."

"How convenient," Joe sneered. "And you didn't question that fact?"

"I sent Pia...to round up the guards. Slipped out the gate...wanted to keep their trail."

Joe wound the chain rope over and over his fist, coming closer. He leaned down, close enough so Max could see the golden discs of his eyes and his vampire fangs. "And did you find them, ole buddy?"

"I think so."

The chain held by Dylan tightened.

Max cursed. "I transformed. I remember impressions...of wolves. Several surrounding me...after I'd chased them a while."

"You were surrounded by wolves?" Joe asked, his voice low and deadly. "Must have been a family reunion. You don't have a scratch on you!"

"I...don't...know why...they wouldn't fight me," Max panted, trying to draw in air past the constricting metal. "I smell blood."

Joe slammed his side. "Nice try, fucking wolf. Tell me you don't know Darcy's dead!"

Max felt lightheaded, ready to pass out, but turned to stare. "What the fuck?" His throat closed so tight, the words were forced.

"She's dead, *were!*" Joe shouted, his face red, tears filling his eyes. "And I'm gonna fucking kill you myself!"

"You think I—" The look in Joe's face said he didn't care if Max had been the one to hurt Darcy or not. He wanted blood.

"Pia?" Max whispered. "Pia's...all right?" He struggled to get to his feet.

"Stay on your knees and clasp your hands behind your back." This came from Navarro, who'd watched the whole inquiry in silence. "Loosen the chain a little, Joe. I don't want him dead...yet."

Max glared at his rescuer, but complied with his orders, and when the chain relented, he dragged air into his burning lungs.

A radio squawked. "Dylan!" Emmy's voice broke over the air.

Dylan unclipped a radio from his belt with his free hand. "What's up, Em? Did you reach the limo?"

"Yeah." Emmy paused to clear her throat. "But tell Navarro the driver and Sidney are both out cold. And Dylan, Dr. Deats and his colleagues are gone."

"Mother-fuckin' bastards," Joe swore.

Dylan aimed a deadly glare at Max and spoke into the radio. "Hotfoot it back here—"

"Already pulling through the gates, baby."

Navarro's eyes closed momentarily, and then he stood. "Bring everyone here," he said, enunciating so precisely the Spanish inflections in his voice sliced the air. "Lock down this place. And then I want everyone in this room. Get this dog some clothes." He left in the direction of the front of the house as tires squealed in the distance.

Max slumped to his knees. "Darcy was killed by a wolf?"

Joe didn't answer, but his breaths grew choppy.

"I swear, I didn't know. I wasn't part of this."

"Save it for someone who gives a damn. Far as I'm concerned, you're a walking dead man."

Chapter Three

જી

Clothed, but still chained like an animal, Max waited as the others gathered in the living room.

Navarro carried a blonde woman inside and deposited her on a sofa. He kept her head in his lap while she slept off the effects of the drug used to incapacitate her and the driver while the three scientists were taken.

Max figured she must be Sidney, Navarro's new woman, by the tender way he combed back her chin-length hair.

Would he ever have that pleasure again? His fingers curled into fists, and he didn't relax until Pia descended the curved staircase, her face pale and tear-streaked.

She held his gaze, sorrow and fear trembling on her lips. Then her gaze dipped to the chain around his neck and anger sparked in her eyes.

The human guards had been found alive, lying atop one another in a corner of the courtyard, also sleeping off drugs. With a new crew patrolling outside, Quentin and Darcy were the only residents missing from the meeting.

Max's stomach clenched as the magnitude of his failure hit him. Darcy was dead because he'd fallen for the pack's ruse. They'd drawn him away from the compound with a calculation far too sophisticated for a random act. They'd deliberately pulled him away, leaving the pregnant women, Darcy and Lily, vulnerable. And he'd fallen for it. He'd abandoned them when they'd needed his protection most.

In her condition, the gutsy woman who'd been his teammate on the Special Unit's task force hadn't stood a chance. He could well imagine how Darcy had been attacked, mauled by one of his kind. The images replayed in his mind, sickening him to the point he was ready to suffer the group's rage.

His head hung low, his body weary beyond words. His relief at Pia's presence only momentarily lifted the shadows crowding in to suffocate him.

"We have to assume Zachary Powell was behind the plan," Navarro said, his expression stony.

Lily wept softly, sitting on a sofa with Pia's arm draped over her shoulder. "Christ, did you see Darcy?"

Pia shook her head. "Quentin wrapped her body in a sheet, and took her to their quarters." She drew a shaky breath. "He won't let anyone inside."

Joe yanked on Max's chain, his expression cold and set, his eyes dry now and deadly.

Max wondered if Joe even remembered that once they'd been tight. Close as brothers. Before Joe had been turned into a bloodsucking demon. And before he'd learned Max was a born werewolf. *His born enemy.*

"Is it really necessary to keep him chained?" Pia asked, glaring at Joe. "He didn't have a damn thing to do with this."

"Says who?" Joe's voice was low and filled with scorn. He swept the room with a glance. "He joined a little gathering outside The Compound. Told us so. If he'd been on our side, he would have taken out a few. Do you see a scratch on him?"

Pia's lips tightened and Joe wondered if the others' condemnation was shaking her loyalty.

"He and his kind killed my child." Joe's lips curled back in a snarl. "They fucking ripped open Darcy's belly to get it."

Max's gut roiled at hearing how Darcy had died. No wonder Joe was ready to skin him alive. "Pia, maybe you shouldn't be here."

Her face blanched and her eyes filled. "Not Max. He didn't do it."

She shook her head in denial, but another's voice spoke for her.

"No, he didn't do it."

Max jerked his head up at Navarro's quietly spoken words.

"But he has an idea who might be involved."

Navarro stared so intently Max felt the vampire burrowing inside his thoughts. The hairs on the back of his neck lifted, and Max tried to close his mind. The vamp was a goddamn psychic! He could almost feel him sifting through his thoughts, searching for the clues that would betray Max's blood oath to his own kin. He tried not to think of his brother and the pine thickets of his home. Tried to return the unblinking stare without giving away secrets that would endanger his whole clan.

"You've seen something," Dylan said softly.

"I see confusion and grief," Navarro replied, "and enough anger that Joe had better not take his eyes off his friend for a second. I also see family." Navarro canted his head, his eerie stare unwavering. "A golden wolf."

Max bared his teeth and growled.

"You wonder whether your clan is involved."

Max swung his gaze to Pia, anything to give the vamp another image and throw him off his current path.

Pia's heart-shaped face wore a pinched expression. Her brown eyes were enormous, but her gaze held his, her heart in her eyes.

Max's chest grew tight. He hated having her see him like this. Chained like a rabid dog. Never had their differences been so sharply drawn into focus. She stood firmly in the vampire camp. He wore a damn collar.

At least, she was safe. The panic he'd felt when he wasn't sure whose blood scented the air, had eased. She'd have others around to console her. Other than Pia, not a soul would regret his death. His own family thought him a traitor for loving a vamp and working alongside others. They reviled him for failing to bring them the breeder, Lily. Or, at the very least, to kill her before she bore Joe's children.

"As unsettling as their breach of our security," Dylan said, clearing his throat, "is the fact they took Dr. Deats and his associates. Why would werewolves need geneticists?"

"They are in league with Zachary Powell," Navarro murmured.

Max shook his head vehemently. "Never! They wouldn't conspire with a vampire." *Navarro has to be wrong!*

"But they have," Navarro said, his gaze dropping to the woman who stirred against his lap. His lips thinned. "They knew we were arriving with the three scientists. It's certain they wanted to take Lily, too, but they had a second aim. Zachary Powell orchestrated this."

"If that's true," Dylan said, his jaw clenching, "then we have a war."

"We are at an impasse." Navarro studied each person assembled in the room. "We must know where the scientists have been taken and for what purpose." His gaze finally came back to Max. "We will need your help to do this."

A reprieve? Max's breath caught in his chest. Was it possible he might escape death tonight? He shook his head again. "I won't betray my people."

"Perhaps your kind doesn't know what sort of vampire Zachary Powell is. You need to tell them." Navarro nodded. "Both our species must cooperate to defeat him."

Relief flooded his body as Navarro's intention became clearer. "I agree," Max said without looking up. "He's a danger to both our communities and risks the balance we maintain with humans." He raised his head. For the first time since awakening, hope and purpose filled him. "I can help, but I want these chains removed."

Navarro studied him for a long, intrusive moment, and then nodded.

Dylan unsnapped his lead.

"I don't believe this." Joe held up his fist with the silver chain glinting in the lamplight. "You think you know what's in his mind? That he'll really help us? He hates us."

Pia rose from the sofa and circled behind Max to unclasp the collar from his neck, and then trailed a finger on his skin. "Max doesn't hate you, Joe," she said, holding Max's gaze.

Max snorted.

Pia rolled her eyes and glared. "And he never wanted Darcy harmed. Don't let your grief cloud your judgment."

When the collar loosened, Max grabbed it and flung it to the ground, and then rose swiftly to his feet. "I'll go to them. I'll tell them what I know. *My clan* isn't involved. But they may be persuaded to use their ties with other groups to find the wolves responsible for tonight's attack."

"And what then?" Joe asked. "Will they be punished for what they did? They were only warring with the enemy."

"They killed a pregnant *human* woman," Max gritted out.

"Leave before morning," Navarro said, still combing through Sidney's hair as her eyes blinked dreamily. "Joe will accompany you. Dylan stays here."

"No! With the chip on his shoulder," Max said, jerking his chin toward Joe, "he'll be dead the moment we step into *were* territory."

Pia clasped Max's hand. "I'll go, too."

"No, Pia," Navarro murmured. "You remain in the compound—incentive for Max's return."

"You think you need a hostage?" Pia asked, her brows lowering.

Max squeezed her hand. "I want you safe."

Pia snorted and tried to tug away her hand. "Stop the macho horseshit." She turned to Navarro. "You're sending the two of them off alone? They'll kill each other."

"They will cooperate," Navarro said in the same level tone.

"I won't leave Lily," Joe said, glaring daggers at Max. "They may come back for her."

"You will leave her," Navarro said, his voice growing clipped. "I'll personally watch over her. Her children are precious to us."

Lily's lips pouted, her expression growing mutinous. "Our children aren't anyone's business but our own."

"You bred with a vampire," Navarro said, his unblinking gaze swinging to Joe's wife, "an act unheard of for centuries. You have invited scrutiny."

"This is nuts. We're just people," Lily said, struggling to rise from the sofa. "Okay, so you're dead people. But we didn't know we were starting the next Armageddon."

Navarro's mouth held the ghost of a smile. "Joe, your wife will get along famously with Sidney—when she fully wakes."

Sidney's lips curved into an answering smile, but her eyes dipped closed.

Joe sighed. "I'll do what I have to. If it makes us safer, and if I can find the wolf that killed Darcy, I'll be satisfied." He rounded on Max and tossed the silver chain at his feet. "But I'm sticking to you like a flea on a dog's ass."

Navarro shook his head. "Don't kill each other until this mission is done. You have use of my jet. Pack and say your farewells."

* * * * *

Max followed Pia, crowding behind her into the room, not allowing her a moment to regroup before he was on her, pressing his aching cock against her sweet ass.

He rucked up her skirt, reaching beneath for the sliver of silk shielding her pussy. "Baby, I can't wait. I have to be inside you now."

"Hurry," Pia sobbed.

He tore away her underwear and pushed her facedown, bent over the mattress. "Open up, baby." Smoothing his hand over her naked backside, over the soft globes of her ass and between, he kneed apart her thighs. "I need you higher."

Pia moaned and knelt on the edge of the mattress, widening her legs, letting him see everything he craved to cram himself deep inside. She sobbed and her head sank to the bed. "Hurry please, Max."

He unzipped his jeans, and from one breath to the next, slid inside her melting warmth. "Goddamn, Pia," he said, his voice harsh. He stood over her, one arm braced on the mattress, as he pressed inside, shoving past muscles already constricting and pulsing with arousal, massaging his shaft until he was ready to blow. He cursed. "Gotta slow down."

"Do, and I swear you'll be sorry." Her voice was thin and high.

He grunted, unable to tell her everything he felt. "Been hearing a lot of that lately," he grumbled, glad to be alive and thanking God he had one more night with this woman. He withdrew partway and slid back inside, setting the rhythm of their upward climb, sharp and fast.

"That's better. Oooh, just like that!" Now her voice was urgent, crooning.

His thighs slapped her bottom and upper thighs, harder, louder, and he bent over her, surging in powerful glides that rocked her body. He reached beneath her and palmed a breast, wanting to connect with her every way he could, cock, body, soul. Hell, if he could climb inside her he wouldn't be close enough. He never wanted to leave.

He squeezed her breast, grunting again when she squealed and slammed backward, her cunt clamping hard around his cock.

He couldn't hold back a second longer.

"Now Max, I'm coming now!"

He growled and pounded into her, his strokes so powerful she toppled from her knees. He followed her, hammering faster, climbing onto the mattress, dragging her up by the waist to hold her where he needed her.

Pia's hands fisted in the coverlet and she writhed, her face pressed into the mattress, her breaths coming in short gusts with each stroke.

When the moment came, his orgasm swept over him like a dark wave, blinding him and sucking the air from his lungs. Cum gushed, emptying his balls, flooding her cunt with the salty spray of his release. He bit her shoulder to anchor himself until the storm passed.

For long moments afterward, he continued to rock against her, loath to see their joining end. *So little time left.*

"Max," Pia whispered.

He murmured and kissed the indentations he'd left on her shoulder.

"Max, you'll come back for me, won't you?"

He stilled, his arm tightening around her waist. Knowing the vampires' penchant for bugging rooms, he kept his response cryptic. "I can't make any promises. I'm not sure what I'm heading into."

Her breath caught. "I love you."

Max slid out of her body and rolled her toward him, settling her close to his side. "If I'm left a choice, I'll come back for you, Pia." He pushed back a lock of hair sticking to her moist cheek and cupped her face, memorizing its heart shape and the golden brown of her eyes. Then he glided lower over her soft, slender curves, amazed as always that she could take all of him. And not just his body.

He remembered too how defiant and passionate she'd been when he'd fucked her with a wooden stake. She'd trembled and moaned, trusting even before she knew him well not to harm her. "You believe me, don't you? That I didn't have anything to do with what happened here tonight."

Pia's eyes welled with tears. "You know I do. I know better than anyone what's in your heart. You couldn't have wanted anything to happen to Darcy or her baby."

His jaw clenched. "I know I don't say it much, but I love you, baby." He leaned down and kissed her tenderly.

If there was a god, he had one helluva warped sense of humor. He'd given Max the only woman he would ever love — and made her a vamp. Lifting his head, he stared into her moist eyes. "Again?"

* * * * *

Max cranked up the radio in the rental car.

"For fuck sake!" Joe said from the backseat, where he lay with a blanket covering all exposed skin. "Will you turn it down? I'm trying to get some sleep back here."

"What'd you say?" Max shouted, a grin stretching his mouth. He'd had as little rest as Joe, but had the advantage — his body wasn't ruled by the daylight.

The seat behind him jolted.

"It's almost dusk," Max called over his shoulder, smirking. "Quit your fucking bellyaching. You should have fought Navarro's order a little bit harder if you didn't wanna come."

"Didn't know I was coming to Mayberry-fucking-RFD," Joe said, sounding grumpier by the minute. "It might help if you'd turn on the freakin' AC, too."

As soon as they'd left the Asheville airport, Max had rolled down the window. The scents from the North Carolina forest had been irresistible after years of salty sea air.

Soft, dappled light sifted between the oak and chestnut tree canopy above. Thick forest, still green despite the onset of fall, smelled of resin and greenery and the smaller insentient wildlife. Cooler here than South Florida, the air still held more than a hint of the warm humidity that sweltered all summer long.

Another powerful jolt from behind tightened the seat belt across Max's chest.

"AC dammit, Max!" Joe shouted.

"Thought you bloodsuckers preferred the heat."

"We do. But the backseat's a goddamn oven!"

Max's seat jounced again and he relented, rolling up the window and turning on the air. "Keep your shirt on. We're almost there."

The mile marker whisked by, and Max straightened in his seat. He'd pushed aside his growing anxiety, but the moment of truth was fast approaching. He wasn't at all sure he'd receive any friendlier a reception from the folks of his hometown than the vamp in the backseat.

In fact, he might be biting a silver bullet within the hour.

"Where do you think Quentin took her?" Joe's voice was more subdued this time, the words sounding gruff and forced.

Max knew exactly who he meant, but didn't really want to talk about it. Each time he remembered the description Pia had given him of Darcy's grievous wounds, he cringed inside and his heart ached. He wished he hadn't let his prejudice get in the way of their long friendship.

So she'd fucked a vamp—so had he.

In the end, there just hadn't been time to mend fences. He'd been harsh and judgmental. He'd hurt her, and he'd wear the guilt like a sodden coat for the rest of his life.

That the same rationale ought to apply to his relationship with Joe occurred to him, but Max wasn't ready to forgive Joe for embracing his inner demon just yet.

Not when Max had resisted his darker side for so many years himself to exist among vamps undetected. He'd learned a thing or two about his human side.

The darkness was a soul-eater.

His hands tightened on the steering wheel. "Where do vamps take their dead lovers? Maybe he'll do us a favor and dig her a deep grave and crawl inside with her."

"Dammit, Max!" Joe said, his voice hoarse. "Don't you care? This is Darcy we're talking about. He should have let us give her a decent burial."

"You pissed because you didn't get to kiss her goodbye?" He knew it was a low blow, but he couldn't resist sinking the stake deep.

"You goddamn were-dog! Navarro should have let me put you down when we had you collared."

Max's smile was grim. "His mistake."

He passed the city limit sign for Dark Mountain and slowed down, taking a right at the first intersection. He'd been gone a long time, but some things never changed.

The white bell tower of the courthouse rose high enough to peek between the tall trees. The red-brick courthouse and jail abutted each other—a short walk from the judge's gavel to a cell.

The law was the center of power in Dark Mountain. And his wolf clan held every elected office. The job of sheriff fell to the ranking alpha male. No election for that position—rather a blood fight. The last male standing earned the tin badge.

While Max might have liked a less conspicuous arrival, he didn't have the time to ease into town. Better to head straight to The Man himself…

He pulled into the handicap slot closest to the doors and put the sedan into park. "Sun's not too intense now. Lose the blanket—no use giving yourself away before you even get to the door."

"And you don't think the sizzle will do that?"

Max unbuckled his seat belt and glanced into the rearview mirror. "Don't be a pussy."

Joe pulled the blanket from his head, his expression sour. "Just make sure the doors aren't locked."

"You trust me not to hold 'em closed once you're out of the car—after you zapped me with a fucking Taser?" Max asked, lifting one eyebrow.

Joe's glance narrowed. "Can it, Weir! We have a mission. Or have you forgotten Pia waiting back at The Compound for you?"

"I'm not forgetting a damn thing." He turned and opened his car door. "Let's do this."

Max climbed out of the car and strode to the double-doors, thrusting them open, not sparing a glance behind him to see whether Joe followed him into the foyer.

The door behind him whooshed, accompanied by the odor of singed flesh. "Could we have stopped someplace *less infested*?" Joe hissed. "It reeks of dog here."

"Scared, Garcia?" Max drawled, while his own heart rate thumped faster.

"Screw you!"

Max pushed through the inner doors and walked down the line of metal desks. The few officers not on patrol turned, their senses alert.

A few had been deputies when Max had run the store, but their expressions weren't welcoming now. Their gazes narrowed and he knew hackles rose.

One deputy hit the intercom switch. "Sheriff, you won't believe who just crawled through the fuckin' door—"

Max gave Todd McGwyre a lethal glare and continued to the oak door at the end of the row.

Behind him, chairs scraped the floor and booted footsteps closed in.

There would be no retreat.

The door swung open and Max's breath caught. *Oh shit, one more complication.* With his heart squeezing inside his chest, he braced himself. "Hello, brother."

Chapter Four

ॐ

With his hackles rising, Alec eyed his older brother, barely sparing a glance for the vampire at his side.

Is he so arrogant he thinks I won't kill Garcia where he stands? Yeah, he knew who the vamp was—he'd shared a beer or two back in the days before Joe joined the fanged brotherhood. Before he'd become "the enemy". But he could dust the bastard later. Instead, he narrowed his gaze at Max.

What was Max thinking, entering were territory when he'd aligned himself with the other camp? He'd fucked a vamp female and not by accident. He decided to cut him where it hurt. "Put the vamp in the pit," he growled, looking over Max's shoulder to his deputies.

"Back off!" Max glared behind him, halting the deputies, then shared a charged glance with his buddy.

That little look riled Alec even more. Max had chosen an enemy over family. "You aren't in charge here," he said, his voice low and lethal.

Max's eyebrows lowered, and his shoulders bunched. "This isn't about us. This isn't about The Wars either. It's bigger, little brother. We've come to ask your help."

Alec's lips lifted in a snarl. Max's life was in his hands—and he knew it by his wary stance. The knowledge was gratifying after the way Max had turned on him in Vero when he'd taken the battle into his own hands. But curiosity about Max's "problem" and the need to prolong the satisfaction had Alec raising a hand to stay the deputies surrounding the two interlopers. "Put them both in the pit."

Max's hands curled into fists. "We don't have time for this shit."

Alec snorted. "Sure you do." He nodded to Todd and another deputy who clamped handcuffs to the men's wrists.

He was disappointed when neither resisted. So rather than stay there and let Max's frustrated glare undermine his authority, he swept past them and strode down the long aisle to the doors and out into the parking lot.

Darkness had fallen, and a hot breeze stirred the trees.

A pickup turned into the lot, lights arcing, and his body roused instantly — urgent and hard. *Stasia.*

The driver's door opened and slammed, and Stasia's light footsteps slapped the pavement. She drew around the end of the pickup and planted herself in front of him, hands on her hips. Her dark gaze pinned him and fevered color filled her cheeks. "Is it true? Did Max bring a vamp here?"

Alec smothered his irritation she hadn't bothered to offer him a greeting first before launching a conversation about Max. The oversight only reminded him that once, a long time ago, Stasia had shared his brother's bed, too. When he'd been top dog.

Alec ran a finger along her cheek, his gaze falling to her mouth and that full upper lip that formed a permanent pout. "Are you asking because you're curious or because you're worried about your old boyfriend's safety?"

She slapped away his hand. "He's fucking a vamp! What interest would I have in him now?"

Her vehemence sounded a little forced to his ears. Alec gripped her upper arms and dragged her close, bending to glide his lips along her cheek. "I don't know. Why are you so hot about it?"

She stiffened. "I'm not. I just can't believe he'd be so stupid."

"Forget Max. Run with me tonight," he whispered.

Her head jerked back and she glared. "Will you tell me what he's doing here?"

Will Max always be between us? Alec let her go and raked a hand through his hair. "Stasi, must it always be a transaction?"

Her gaze faltered.

Another sin to lay at Max's feet. When the warlairds had called for volunteers, Max had been so eager to infiltrate vamp territory he'd left Stasia without a backward glance. What remained of her heart was a hollow space she guarded like Fort Knox.

At least her hormones were still ruled by the moon. "Run with me," he repeated, his hand slipping beneath her T-shirt to cup a heavy breast.

Her breath caught, and a hardening nipple poked against his palm. "Is our clan alpha asking?"

Frustration made him mean. He squeezed her breast hard. "Yes, damn you."

She shrugged from his embrace and pulled her T-shirt over her head. "Can't say no, can I?" she drawled, her gaze boring into his.

Alec trembled with rage. *Does she think to shame me into rescinding my invitation?* While he seethed deep inside, he reached for the button at the top of his uniform shirt and flicked it open. "Just strip," he commanded.

The parking lot lights illuminated them, so that anyone looking out the station windows could see them both tearing away their clothes. Alec didn't care. His body tightened, reacting to the rage his brother's return and Stasia's continuing rejection had built. Through the blood challenge a month ago, he'd won the right to choose his mate—choose as many as he wanted. He'd have her whether he was her first choice or the very last. *Damn her!*

Naked, he felt the breeze lift the hairs sprouting from under his skin. He watched hungrily as she pushed her jeans down her slim, muscular legs and flipped them into the bed of her pickup truck. Her long brown hair curved around her shoulders and her full breasts below. Her eyes, with their slight upward cast, glinted mysteriously in her oval face.

The start of her transformation shone in those eyes, light reflecting against the golden irises. "Think you'll catch me?" she said, flipping her hair over her shoulder, not caring she'd just bared her breast to his view.

Alec growled and let his change flow rapidly. When he dropped to his paws, his intellect faded, replaced by a hunger that burned in the wolf's loins.

The wolf raised its head and howled, and when the woman melted and shimmered into a lean, brown-furred bitch, it loped across the parking lot and into the forest beyond.

* * * * *

Alec rolled from his side to his knees, leaves sticking to his moist skin. Beside him, Stasia stirred and sat up. He cursed. His cock was limp and wet, and he had only fading memories of mounting her body.

"Well, that was quick," she said, shaking out her hair, a trace of mockery in her voice.

He flushed, angry she'd prodded him into taking her in his wolf-skin, again. Frustration, sharp and fierce, rushed through him. He sprang on her, forcing her back against the carpet of leaves. When he stretched over her, pinning her limbs beneath his, he held his lips a fraction of an inch above hers. "Did I disappoint? I can remedy that," he drawled, slipping a knee between her thighs.

"I wasn't disappointed," she blurted. Blood pulsed at her temple. Her nostrils flared.

Was she wary or aroused? "No?" he said, dipping his head to drag his lips across hers. "Then you came?" he asked, his tone silken.

She arched, trying to lift him. "I don't remember," she ground out.

"Can't have you wondering." He centered his hardening cock between her thighs and nudged between her slick folds.

"Alec! Enough!" Stasia tried to roll to the side.

He braced his legs, resisting. His gaze was unwavering — as was his intent. He had her attention now.

After several moments of futile writhing, she went still beneath him and glared. "Don't you think we should get back? Max and that vamp — "

"Are being taken care of."

She pushed at this chest. "You said you'd tell me why he's here."

"And I will — when I know," he drawled.

Stasia gasped. "You don't know?" Her voice rose. "You led me on!"

His gaze pierced hers. "You thought you could get what you wanted by giving me sex."

Her brow creased as she scowled. "So what? I have to do it anyway."

"It's not enough, Stasia," he said, his throat tight, fighting the overpowering need she inspired. But why her? He nuzzled under her jaw and growled, "I want you howling in my arms."

"I already did," she gritted out.

"I don't think so." He nipped her earlobe. "I would have awakened with the sound ringing in my ears, I've waited so long."

She shoved him. "Let me up."

Her scent was strong, ripe — arousal perfumed the cream seeping from her body. She could deny him until Christmas, but he knew her body wanted this.

He settled more heavily onto her. "Not yet. I'm still hungry." He nudged her again, but when her legs pressed in at his sides, trying to close access, he pulled away. They both knew he was stronger and he could overcome her physically, but he wanted her participation this time. He rose up on his arms and quickly moved down her body, nipping her collarbone and the top of her breast as he went.

Frantic now, she slapped his shoulders and pulled hard on his hair, but he clamped his lips around a spiking nipple and bit.

Stasia cried out and clawed at his back. When he didn't let go, she yanked harder on his hair...but her legs rubbed restlessly against his.

Alec growled again, this time in smug satisfaction. He'd finally found the key to her passion. *The little wolf-bitch wants to play games.* Releasing her nipple, he pried her hands from his hair and stretched them above her head. "So you like it rough, baby?"

"Bastard. I don't like it any way with you," she spat, her body shivering beneath his. Her expression was fierce and unrelenting, but her pungent arousal scented the air.

"Liar," he whispered. "Was Max rough? Is that what you miss?"

Her mouth tightened. "I don't miss Max! Get off me."

He rasped his chin across her nipple. "Not until I have my due." Then he opened his mouth wide and sucked as much of her plump breast into his mouth as he could hold. With one hand holding her wrists away, he dragged the other down her body, following the honed and rippling muscles of her abdomen and hips. Arching his middle over her, he made room to sink his fingers between her legs and into her silky, slick cunt.

Her body betrayed her instantly. Stasia's hot pussy released a stream of molten excitement that coated the fingers shoving deep inside her.

Alec groaned, pleased beyond words at her response. His own body reacted to her quickening pulse with a hardening that threatened to release the wolf. He let go first of her breast, then her hands and scooted farther down her body. When his nose nudged her pussy, Stasia whimpered, but her thighs spread wide.

Pulling out his fingers, he parted her dripping flesh and tongued the edges of the thin quivering lips, while dipping between to lave the cream her body offered. His tongue lapped inside, sliding over the silken folds, stretching to caress her inner walls as her hips jerked and rolled beneath his mouth.

He spread her sex wider and pressed a thumb to pull up the delicate skin that shrouded her hard clit. Exposed and engorged, it ripened further as Alec rubbed his thumb in ever tightening circles. A sliver of moonlight revealed the swollen pink lips below were darkening as her passion increased.

"Too much. Alec, it's too much!" she keened.

He tongued her clit and murmured, "Sensitive here, are you?"

"Please, Alec," she sobbed. "Please stop."

Regret thrust a shard of ice into his chest. "Can't, baby." *Even if I could.* "I'm hard as a rock—ready to explode if I don't have you now."

"I hate you," she said, her voice hoarse.

"Do you?" *Maybe she does.* "I don't give a damn. Long as you want me," he lied, plucking her clit between his thumb and finger.

Her belly and legs vibrated, and she hiccoughed. "I don't want you."

"Liar." Alec crawled up her slender body, sliding his skin over hers, eliciting shivers as his chest hair grazed her inner thighs, her belly and her breasts. "Little liar," he whispered again, settling his hips between her widespread legs.

When his cock poised at her sucking entrance, he rose on his arms and stared down into her moist eyes.

"Just get it fucking over with," she said, her voice and face tight.

With her pussy caressing the head of his cock, a flush of anger heated his skin. The little bitch would never give him an inch — but he could take — and she'd love it. To prove his point, he speared into her, hard and sharp.

Stasia gasped and convulsed around him, her cunt rippling, squeezing — her channel tightening along his shaft to pull him deeper.

He lunged his hips, tunneling deep, and then arched to withdraw and slam back inside. The tug and pull became relentless, instinctive motions — again, again, and again.

Her silken sheath caressed his shaft. Her hips tilted to take him deeper still. Her hands clutched his buttocks, her nails spearing his skin. All the while her head thrashed restlessly as she snarled her defiance.

Inflamed by her growling response, he pounded into her tight cunt with little rhythm or grace — just answering a need to mark her, stretch her — brand her as his with each deep, hard stroke. And yet, he wanted to be deeper still.

He pulled away and flipped her onto her stomach.

Stasia came to her knees and bolted forward to escape, but Alex understood now. He grasped her hips and steadied her for just a moment, and then slammed inside her again.

She screamed and clawed at the ground in front of her, cursing his name.

But Alec hammered at her, so sharp his belly and thighs slapped her skin, the sound joining the wet slurping of their sexes gliding together, and their moans as they raced to the finish.

"Alec —"

"Baby, I want your howls."

"Never! Bastard, stop!" she sobbed.

Alec had a moment of doubt, so anguished was her cry — but then she howled, her pussy clasping his cock hard as she slammed back to meet his strokes. Her inner muscles dragged at his dick, sucking him into her body. *Let her try to deny she wants me now!*

His knees ground into the dirt, his thighs hardening to stone as he hammered faster.

Stasia's cries grew choppy, breathless, and her shoulders slumped to the ground.

Alec reached around her belly, fingers plucking a breast and tapping her clit.

Her bottom lifted into his hips, giving him deeper access, and she squirmed to press as close to his groin she could get.

Christ! She was tight and hot as hell. Cream smeared her thighs and his.

Then his balls erupted, pushing cum through his cock to jet deep into her body. His howl joined hers, wrapping tight around her cry as his body hunched over hers—ending when his teeth gripped her shoulder.

He held her like that for long moments afterward, rocking his hips against her bottom, his arms encircling her belly so tight she gasped for breath.

When her arms shook with the effort to hold them both up, he relaxed his grip and disengaged his teeth. "Are you all right?" he asked, rubbing his cheek against her shoulder.

She nodded, her chest expanding with her deep breaths. "Now will you get off me?" she said, her voice shaking.

She'd done it again. Made him feel like a ravaging beast when he knew this was exactly what she wanted. His fingers bit into a breast, punishing her for rejecting him again. "Why, Stasia?"

"I'm going to be eating dirt if you don't get your weight off my back."

Still stuffed deep inside her, he lifted and sat back on his haunches, bringing her with him. "You know that's not what I meant."

She remained stiff and unyielding in his arms. "I should ask you the same thing. Why?" She drew in a deep, jagged breath. "I'm not what you've been searching for. I'm not really what you want."

Alec gripped her chin and turned her so their gazes met. "What the fuck are you talking about? What do you think I'm doing here?"

She lifted an eyebrow, disdain curving her lips. "Getting a workout? Maybe, getting a little revenge on Max?"

"That's not true," he said, frustration roughening his voice.

"No?" Her gaze swept down to where his hands bracketed her chest and slowly back up again. When her glance met his, raw, painful anger shone in her eyes. "Then tell me you haven't been looking for a way into the vamp headquarters to get at that breeder."

It was an effort to keep his gaze level. "I haven't been back," he hedged.

"That doesn't mean you haven't been keeping tabs. You're just waiting for her to drop her vampire cubs before you take her."

"If I take her, that won't mean I want her. I have to do it."

"And what about me? When you have her in your bed, where will that leave me?"

Did she care, or was pride the source of the ragged note in her voice? "I won't abandon you," he said softly.

Pain, raw and honest shone in her dark eyes. "Then tell me you don't need her."

"I don't want her," he said, holding her gaze. "But the clan needs her womb."

"Why does she have to bear *your* children?"

"Because I'm the alpha. And because I'm strongest, I'm the best hope for our clan's existence."

"And if I were a breeder, would you need her?"

The poignant note in her voice caused a tightening in his chest. "Well, you're not. You'll never bear children. Should I ignore our ways? I'm not my brother. I won't turn my back on my clan." He cupped her chin, not letting her turn from his gaze. "I won't turn my back on you."

"But you left before…with Max." Her expression was defiant, but that sexy upper lip trembled.

He stroked her lip with his thumb. "I didn't have anyone keeping me here."

She drew back her head, ending the caress. "Did you love me then?"

His glance slipped away. "I cared. I didn't like that he left you without ever looking back. It was harsh, but at the time we both had a mission."

Her gaze narrowed. "You liked to watch us make love. Me and Max. And not just once."

His arms tightened around her. "Didn't look like love to me."

"Does this look like love?" she said, pointing to the indentions in her shoulder.

His hands bit into her belly, but he didn't answer.

"Tell me," she said, her voice roughening, "do you love me now?"

Alec drew in a deep breath. He'd never lie to her—even if it hurt. "Stasia, I'll marry you."

Her eyelids dipped, concealing the thoughts that shimmered in her almond eyes. Her lush upper lip lifted in a snarl. "No thanks. Our bed would be too crowded," she said, her tone flat. "Besides, I think I deserve more than obligation."

"I'm not looking for a breeder for a wife. But I must honor our ways, protect our destiny."

"Fine. I understand," she said, her voice tight. She pried away his hands and he let them fall away. "Same time tomorrow, Sheriff?"

Frustration, and more than a little guilt, had him heaving a deep sigh. "Dammit, Stasia."

"Can't have it both ways, Alec. You either love me or you don't. You marry me or you seek your breeder. In the meantime, you owe me answers." She rose off his lap and lifted her nose to the air. "I wonder how far from the station we are."

He took a deep breath, not finding it easy to return to prosaic conversation with his waning cock growing cold. "We have a long walk back."

"Damn, and I'm sticky," she said, thrusting a hand between her legs, a look of disgust wrinkling her forehead.

"That I can do something about." His hands reached up and gripped her ass, pulling her toward him.

Her footsteps were leaden, but she came, her chin lifting to show her resentment.

This time, Alec's hands coaxed rather than demanded, until she stood, legs braced apart, her pussy poised before his mouth. He bent to take the longest rivulets of liquid that leaked down her legs, working his way upward.

Her rigid stance relaxed and she swayed, angling her legs apart, begging him silently to come to her center.

Relief, and an emotion he'd sooner tamp deep inside, swept over him. He sucked her hot, swollen lips into his mouth, bathing them with his tongue, then cooling her hot flesh by blowing softly over them — offering an apology he couldn't voice.

When her fingers threaded through his hair, he accepted the invitation without comment and licked between the folds, parting them gently. He massaged her pussy while he drank, thumbing her clit until she moaned and pulsed her thighs and hips, sliding her cunt against his mouth and tongue, faster and faster.

Alec resisted her growing insistence and drew out her arousal, sucking on her until she squirmed and begged.

The begging earned her completion, and he fluttered his tongue on her clit and suckled it, not stopping until she groaned and collapsed against him.

Alec hugged her body, resting his hot cheek against her belly until she remembered who he was, and drew back.

Finally, he stood and grasped her hand to lead her from the forest. "Now you've earned your answers."

Chapter Five

ဆာ

Stasia McGwyre fumed as she drew her blue jeans over her hips. Still sticky and hot, she knew the guys in the station would smell the scent of sex clinging to her body. They'd share smirks and knowing glances and think she was still the dutiful little bitch to the clan's alpha male.

She'd been there. Done that. With Max when he'd had his choice of mates.

When her brother Todd had been the ranking male, her stature as one of his familial females had raised her above the sniffing of the local dogs. Now she was back to square one.

And all because another Weir crooked his finger to make her his.

Alec finished dressing and leaned against her pickup, watching as she drew on her boots. Her fingers shook and her stomach jumped, afraid to lean over and present a view he couldn't resist exploring. It didn't take much to turn on the horn-dog.

She berated herself for betraying her attraction in the woods. Having fought hard to wrest control of her passionate nature, she hated Alec for the ease with which he'd knocked down her walls.

The man who had the power to arouse her had the power to destroy her, unless she could tip the scales in her favor.

"Didn't take you near as long to get those off," he grumbled.

Stasia gave him a chilling stare, but his lips lifted in a grin. She straightened and strode toward the station house without replying. He was trying to draw her into another argument, and she wasn't going to be led. He may have power over her body, but she controlled what went on inside.

It seemed all the deputies on duty, and even a few who worked the early morning shift, had gathered in the station. When Stasia and Alec drew near, their conversation halted and they looked up, excitement tightening their features.

Her brother Todd gave her a quick once-over, and his lips thinned in disapproval.

Stasia glared and tilted her chin, pretending indifference. But she couldn't resist lifting a hand to her hair and wondered if she still had leaves clinging to the strands.

"They're both in the pit, waiting for you, Sheriff," Todd said, a note of insolence in his voice. Todd still smarted at how easily an accountant had bested him in the trial.

Alec nodded, not seeming to notice his deputy's disrespect, and continued past the line of officers. "Get out on the road," he threw over his shoulder. "Make sure we don't have more bloodsuckers making their way into town."

Stasia followed on his heels as he headed away, staying quiet so as not to underline her presence. She had to get into the pit to see for herself.

The steps down into the basement of the one hundred and twenty year-old station house were narrow and lit by a single naked light bulb. The air was moist and smelled slightly of mildew. Stasia sniffed and caught two other distinctive scents below.

One she'd know anywhere if she lived to be a thousand years old. The other, a mix of masculine musk and elusive almond corpse, was a smell she hadn't experienced often, living this deep in were-held territory.

A vampire. Max truly had dared to commit the offense!

Her heart pounded faster, and she had to consciously rein in her were-beast lurking just beneath the surface. She followed Alec past storage cages to the specially designed cell

187

at the end of the basement, fighting the urge turning on the tap of liquid lust that seeped a slow drip between her legs.

Thick steel bars, set deep in concrete, ringed a dark cell. Alec flicked on a light shaded to shine directly into the faces of the two captives.

"Dammit, Alec. Are we still playing games?" Max growled.

That deep-throated rumble made her body weep faster. Stasia couldn't help it. She reminded herself Max wasn't the wolf she'd known before, but her body remembered the sex and her panties drenched.

Unforgettable, harsh, uber-alpha sex.

"Who's playing?" Alec murmured and leaned back against the wall, in mocking indifference. "I'm here. So, talk first. Then I'm going to dust your buddy."

"Now you wait a damn minute!" Max stalked across the cell to stand as close to Alec as steel would allow. "We're here for a reason. This concerns the clan."

"You know the rules, brother. And you knew what you risked when you brought that parasite here." He canted his head. "Hell, you know you're not any more welcome around here than he is...unless he's your peace offering."

"Alec..." Max's voice trailed off in warning.

Stasia wondered at the enmity she sensed between the two. Once, they'd been as close as any two brothers could be. Since returning to Dark Mountain, Alec had kept silent regarding Max other than to say his brother preferred life among the vampires since taking one as a lover.

Stasia had died a little that day. Hope that Max would return to claim her dried up and a bitter anger filled her. She'd been good enough to fuck, but not to love. Despite her pedigree and rank among the clan, her barren womb placed a ceiling on her aspirations.

"Goddammit, let us out of here!" Max roared.

The tension in the basement was thick enough to taste. The heady mix of male sweat and testosterone had her salivating and fighting the urge to sniff the air and drag the scent deep into her nose and savor it on her tongue.

If they'd faced each other in their animal forms, hackles would be raised and teeth bared. As it was, Max's square jaw rippled with rage and Alec's strong back was taut. The rift between the brothers appeared deep as a mountain chasm.

Her interest piqued at their animosity — as did the edge of sensual tension still gripping her body after Alec's surprising aggression in the woods.

Max. Alec. Two dominant alphas from the same ancient lineage.

Perhaps they shared more in common than she'd originally thought.

Stasia's glance rested on one then the other, measuring, assessing. The Max she remembered hadn't changed — he was still a mountain of ridged, tensed muscle. She'd cupped the hills, licked her way along the valleys and scaled sheer agonizing pleasure when she'd sheathed his enormous cock.

Tonight, Alec didn't seem so lost in his overpowering shadow.

Physically, both were tall and broad-shouldered, although Alec was leaner of frame. In the glare of the bright bulb, both their faces were harshly etched — both their bodies were held rigid and wary as they circled — only stopped short of a true challenge by the steel cage.

But where Max was dark as a moonless night, Alec was a blond Viking. How he'd hidden that brawn beneath an accountant's bland façade during his time in vamp territory was a wonder. Stasia swallowed to wet her dry mouth and shifted to ease the ache between her legs.

"Alec!" Max gripped the steel bars so hard his shoulders flexed. "You know I wouldn't have brought him here if this wasn't an emergency."

189

"Law is law—written for a reason. You taught me that," he drawled. "Would you really have me ignore a century and a half of tradition on your word? You promised us the breeder. How's that going?"

A growling hiss sounded behind Max and the vampire stepped out of the shadows. "Something else you failed to mention, dog-breath?" he lisped around his fangs.

Max rolled his eyes. "Not now, buddy. You know he's only trying to rile us."

"Well, it's working."

Stasia's glance roamed the vampire. Leaner than either wolf, his pitch-dark hair and round brown eyes betrayed his Latino heritage. Exotic like a poisonous snake—he drew her fascinated glance. His fangs curved over his lower lip and the exaggerated ridge of his brow cast a sinister shadow over his eyes. She'd seen vamps before, but not in a long, long time. He was delicious, forbidden—and sexier than she should allow.

Her legs tensed closer, trying to shut off the arousal that wafted like a pungent cloud around her. But her nipples beaded hard against her shirt. It was all Alec's fault!

If he hadn't given her the roughness she craved, she'd be in control. Her body still resonated from the unexpected pounding it had received. She stepped deeper into the shadows, hoping he'd end the interrogation quickly so they could slip back up the stairs and leave before she embarrassed herself.

"Stasia."

She jerked as Max's gaze drifted past Alec's shoulders to seek her in the darkness. "Hello Max," she said, hating the breathless sound of her voice.

"You shouldn't be here, sweetheart."

"She's with me," Alec said, his jaw tensing.

"I can see that." Max's narrowed gaze settled back on his brother.

Stasia dragged in a ragged breath. "This is a little awkward," she said, injecting a note of humor she was far from feeling.

"Hope you know what you're doing, baby girl," Max said, his gaze remaining on his brother.

"You think I have any choice in the matter?" she asked, her voice tight. "Like I ever did?"

Max's gaze came back to rest on her and he nodded. "I'm sorry about that." He drew in a deep breath. "Meet Joe Garcia," he said, and glanced back into the darkness behind him where the vampire prowled. "This is Stasia."

"An old friend?" Joe said, one dark brow lifting in sardonic amusement.

"Something like that," Max muttered, but his gaze never wavered from her.

The hint of apology that crimped the sides of his mouth nearly made her lose control of her tightly leashed anger. *He feels sorry for me?* She shook her head, letting her hair settle around her shoulders and stepped closer to Alec, lifting a hand to caress his shoulder. "I don't need your approval—you're not the clan alpha anymore." She stepped closer, pressing her breasts to Alec's back as her hand trailed around his belly.

Alec's breath caught. "Stasia…" he warned, his body tightening beneath her touch. "Maybe you'd better wait in my office."

"Gonna be long?" she asked, leaning closer to aim the whisper up into his ear. She liked the way the two behind the bars watched her play—their nostrils flared, no doubt to catch her ripening scent. Max's gaze narrowed to fierce, feral slits.

Alec's head swiveled and his lips hovered just above hers. Anger flared in his hard glare, but she didn't care. She had his attention. She had all their attention. Not because she was an available were-bitch—she was a bone between two fierce dogs. "Upstairs," he ground out. "Now."

Her hand drifted lower, grazing his beltline and she laughed, low and husky. "Anything you say. It's not like I can refuse, hmmm?" And because she'd accomplished what she'd set out to do—determine whether Max was still…interesting and annoy the hell out of Alec—she left, swaying her hips and leaving her scent to tease their nostrils. She laughed again, letting the sound echo in the silence behind her and made her way up the stairs.

Todd waited for her at the top. He gripped her elbow and jerked her through the door, shutting it with a slam. "Little bitch, did you do them all?"

Stasia jerked away from her brother and scowled. "It's none of your business anymore who I do."

He leaned close, trapping her between his arms against the door. "Who you fuck will be my decision very soon," he growled. "So don't piss me off."

She snorted. "He kicked your ass the last time. You really wanna go back for more?"

Todd's cheeks flushed an angry red. "Is the vamp still alive?"

She nodded and let a little smile play at the corner of her lips. "He's playing with them now."

His expression grew impossibly darker and tense. "Did Max say why he came back?"

Stasia's lips twisted and she pushed away the arms confining her. "I suppose they're talking about it now."

"You didn't stick around to find out?" he hissed.

This time she blushed. She'd been so busy getting horny, swimming in testosterone, she'd blown her chance to learn what was going on. "Alec sent me to wait. I guess he'll tell me all about it when he comes back up."

"You think just 'cause he fucks you he'll tell you everything?" he said nastily.

She lifted her chin. "Yeah, he will." He promised he would. *And I'll fuck him again to make sure he doesn't go back on his word.* Of course, as hot as her cunt was now, she'd fuck him just to ease the ache—not that she'd let him have it without a fight. Her body craved more of his sweet violence.

Todd stomped to his desk and picked up his deputy's hat. "I have to get on the road, but you find out what they're doing here. By the way, who's staying with Sissy tonight?"

"Mrs. Hughes said she'd check in on her. She's plenty old enough to be on her own at night."

"She'd have to be with a slut like you for a sister."

Stasia had heard that slur so often she no longer flinched.

"You find out what's going on here. I'll see you later."

"Sure thing," she said and sauntered toward Alec's office to wait for him to come.

* * * * *

"Listen to me, Alec," Max said his expression turning from irritated to deadly earnest. "What I tell you has to stay between us for now—until I can speak to the warlairds."

Alec shook his head. "Do you really think they'll grant you an audience?"

His fists tightened around the bars. "If they aren't the ones who agreed to an alliance with a homicidal maniac—then yes, they will."

Alec's heart stilled, then pumped a slow, thudding beat. "What are you talking about? Still having problems with weres in Vero?"

"No, we just about have your mess cleaned up."

Alec felt heat fill his cheeks. "All I wanted was the breeder—you know we need her."

"I understand, but she's taken and already bred. Get over it."

The vampire lurking in the darkness beyond the light, growled.

Alec aimed a glare at Joe Garcia. "After she drops her cubs…all bets are off."

Max held his hand up when the vamp's growls deepened. "Someone else wants her worse than you do."

"Another pack?" Alec shrugged. He really didn't care. The warlairds had promised the woman to him. Whoever took her would have to relinquish her to the Dark Mountain clan.

"Looks like it." A muscle flexed in Max's jaw. "But the thing that makes this personal is the wolves who tried to get her killed Darcy Henry. She was my friend, a human—and pregnant. I want the hides of the wolves responsible for it. I'm demanding that satisfaction from the warlairds."

Alec felt his stomach clench—he'd liked the woman. So Darcy had poor taste in lovers, she hadn't deserved to die. "You think it was one of the clans? Not just a few rogues?"

"Their attack on The Compound was organized. They worked like a team. Not like rogues in their first bloodlust."

"You don't think our clan was involved—"

"No. That's why I need to speak to the lairds. They can find out who crossed into the forbidden territory."

"It couldn't have been any deep-cover operatives, like we were. They'd never bring that kind of attention to themselves."

"Exactly." Max released the bars and raked a hand through his hair.

For the first time, Alec noted the weariness etched deep in the lines surrounding his brother's mouth.

Max's gaze, empty of all resentment, looked hollow. "But it gets worse."

Alec heard the despair in Max's voice and stiffened. This couldn't be good if it frightened his stoic older brother.

"Whoever the wolves are, they made a pact with a real devil—a winged vamp who's bent on taking the breeder for his own purposes. And he's not playing nice with his own people. He's kidnapped scientists — geneticists who can help him grow more winged demons in a Petri dish using the breeder's eggs. Zachary Powell isn't wrapped too tight. If he gets his hands on her, it's a whole new war. He won't honor any ancient treaty — he won't play by the rules. Our peaceful coexistence with humans will be over and we'll all be hunted to extinction."

Despite the chill his brother's stark pronouncement sent quivering down his spine, Alec snorted. "A plague of locusts, rivers flowing with blood...what? Armageddon? Like any werewolf would make a pact with a demon like that!"

Max leaned close, his forehead halted by the bars. "It's already happening," he said, his lips twisting. "He has the three men who can make all this come to pass and he was at the breeder's doorstep last night."

"Sounds like a fairy tale to me. Something the vamps dreamed up to fuck with our heads and draw us out of our territory."

"Dammit, Alec! They killed Darcy. You knew her. She didn't fucking deserve to die that way. A goddamn wolf ripped her baby out of her."

Alec stood in rigid shock. "That would never happen."

"Well, it did."

"You saw it for yourself?"

"No, but he did," Max said, tilting his head toward Joe.

Alec narrowed his gaze. "And you believe him? What if they're using you? Feeding you a goddamn story?"

Max reached between the bars and clutched Alec's shoulder. "You've got to listen to me. Put aside your prejudice for just one goddamn minute. Consider if what I say is true. Life as you know it will cease. You won't have this cozy little town with your hot little were-bitch to fuck. You'll both be living like animals in the woods, hunting deer and mice to survive. And every redneck with a rifle will be hunting you for your hide!"

Alec jerked away from his touch, cold, mind-numbing shock threatening to overcome him.

It could never happen—not again. Not another bloody pogrom. The wereclans had been decimated before they'd fled the Old Country. They'd learned to coexist—they'd banded and accepted law, agreed to be governed by the lairds. They were civilized, sentient. How easily could all that be lost?

Alec swallowed against the horrible possibility and straightened. "I'll send a message to the overlaird. You'll get your chance to convince him. But prepare yourself. He'll probably still demand your death...and his," he said, lifting his chin toward Joe. He turned on his heel and walked away. His head reeled with all he'd heard, and his stomach churned over what the overlaird would do to his brother. It was too much to take in, and at the back of it all was the need to find Stasia. Now!

Already his body tightened. Every ounce of desperation, anger and need seemed to flow straight toward his cock, making his muscles rigid with the need to cram himself inside her, conquer her—mark her so anyone looking at her would recognize his claim.

She'd flaunted herself before Max, before Joe, her avid gaze drinking in their physiques. She'd compared them to him. He'd make sure she didn't find him wanting.

The key to her passion was submission—rough, even cruel, forced submission. He should have known. He'd watched her with Max all those years ago—witnessed the way his brother had handled her.

At the time, his stomach had turned at the frenzy of violence that overtook Max when he'd forced her, ripping away her clothing, restraining her hands and legs with his weight as he'd entered her in hard, pounding thrusts.

But Alec hadn't been so naïve that he'd missed the clues to her arousal. The biggest being her pungent scent. While she'd screamed and clawed at Max, she'd ripened, her nipples had tightened to hard points, and her howls rang in his ears as she'd writhed beneath Max.

Unable to intervene unless he was willing to challenge his brother in trial, he'd bit back his objections and watched while Max ravaged Stasia. Hidden in the brush, he'd crept closer, his greedy gaze eating up the glimpses of her honed body—pale skin rippling over muscle, her dark bush framing slick, swollen pussy lips, and pink-tipped tits that jiggled with each hard thrust. He'd admired and envied her fiery passion and the fact that she'd never conceded easily to Max's domination.

However, when it was his turn to claim her, he'd made the mistake of thinking she might prefer a wooing over a rough claiming. He'd coaxed and seduced—and when that had failed to earn her acquiescence, he'd commanded.

Stasia had responded with a little more heat to his demands for sex, but her surrender was only a pale shadow of the passion she'd relinquished to Max.

If Alec had never watched them together, he might not have known the difference, but he had. And his failure to bring her fully to completion—trembling, begging for his touch—ate at him.

Tonight, had been different. He'd acted on his frustration—and yes, a little jealousy that Max had been able to make her howl so easily. He'd scared himself with her. The violence that gripped him had nearly taken him past the point of control.

As he climbed the stairs, each step drawing him closer to the she-bitch who burned a hole in his gut for want of her, his body grew rigid, his fists clenched. His cock filled to bursting and crushed against his zipper.

He'd give her seconds to strip or he'd tear away her clothes. He didn't care if she had to walk naked to her truck afterwards. That humiliation would put to rest anyone's doubt about who she belonged to. With her thighs glistening and the scent of her sweat and their combined cum leaving a trail behind her, she'd be linked with him—irrevocably.

Alec would never give her up. Even if the breeder shared his bed, gave him children. Stasia would be the one to bring him to arousal—the one he was driven to mount and command.

As his hand reached out to the door of his office, all thoughts of the men in the pit below emptied from his mind. The woman with the silky brown hair and lithe body filled his mind and his balls. He couldn't wait to see those pouting full lips close around his cock.

He flung open the door and his eyes widened. Stasia's pert, naked bottom faced him as she lay draped over his desk. Her plump pussy lips were visible between her legs and gleamed with moisture.

It was all he could do not to drop to his knees behind her and lick her like the dog he was. Instead, he closed the door quietly behind him and adjusted his cock in his trousers.

He'd figured out the way into her heart and passion—he wouldn't blow this chance by cramming his dick inside her now—no matter how much he ached to slide inside her juicy cunt.

Stasia rose on her elbows and gave him a glance over her shoulder. Her steady gaze and the tilt of her chin held a challenge. "I'm being the dutiful bitch now, aren't I?"

"Stasi—I'm not very pleased," he lied. "Now I'm wondering whether you're spreading your legs because you want more of me or because you're all worked up seeing my brother down there."

One dark brow rose, mocking him. "What the hell does it matter? I'm here and I'm horny. You've never cared before." She lifted her bottom and wiggled it. "Fuck me, Alec. Maybe I won't give you another chance."

Despite the gut-churning need to follow the movement of her ass, he kept his gaze glued to hers and narrowed his eyes. "You forget who's in charge here. I think you need a little reminder whose cock is gonna fuck you."

She swallowed and licked her lips, her expression a little less sure of herself. "Now, how will you ever know who I'm creamin' for? My thoughts are my own, Sheriff."

Alec stalked toward her, knowing what he had to do to make her his. No more tender seduction. No more cajoling or commands born of frustration. If the only thing she respected was power, he'd show her who held it.

His hands slipped his belt free from its loops. "Baby, I'm gonna mark your sweet ass so every time you sit, you'll only think of me."

Chapter Six

∞

"It'll be my cock reaming your sweet ass—my name you howl," he said, his voice pitched low, each word fired like bullet.

As he strode toward her, Stasia shivered at the hard jut of his jaw and the fullness tenting his trousers. *Please, please, fuck me now.* But she held back the words, secretly dying to see what he'd do next. This Alec was an unknown. Where she'd led the malleable man on a merry chase for weeks, this one looked as flexible and moldable as cold steel.

He doubled the belt between his hands and jerked apart his arms, snapping the belt with a crack that echoed like a rifle's report inside his office.

Her heart thumping with trepidation and excitement, Stasia eyed him warily. "I don't know what you're thinking, Sheriff, but that belt better not come anywhere near my ass, or I'm walking!" Her threat rang hollow, even to her ears, especially since it was delivered with a quavering voice. Not that she was truly scared. Oh no!

He cracked the belt again, and she jerked. Her traitorous pussy clenched and wept. For a moment, eying his tense jaw and hard gaze, she wondered if she'd pushed him too far—and whether he really had the guts to follow through with the threat.

Unsure and unnerved, she wriggled up, trying to find the ground beneath her dangling feet when the first sharp slap struck her quivering bottom. "Ow!" she howled.

His hand shot out and shoved her back over the desk and he leaned over her, the hard ridge of his clothed cock burrowing against her pussy. "Not 'til I say so, sweetheart.

You've been a very bad girl." He drew away sharply when she flexed to tilt her pussy and deepen the caress.

Stasia moaned her disappointment and struggled up, her breath catching at the next stinging snap. "Bastard! I'm not a child for you to punish."

"No, you're not. You're my woman—and you won't forget it after I'm through with you."

The hard, unyielding tone of his voice set her pulse jumping and she nearly swooned when he striped her bottom with several more burning slaps of leather. "You think I'm gonna fuck you after this?" she shrieked, her anger a pretense. "You're crazy! You low-down mother-fu—ouch!"

"You'll address me with respect," he said, his voice cold and hard. "I'm your master, Stasi. Say it!"

The belt rose and fell, not hard enough to raise a welt—part of her acknowledged the care he took to avoid really hurting her, but another part reveled in his dominance and wanted more of his violence. "Never! I don't belong to anyone, bastard!"

"Wrong answer." He swatted her again, this time grazing her tender pussy.

Stasia's breath caught on a jagged sob and she sank against the desk, gripping the edge as deep inside her desire coiled tight, liquid fire spilling from her body. The next stinging glance against her cunt had her curling to rub her breasts on his desk pad, scraping the aching tips on the edge of the papers. She mewled and squirmed as the next stripes fell, warming places not yet touched by his careful punishment.

A hand caressed her bottom. "Your butt's all pink and hot." A finger dipped into her pussy and her inner muscles clamped around it. "Jesus, you're hot. Ready to call me master, or do you want more?"

"You can go to hell!" she said, sniffling, her ass and pussy on fire. But her heart was tearing open. No one had ever cared enough to figure out what she needed. No one had ever wanted her this much.

The belt landed on the desk beside her face and he leaned over her again, nudging apart her legs roughly with his knees and reaching for her hands. His heavy weight pressed her into the desk, but before she could choke out a protest, he wrapped the belt around her wrists and cinched it tight.

She bucked against him, alarm lifting goose bumps across her skin and spiking her nipples painfully tight. A frisson of fear seeping through at the calculated way he was forcing her submission. How far would he really take this? "Let me go now, bastard!"

"You don't make demands. You serve me, got that?"

"Fuck you!" She bucked again, but only managed to center his cock along the seam of her pussy. "Ah!" She convulsed, the first spasm of an orgasm overwhelming her. She squirmed to rub harder against him.

"You need to learn your lesson," he gritted out and lifted his hips away.

She nearly wept with frustration until she heard the scrape of his zipper. Oh God! *He's going to fuck me now. Yes!* She squeezed her eyes tight and held her breath.

The blunt head of his cock pushed between her folds and air hissed between his teeth. But he didn't sink deep the way she thought he would—the way she craved.

His cock sank only inches, enough to wet the head in her juices, and then he pulled away, only to tease her with another shallow dip inside.

"No!" She bit her lips to halt the litany of curses she wanted to scream.

His mirthless laughter gusted against her ear. He licked her earlobe and stabbed into her ear, making her shudder with delight. "Think I'll let you have it?" he whispered. "You want me to fuck you? Your pussy's crying for me to come inside. It's clamping so tight around my head, you can't lie about what you want."

"I want you off me," she gritted out.

"Say my name, Stasia."

"Stop playing with me!"

"Be a good girl." He nipped her shoulder in exactly the spot he'd gripped her earlier that night. "Say my name, like you really want me."

"Fuck you!" she sobbed.

He dipped his cock back inside, a teasing probe that stretched her, making her pussy tingle and ripple. "Say it."

God, she'd come if he just pushed a little deeper. Could she goad him into doing it? "I don't care whose prick's inside me — you're just any old cock!"

"Liar," he drawled. "Shall I leave you here, draped over the desk like a whore and invite one of the deputies to fuck you hard, like you like it?"

No, no, no! God, just you! Unable to hold it back, her shoulders slumped and her breath sobbed. "Don't —"

"Shhh…" He stroked inside, a little deeper this time and a hand soothed over her hair, petting her gently. The tenderness of his touch almost did her in completely. "I couldn't let them have you. I already told you. Mine's the only cock that's ever gonna fuck you again."

He glided out and in again, and tears of relief fell to the desk. She took a deep steadying breath, savoring the sensation of his comfort now the storm was past.

Only he halted. "But there's still the problem of your punishment."

Stasia stiffened beneath him, wanting to howl, to scream the walls down. "Why are you doing this to me?" she wailed. "You don't love me."

"Who says, baby? Don't I love you enough to want what's best for you?"

"You think you're what's best for me?" she asked, her voice rising on a note of hysteria. He continued to hold himself still inside her while her whole body shivered and cramped with need.

Alec planted a kiss on the side of her cheek and nuzzled her neck. "Don't you know it by now? I know all your nasty secrets, your dark desires." He whispered directly into her ear. "I'm the only one who can give you exactly what you need."

Her forehead settled on the desk. She hid her expression, unwilling to let him see how shattered she felt. "And what do I need?" she asked, not recognizing the thin, faint sound of her own voice.

"To be punished."

Fresh desire leaked from deep inside her to surround his cock. His laughter this time sounded strained as he lifted from her back. "Hold that thought, love." His fingers glided over her ass and his thick thumb trailed the crevice separating her cheeks.

Stasia moaned a protest when he circled her sensitive asshole.

"You're tight here, Stasi. I noticed that right off when I played with it earlier. Didn't Max ever fuck your ass?" he whispered, fingering her opening.

"No," she groaned. "He was always in a hurry."

"I'm not rushing your punishment. I told you I'd ream your sweet ass — I keep my promises."

His hips drew away and he withdrew his cock, leaving her pussy empty and aching. The cool air licked at the sweat that had gathered where their bodies met and the moisture clinging to her engorged folds. She heard the rustle of clothing and boots dropping to the floor. Her heart thudded, dull and heavy, picking up in pace when his hands smoothed up the backs of her thighs and beneath her belly to pull her bottom past the edge of the desk.

He held her up, clasping the notches of her hips and tunneled his cock between her buttocks, nudging harder when he found her tight hole.

Stasia hadn't the will to defy him anymore. She wanted him — desperately — any way he wanted to take her. She strained to open her legs and spread her cheeks wider to let him slip deep between. A drop of liquid plopped into her crease and his cock circled, rubbing the moisture into the puckered ring of tissue.

Then he was there, pressing hard, working his hips side to side to screw into her, pushing inexorably against the strong muscles poised to prevent his entry. His blunt cock head pressed forward until she felt her asshole stretch and burn. She whimpered. "You won't fit."

"I'll fit," he said, his voice tight. "It'll hurt all right, but that's part of the punishment. You have to love the pain first." He flexed his hips and pushed harder and suddenly her sphincter gave and he sank into her, stretching her asshole as it opened just enough let the crown inside.

A strangled scream ripped from her throat, and she sobbed on her indrawn breath. "It's too much!"

More spit dropped and he circled his hips, pumping in shallow thrusts, just enough to work the lubricant inside her hole. Then an arm curved beneath her belly and a hand snaked around to sink between her legs. He thumbed her clit and worked two fingers into her greedy cunt, but thankfully he didn't tunnel any deeper into her ass.

A ragged moan escaped and she held her hips still, afraid any movement would drive his cock deeper. However, she strained to savor the fullness entering her pussy. "Fuck my cunt, Alec. Please, please fuck my cunt."

"Easy, girl. I'm gonna start moving again."

"No, no. Just your fingers. Please."

"Can't stop now, baby." His groan sounded like it came dredged up from his toes. "Feel what I'm doing to your hot, tight pussy?" He finger-fucked her faster, harder—all the while thumbing her clit.

Stasia's whole body trembled on the verge of ecstasy. "Deeper, please. Fuck me harder."

"Like that?"

She nodded, keeping her head tucked low in submission—anything to keep his hand working inside her pussy. *Christ, I'm so close!*

He dug deeper between her legs, "Relax your asshole, baby. Let me inside. I promise it'll be worth the pain."

"Can't. It burns!" she said, her voice tightening as she drew closer to the edge.

"What burns?" he whispered. "Your cunt? Baby, you're melting around my fingers." He pulled out and thrust three fingers inside her now, screwing into her, scraping her inner walls with his knuckles until she couldn't help but writhe and arch beneath him.

Her whole body shivered and sweat broke on her forehead and upper lip. Her nipples chafed, engorged and aching, scraping against the edge of the pad.

His hips pistoned once and his cock slipped deeper into her ass. "Yes!" she shouted as another ripple convulsed along her channel to caress his fingers. Her ass relaxed its tight grip on his cock and he glided deep inside, stealing her breath.

With her pussy and ass so full she couldn't breathe, Stasia collapsed onto the desk and rolled her head from side to side, surrendering to his harsh mercies.

Alec shuddered behind her and ground deep into her ass, lifting her bottom as he pumped in and out—burning her ass, ratcheting up her desire until she felt brittle as thin glass, ready to shatter at any moment.

"OhGodohGodohGod!" she chanted.

"That's it, baby. Take it!" he said, slamming his hips against her bottom. His fingers shoved deeper until she swore his whole hand slipped inside and twisted.

She came howling his name, prickling light exploding behind her clenched eyelids, her body stretching taut as a bowstring.

When at last he shuddered and cum spewed inside her ass, Stasia wept. Alec had conquered her, claimed her in way no man had ever done.

Somehow, he'd guessed her darkest needs and used every one against her to prove his mastery of her.

She was his whore, his slave, his bitch. She thought she might even love him.

"I can't breathe," Stasia whispered beneath him.

Alec roused from where he lay slumped over her back, naked, replete—they were still joined like two dogs tied, panting. He kissed her shoulder, knowing an apology would be inappropriate and possibly a setback in her "training".

Weary to his soul, and feeling more than a little shocked at himself and her, he lifted off her and slowly pulled his cock free from her ass. Each inch away from her tight heat deepened a feeling of loss.

When at last she'd surrendered and welcomed him into her body, he'd felt connected, part of her. Now he noted the stiffness of her shoulders and the shallow little breaths she took as the tension returned.

"Don't move from that position," he said, keeping his voice harsh. "I'll be right back."

He didn't bother to wait and see whether she obeyed. He thought his domination was so fresh she just might obey—at least for now. But there was more he wanted to do for her. Ways he could say he was sorry without diminishing her respect for his strength.

He'd never been into the BDSM scene, wasn't even sure if that's what they were doing here, but he'd recognized her need to be subdued instinctively. Stubborn, beautiful, brave…but deep inside she craved to give up control, to be taken by a man. One strong enough and sane enough not to use her surrender to do her harm.

Running the tap in his private bathroom, he grabbed a stack of paper towels and wet them, then returned to find Stasia in exactly the same position he'd left her. Her bottom was still bright red from her spanking and her pussy was swollen and dripping.

He parted her buttocks and cleaned her, then used fresh towels to scrape the cum from her inner thighs.

Stasia remained silent, acquiescent, and still leashed by the belt cinched around her wrists.

Then he knelt and lapped at her pussy. Licking softly and blowing to cool the heat emanating from her swollen, abused flesh.

Stasia sighed. "That's nice." She sounded a little hoarse.

Alec kissed her clit and gave into the urge that had gripped him the moment he'd stepped into his office and spied her bottom wagging at him. He suckled her pussy, drawing her lips into his mouth, drinking their spent excitement. When she squirmed, he licked along her seam in long soothing strokes, spearing deep to lap at her inner walls until her soft cries filled the air again.

After she orgasmed sweetly against his tongue, he removed the belt and drew her into his arms. He sat with her draped across his lap on the floor, his back against the desk.

"What are we going to do, Alec?" she asked sleepily.

Reminded of his brother below, hours from certain death, he clutched her close and kissed her moist temple. "Baby, I haven't a clue."

* * * * *

"I'd never have pegged Alec for the kinky sort," Joe drawled from the cot snuggled against the far wall of the cell.

Max snorted, glad the sounds of the sexual battle coming through the floor above had finally stopped. "He'd have to be to keep Stasi happy." He eased apart his legs to relieve the ache. Stasi's mewling cries had brought back pleasant memories.

"I take it you two were close?"

Max's lips curved in the darkness. "Fucked like bunny rabbits."

"So why'd it end?"

Max shrugged and leaned against the bars. "I had a job to do."

"Killing vampires."

Max shot him a glance over his shoulder. "That wasn't the main directive. That was just an added bonus," he said, a grin stretching his lips wider.

"Think he'll really get us that interview?"

"Yeah," he said, distracted by an unidentifiable sound coming from the direction of the stairs beyond the row of storage cages.

"They're gonna kill us, aren't they," Joe said quietly.

"Probably." He cocked his head, straining to hear.

"Did I ever tell you that you talk too much?"

Max snorted again. "Never."

"You're one miserable bastard. I know I told you that before."

"Yeah. A time or two."

The distinctive scrape of a footstep sounded from the other side of the basement—followed by a low feminine curse.

Max stiffened. "I don't fuckin' believe it," he muttered.

Joe rose from his cot to stand beside Max as the patter of footsteps drew closer.

"Pia…" Max pitched his voice low in warning. "I don't know what you think you're doing here, but you can turn your sweet tail around and get out of here now!"

Pia strode into the light and peered through the bars at him. "We're here to spring you."

"We?" he growled.

Emmy stepped from behind her and fluttered her fingers in a little wave. "Yup, we. Me and Pia. Somehow, we knew you two would wind up in a mess of trouble. We're here to break you out of the hoosegow."

However much he'd wanted to see Pia's sweet face one more time, hot anger poured over him. "All you're going to do is get yourselves killed. This place is crawling with werewolves who'd love nothing better than stake your asses in the sunshine."

"But we have the key!" Emmy said, dangling a ring of keys from a finger.

Exasperated, Max rubbed a tired hand over his face. "I'm not going to ask how you got past the cops upstairs."

Pia's amused glance slid over him, like she was drinking him in one satisfying gulp. "Probably better you don't know. You'd just get upset."

"You think I'm not?" he growled.

"We stole Joe's Taser gun," Emmy gushed, completely oblivious to the fury building in Max's tense body. "It's amazing how well it works on wolves—they didn't even twitch. 'Course the two goin' at it in the back office never noticed." She tried one key, then another, finally finding one that turned the tumbler of the lock.

Pia swung open the door. "Aren't you even going to say thanks?"

"Thanks isn't exactly the word I was thinking of." He grabbed her shoulders and kissed her hard, then shoved her back. "Stupid, careless, insane—"

"I take it Navarro didn't sanction your little road trip," Joe murmured.

"'Course not." Emmy wrinkled her nose. "He thinks we're conducting mop-up in Melbourne. Someone reported sightings of werewolves down the road."

"Dylan let you two go out on patrol on your own?"

A shadow crossed Emmy's face. "He was a little distracted. Quentin's disappeared...with Darcy's body."

Joe jostled past Max and grabbed Emmy's hand. "Come on, buddy. We have to get these two out of here."

Pia grabbed his arm and tugged. "Come on, Max."

Regret, sharp as a knife blade sliced through his chest. "I can't, baby. I have to stay."

She shook her head, dismay dampening the excitement that lit her eyes like Christmas lights a moment ago. "They put you in a cage, Max. You can't stay now."

Max wrapped her in his arms, knowing this was likely the last time he'd breathe her sweet perfume or burrow against her softness. Their first goodbye had been hard enough, this one was going to kill him. "Baby, I have to stay—and you need to get the hell out of Dodge. The wolves are out tonight, hunting vampires. Don't make this any harder. Go!"

Pia's arms clutched him tight, her body trembling against his. "I don't want to go without you. I don't think I could live."

Max smoothed back her hair and pressed a kiss to her forehead. "Baby, I have the best chance of surviving. I'm one of them. I still have my mission to fulfill. If they catch any of you, you're dust. Now get out of here."

"He's right, Pia," Joe said. "He's the only one who stands a chance of living past tonight."

Max opened his arms and stepped back, closing the cell's door between them.

Pia gripped the bars and leaned toward him. Max couldn't resist one last kiss and pressed his lips to hers. "Go, baby."

Joe lifted his closed fist and bumped it against Max's fist still gripping the bar, sharing one charged gaze. "Later." Then he pulled Pia away and followed Emmy's retreating figure.

Max waited agonizing minutes while he strained to hear sounds indicating the wolves above had discovered them. Instead, he heard a car pull away in the distance and relaxed.

Alone in the darkness, he sank on top of the solitary cot and covered his face with his hands, breathing in the fading scent of the only woman he'd ever love.

Dirt landed at his feet and he jerked up his head to find Alec brushing off his hands. His bare chest gleamed bright, his trousers were open and sagging at his waist.

"Did they make it out of town?" Max asked, his throat so tight the words ground like sticking gears.

"Yeah, radio's quiet."

Max nodded to the dirt at his feet. "Think the others'll buy it?"

"He tripped onto my stake. Yeah, they know I hate the bastards."

Max swallowed past the lump choking the back of his throat. "Why?"

Alec's jaw tightened, a muscle rippling along the curve. "I finally figured out what you have with Pia."

Max gave him a slight smile. "Yeah? And what's that?"

Alec shrugged, not really wanting to spill his guts. He cleared his throat. "You aren't...whole without her, are you?"

Max shook his head, staring into the darkness.

Alec stared at the wall too, watching his brother from the corner of his eye, waiting for a reaction. "Stasi drives me nuts, makes me madder than any other person on the planet but I can't imagine being without her." That hadn't been so hard to say.

"Do you love her?" Max asked, spearing him with his gaze.

Alec's throat tightened. He thought back over his stormy relationship with Stasia and realized the strain between them had started a long time ago—when Stasi still belonged to Max.

For the longest time, he'd thought he wanted her because of Max, because he'd been jealous. But now, he knew he'd cared about her all along. Seeing them together, seeing her love for his brother, had twisted his insides. "Yeah. I guess I do."

Max raised one dark eyebrow. "She's not an easy woman to be with. She keeps secrets."

Alec snorted. "If she was easy, I probably wouldn't have looked twice at her." He drew a deep, ragged breath. "I've never been…the way I am with her. Sometimes…I think, I could hurt her."

"She likes it wild," he said, nodding.

"Do you ever think about her?"

"You asking me if I'm still carrying a torch for Stasi?"

Alec straightened. "I guess I am."

"No, little brother. I never loved her."

Alec blew out the breath he didn't know he'd been holding. "Good. 'Cause I'd fight you for her."

The corners of Max's mouth curved upward. "Think you could take me?"

Alec grinned back. "Let's never find out."

Chapter Seven

§

"He let that vampire bastard go!" Todd said, slamming his fist against the kitchen table.

Stasia jumped and slid out of her chair to face him. A lifetime of experience taught her never to stay within striking distance when her brother was on a tear. "That's not possible, Todd. He dusted him and the vamp who tried to free them. Alec hates vampires. Besides, I was there. Don't you think I'd have noticed a little thing like Joe Garcia sneakin' out of the station house?"

His dark glare held a world of scornful fury. "You were so busy getting your brains screwed out, you wouldn't have noticed if a tornado dropped on top of you!"

"Keep your voice down—Anna's still sleeping," she hissed. "And I was not screwing at the station house!"

He stalked toward her, crowding her back against the counter, gripping it on either side of her hips to trap her. "How do you think the other one snuck up on Danny and Garret?" he asked, his hot breath gusting over her face. "Those two had their ears glued to the fuckin' door listening to the two of you goin' at it!"

Stasia's face flushed hot—so much for keeping her embarrassing proclivities private. She pushed at his arms and grew alarmed when he wouldn't release her. "I'm telling you, Alec wouldn't let a vampire go. Maybe Max, but not a bloodsucker."

"And I'm tellin' you that's exactly what he did," he spat, from between gritted teeth. "He knew that Mex'can asshole was gonna be dusted and he let him out."

"Cuban," she said faintly. "Alec said Joe was Cuban."

"I don't give a fuck. And you shouldn't either. Or are you lusting after vampires now?"

His hips brushed hers and Stasia lifted her knee in warning. "Back off, Todd! I hate the bastards same as you."

"But you like bein' Weir's whore, don't ya?" he said, his lips hovering just above hers.

Her eyes widened and she pushed against his chest. "I'm not a whore!"

Todd dropped his head to sniff along her shoulder and neck and then drew back to meet her gaze. "You think he's gonna marry you? You may stink from his loving, but you can't give him cubs. Your womb's useless."

Stasia bit her lower lip to prevent it from trembling. Hearing her brother spew acid on her wounds, only deepened the hurt she already felt. He was right. Alec still wanted the breeder in his bed.

He lifted one hand and she flinched, but he only trailed a finger along her cheek. "What if I told you there might be a way to change your destiny, little sister," he said, his voice smooth as silk.

She turned her face away. "What are you talking about?"

"What if there was a way to make you able to breed?"

"Since it's not a possibility, I'd rather end this conversation." She slid out from under him and circled the table. Line-breeding might be acceptable when the pack was thinned, but incest still made her skin crawl. Brother or no, she'd never submit. "I've got better things to do. And you know I don't like you touching me."

"I love you, Stasi. I'm the only one who does." His voice lost its mean edge and his face softened, giving her a poignant glimpse of the littermate she'd adored as a child. "You think I'm happy with the way he treats you? Don't you think I'd do anything to make you happy?"

Tears welled in her eyes. Weary to her toes and desperately unhappy, she shrugged, just wanting the discussion to end in a hurry so she could lock her bedroom door and sleep. "I don't understand what you're saying, Todd."

"Those vamps have found a way to breed more born bastards—winged vampires. Don't you think if they can do that, they could make you a whole woman?"

Stasia's body trembled at the possibility. She could breed—she could give Alec everything he needed. He wouldn't have to bring another woman into their bed. "How...how can we get them to help us?"

Todd stepped toward her and fell to his knees. He put his arms around her hips and pressed his cheek to her belly. "Stasi-girl, I know some folks down south a piece from here. They've got hold of the scientists those vampires are lookin' for."

Her spine stiffened and she grabbed his hair to pull back his face and capture his gaze. "Todd, are they the same wolves who attacked the vampires' compound in Florida?"

His expression grew sly. "Alec tell you all about that? Imagine that. Do you really care about what happened down there?"

Alec hadn't told her—she'd eavesdropped with her ear pressed to the floor of his office. She pulled Todd's hair hard and leaned down. "They killed a human woman," she bit out. "A pregnant one! They broke our laws, too."

"They were fetchin' our breeder. The one that got away from Garret in New Orleans. The human just got in the way."

Stasia shook her head. "There is no excuse! Alec has to know."

Todd's embrace tightened and his expression beseeched her to understand. "Alec's gonna help his brother take the scientists back to the vampires. Think about that, Stasi! His actions will help them breed more of the bastards. We're already losing territory; our packs are thinnin' fast. Alec's gonna betray us."

Her heart raced. Not Alec! He was strong and pure—by-the-rule Alec! "He would never do that," she said, although she felt doubt creeping in due to the strength of Todd's conviction.

Todd's gaze pleaded, his hands caressed her back, soothing her now. "Maybe Alec doesn't understand what they plan. They're gonna build an army to destroy us—wipe us off the face of the earth once and for all."

Stasia shook her head again. "I'll talk to him."

"He's gonna follow his brother, Stasi. He did before—all the way into vampire territory. You've defied him every step of the way. Why would he believe you now? He may not even understand the conspiracy they've hatched, but he's gonna betray us just the same. There's not a damn thing I can do."

Everything he said was true. She'd fought Alec, ridiculed him, acted like a spoiled bitch every time he'd sniffed around her. Why would he listen to her? Her heart squeezed. "He'll be cast out," she whispered. Alec would be alone; she could follow him, there was nothing holding her here...except for her little sister. She could never leave her in Todd's care. Her shoulders slumped.

Todd shook his head sadly. "The overlaird will kill him. Unless...you help me. We can stop them. We can save Alec from himself."

She eyed him, suspicion rearing its ugly head. "You hate Alec. Why would you want to save him?"

He kissed her belly. "I love you more. I want you happy."

"Stop it!" she said, shoving his face back. "You're asking me to betray him?"

He tilted back his head and nodded. "It's the only way to save him. Do you love him?"

Even before tonight, she'd thought she was pretty damn close. He drove her crazy. Made her madder than anyone ever had. But his mastery over her body had finally sealed her love. "He won't ever forgive me," she said, her voice breaking.

"It's the price you'll pay to save his hide. Do you love him enough to give him up?"

A dull, thudding pain pounded behind her eyes. "That's what this is all about, isn't it? You want to separate us."

"I...love...you," he said, tears filling his eyes. "I know you'd never forgive yourself if you didn't give him this chance."

She stared out the kitchen window into the bleak, gathering dawn. "What do you want me to do?"

"What you do best."

* * * * *

"I don't like this one damn bit." Alec slammed the telephone back in its cradle and cast a worried glance across the desk at his brother.

"So, they want someone else to transport me to the meeting," Max said, his voice deadly calm.

"Yeah. Todd." He snorted. "I guess they don't trust I'll get you there." Alec felt a deepening dread that something more was at work here—the hairs on the back of his neck lifted, warning him.

"And you don't trust Todd? I know he holds a grudge against me for mating with his sister all those years ago, but do you really think he'd betray the clan?"

"He's the same weasel he ever was. And big brother, he hates me more. Not only did I take Stasi for a mate, I kicked his ass in the trial."

"I still don't see the problem. He wouldn't dare try anything along the way—not if he ever hopes to win back the pack alpha position."

Alec rubbed the back of his neck. "Still...something doesn't feel right."

"Doesn't mean you can't follow him. You plan on being there, right?"

"It's an open meeting. I wouldn't miss it."

Max's mouth tightened. "Maybe you ought to," he said quietly.

Alec's gaze fell away and he took a deep breath. "If they decide to put you down, I want to be there."

Max leaned forward in his chair. The hard edges of his face were sharper than ever. "Just don't try to be a hero. I knew what I was walking into when I came back."

Alec read acceptance in his brother's flat gaze. "I'm no hero. I leave that role to you." He tilted his head back, fighting to keep his composure. "He'll be here soon."

"Guess this will be it. Maybe the last time we have to talk."

"Yeah." Alec cleared his throat and met his gaze. "I wanted to tell you this for a long time. I'm sorry about what went down in Florida. I don't know what I was thinking."

"You were thinking you wanted it over and you wanted to come home."

Alec snorted. "I guess. I went about things ass-ways. Turning wolves. I thought I could control them." He wished he could walk around the desk and fold his brother in his arms—but Max wouldn't like that. He was stronger than that.

"So, you made a mistake. I did too. I should have explained what was happening, what I was learning about the vampires." The corner of his mouth lifted in a smile. "So what about you and Stasi? You gonna marry her?"

"If she'll have me." And he meant it. Enough playing around. He'd even give her his fidelity—let someone else save the pack from extinction. Anything to make her trust him. Maybe then she'd realized he really loved her.

"Way it seems to me," Max drawled, "you shouldn't ask her."

Alec gave him a startled glance and flushed at Max's rueful grin. "Yeah, it's probably not the best approach—to ask." He grinned at the thought of just how he ought to approach popping the question. Handcuffs might do the trick.

"I'll give you a hint," Max said his voice sliding into a low, teasing growl. "Buy her a collar. She'll love you for it."

Alec didn't like thinking about how well his big brother knew his future wife. "Did you ever…?"

"No! I never took to the time to figure out what rang her bell. I was a purely selfish bastard."

"Good. Don't want her comparing."

A single dark brow lifted about Max's twinkling eyes. "Think you'll come up short?"

Alec narrowed his own gaze. "Not a chance."

His office door was flung open and Todd strode in. "Ready, Weir?" he asked, his lips curling in a snarl as he approached Max. "Hey, he's not cuffed!"

"You don't need 'em," Alec said, rising from his chair. "He asked for this meeting."

"Still, law's the law."

Max shrugged and held up his hands. "Wouldn't want you getting nervous on the drive."

Todd grabbed one arm and twisted it to bring it around behind Max's back.

Alec stepped forward to reprimand him for his unnecessary roughness, but Max shook his head as Todd finished. "I'll be right behind you, Todd. No detours."

"Wouldn't dream of it, boss," Todd smirked. "The sooner this one gets to the town hall, the sooner he'll be pushing up daisies."

Max's jaw tightened, but he remained silent as the deputy led him out of the station house to his cruiser.

Alec followed on their heels, the sick feeling in his belly growing stronger by the minute. He climbed into his cruiser and peeled out of the parking lot, determined not to let Todd and his brother out of his sight.

Darkness was falling fast and he flipped on his lights. When Todd's cruiser left the hardtop to follow the gravel road, his jounced along behind it.

Deeper into the forest he traveled, toward the old town hall—the original building the first settlers had built when Dark Mountain was chosen as the new home for the battered pack. Fresh off the boat and determined to save their heritage and species, they'd sought refuge far from any human settlements, content to make their own insular community until progress had caught up with them.

The newer town hall was reserved for show and political meetings—but the old log building was their true town center. Alec knew the rugged road to the hall like the back of his hand, so he was surprised when Todd veered sharply left ahead of him. He was following so close, he almost didn't hit his brakes in time to miss the pickup at the side of the road.

Its hood was raised. He'd recognize the battered blue paint anywhere. Eyeing Todd's disappearing taillights, he cursed and pulled his cruiser in front of Stasi's truck.

He climbed out and walked back to her truck. Stepping on the foot rail, he peered into the cab, but didn't see her inside. He walked around the back, but still didn't see a trace of her.

Perhaps she'd already gotten a lift. Assuming she was headed to the meeting as well, he strode back to his cruiser.

"Hey there, Sheriff."

Stasia's soft greeting tightened his body instantly. God, would he ever grow inured to her appeal? He hoped not.

He turned and his heart stopped.

Stasia stood naked beside her truck.

He swallowed, fighting for the proper reserve. "Not afraid of hurting your feet on the gravel?"

"I welcome the pain," she said softly.

"I'm guessing you aren't headed to the meeting."

221

"I was planning on being there after they get past the formalities..." She lowered her gaze and added. "If that's agreeable with you."

Christ, what timing. Here she was, giving him the subservience he'd demanded, and he didn't have time to show her how pleased he was.

"Stasi..." He stepped closer to caress the nipple pointing right at him. "I can't do this now. I have to go."

Her head came up, her dark almond eyes pleading. "I was hoping you'd let me service your cock before we go into the meeting. To relax you."

That full upper lip pouted, teasing him. He'd waited forever to see it closing around his dick. "Baby, you know I'd love that, but now's not the time."

Her hand cupped him through his pants, sliding to trace his length. "Five minutes? I can get you off quick, I promise."

A groan nearly escaped his throat. He'd never enjoyed this particular sexual act with her before, although he'd dreamed about it often. He'd been wary of letting her teeth get too close to the most vulnerable parts of his body.

"I can't. Really," he said, trapping her hand beneath his, but not moving it off his cock—it felt too damn good. "Need a ride to the meeting?"

Stasia stepped closer and her tits grazed his chest. "My truck works just fine." Her fingers toyed with the buttons at the top of his shirt. "You sure?"

His cock protested, filling despite his best efforts to will it into remaining tucked against his thigh. "Get your clothes on before someone else comes along," he said, regretting the words came out more harsh-sounding than he'd intended.

Her crestfallen expression had him hoping she'd still be as malleable later.

But the feeling of dread that had ridden his back since he'd received the call, hadn't lessened. "Get dressed, Stasi. Hurry it up!"

She shoved at his chest and flounced away, her bottom jiggling as she walked around the back of her pickup truck and into the bushes to retrieve her clothing.

The sound of another car coming down the road rumbled in the distance and her head popped up, her eyes rounding. "Do you want them to see me?"

Startled by her question, it took him a moment to realize she was still his willing slave, asking whether he wanted her humiliated for his pleasure. "No, Stasi. Get into the bushes and dress. I'll be right here. But get a move on."

The car came into sight surrounded by a cloud of dust and slowed to a stop beside him.

Amos Hughes, an old-timer in the pack, squinted at the truck. "The McGwyre girl havin' a bit a trouble?"

"No trouble at all. She's, um...relieving herself."

His bushy gray eyebrows rose when his gaze dropped to the prominent ridge of Alec's cock. "Sure she is." He winked and continued on his way.

Alec gave Stasia a couple more minutes then stomped into the woods after her. "Dammit, Stasi! I don't have time for games. Where the hell are you?"

When she didn't respond, his heart beat hammered faster and he retraced his steps back to the truck and carefully stretched his wolf senses to hunt for clues where she'd gone. He found her panties wadded in the brush beside the road and put them in his pocket. Unfortunately, her footsteps were indiscernible due to the heavy layer of pine needles covering the forest floor.

So, he followed her scent as best he could without changing to his wolf form.

As the minutes grew longer, his panic rose. He beat the brush and crawled through ravines calling her name. At last he heard a quiet sob in the distance and followed it.

Stasia sat at the base of a tree, her arms wrapped around her legs. Her face was buried against her knees.

223

Concerned, he knelt beside her. "Baby, are you hurt? Why'd you come so far?"

That only made her cry harder.

He lifted the hair that fell across her face and pushed it behind her ears. "Stasia…baby, what's wrong?"

Her shoulders jerked with her next sobs, but she kept her face averted. "You're gonna hate me," she said, her voice thick with tears. "I only helped him to save you. But you're gonna hate me, now."

Alec sat back on his haunches and the haunting sense something was terribly wrong nearly smothered him. She'd deliberately acted as a decoy. But for what purpose? Frustrated and stunned by her betrayal, he bit out, "Stasia, you'd better start talking right now."

"Max…they're gonna stop Max from talking to the overlaird. I was supposed to keep you away from the meeting." She covered her face with both her hands, her shoulders shaking with her wrenching sobs. "But I think I made a mistake. I shouldn't have trusted him."

"Who?" he said gripping her shoulders and shaking her hard. "Who, Stasi?"

"My brother…and the Nantahala wolves…"

"The Nantahala clan?" A chilling thought exploded in his mind. "Are they the ones who attacked The Compound?"

She nodded, tears spilling down her face. "They came to him. Offered to help him regain his position—if he'd help them get an audience with the warlaids."

"The warlairds aren't going to give my position to someone who's helping stone-cold killers! He lied to you, Stasia. They have something else up their sleeves." His hands squeezed hard on her upper arms. "Why didn't you come to me? What the hell were you thinking?"

She shook her head, knowing everything he said was true. She'd been a fool.

"Damn you to hell!" Alec shot to his feet. "Get up, Stasia! Or I swear I'll leave you here. They're gonna kill Max!"

Chapter Eight

ഇ

Stasia quaked in the shadow of his rage. He jerked her up, nearly wrenching her arm from her socket, and took off at a run, dragging her behind him. She tried to keep up, tried to keep her feet beneath her, but he knew where he was going, could see the holes small animals had dug, see fallen branches she hadn't the time to avoid. Each time she fell, he yanked her back to her feet, not once looking back to see how she fared.

She was surprised he didn't leave her in the forest, but maybe he wanted her at the meeting to see what her actions had wrought. And she knew the results wouldn't be good. With her brother involved, it might get downright twisted and ugly.

After Todd's gut-wrenching revelations, she'd been in shock. She'd surprised herself, sleeping so heavily it had taken him pounding on her door to wake her up to lay the trap. She hadn't time to reconsider the plan. Nor to think through Todd's motivations to figure out what he wasn't telling her.

She'd gleaned bits of the information from the conversation she'd overheard between Max and Alec, but not enough to understand the bigger picture.

So, why had she listened to Todd?

Because, somehow, he'd discovered and touched on every one of her vulnerabilities. Her despair that she hadn't been born a breeding wolf. Her lack of self-esteem when it came to her ability to attract and hold an alpha male. Max had abandoned her without once looking back—why wouldn't Alec do the same?

Her burgeoning love for Alec.

Todd had recognized it before she had. His fierce jealousy should have clued her in, but she'd been too busy building defenses against Alec's seduction.

She stumbled over a rock and Alec yanked her to her feet again, never slowing his pace. Suddenly, they were out of the forest and standing beside the road. When he reached her truck, he let go of her hand and gave her one hard stare. "Go home, Stasia."

She shook her head. She couldn't let him go into that meeting alone.

"Go home!" His expression was shuttered, his lips thinned. "I don't have time for any more of your games." He turned on his heel and stalked to his cruiser.

Stasia didn't move until his door slammed shut and gravel sprayed from his back tires. Then she shook herself and scrambled into the cab of her vehicle.

Coward! That's what you are! Too afraid to love him.

But not too afraid to disobey. She started her engine, stomped on the gas pedal and followed his cloud of dust.

* * * * *

Alec's panic wasn't lessened one bit when he found Todd's cruiser parked in front of the meeting hall. He skirted the building, keeping to the shadows in case anyone else was watching and peeked into a window.

His blood ran cold at what he saw.

Max was on the floor. Todd's booted heel rested on the back of his neck, and his revolver was drawn and pointed at the back of Max's head.

Only that wasn't the end of the madness. Men dressed in camouflage hunting gear and cold-weather masks surrounded the council who'd been forced to their knees as well. The townspeople sat erect with their hands gripping the pews in front of them.

"What the fuck?" he whispered, disbelieving.

"What we have here is a coup." Todd's voice rose above the dead silence inside the town hall. "We have a chance to make things right for all wolves, and these old men," he said to the audience of frightened spectators, "want us to give up our last chance at survival."

Alec crept past the windows, ducking low to avoid detection, working his way through brambles to the back door of the building.

"You all heard what we have in our hands now. 'Though they're goddamn vampires, these scientists can give our women back their ability to breed us wolf cubs. They're geneticists and fertility experts. Haven't we had enough misery? Our women have cried for their barren wombs. My own sister was shamed into mating, without a husband, because she can't bear his children.

"We can change this now. We can take back the territory we've lost to the bloodsuckers—"

"But what about our council? Our overlaird?"

Alec squeezed his eyes tight for a moment. "Keep out of it, old man," he prayed. Then he edged up to take another look inside the hall.

Amos Hughes came to his feet despite the clicks of multiple chambers and the barrels aimed his way. "They've already said what these men did was wrong and they would be punished. Are you going to ignore their ruling?"

"They're a bunch of scared old men!" Todd shouted. "They'd sooner quiver in their beds at night than risk comin' up against the vampires."

"You gonna kill 'em?" Amos asked, his shoulders shaking with rage. "We've lived by the order of our laws all the time we've been on Dark Mountain. Would you risk the lives of the people here for your scheme? What if it fails?"

"What if it doesn't?"

Another voice rose at near the doorway of the hall—sweet, but quavering. "Would you really kill our elders, Todd?" Stasia stood in the doorway, her face drained of color. "Would you murder them where they sit? 'Cause it sure looks like that's what you and these men intend."

Todd's expression screwed tight in frustration. "We came to parley."

"If you only came to talk, then why are your friends afraid to show their faces?"

One of the masked men stepped behind her and shoved her with the butt of his rifle, pushing her farther into the room, down the aisle that divided the spectators' seats.

Alec bit back a blistering curse and hurried again to the back of the hall while their voices carried in the stillness surrounding the log building.

"Don't you hurt her!" Todd yelled.

Alec rounded the corner, but was drawn up short by a pistol shoved under his chin. The blonde woman who held it pressed a finger against her lips, signaling silence. He'd never seen her before, but recognized what she was by the fangs curving over her bottom lip.

Stasia's heart pounded so loud she knew the wolf nearest her could hear how frightened she was. Her gaze swept the hall but found no trace of Alec—he had to be outside, trying to figure out a way to prevent what was shaping up to be a bloody massacre.

Max was sprawled on the floor, his hands manacled behind his back and his body slack. Blood seeped slowly from a wound at his temple—but he breathed. So far no one had gotten killed. There was still a chance this could end without an irretrievable act of violence.

As she drew closer to her brother, she noted the wildness in his eyes—a wildness he rarely displayed to anyone other than those closest to him. He'd backed himself into a corner with the warlairds and wouldn't be open to conversation with them, but would he listen to her?

"Todd, you can stop this now," she said, keeping her voice calm despite the terror making her hands shake. "You can order these men to put away their weapons and end this now."

He shook his head, sadness tugging down the corners of his lips. "Baby-girl, it's gone too far. They wouldn't listen, now I have to seize control of this situation myself."

"But think, Todd, when they're all dead, then what? Do you think the people in this room will follow you? We're a law-abiding community. We keep to ourselves; we don't mingle much outside our little town. You know every one of these folks. Do you really think they will follow you? Especially, when they hear about the winged demon these bastards have allied themselves with?"

His hand tightened its grip on the pistol. "Doesn't really matter if they do. I probably won't be here. But I can still help them from a distance. I can bring them the therapies they need to make their womenfolk whole. I can make you whole, Stasi. Someday, all of you will thank me."

Convinced he wasn't going to surrender, she determined to keep him talking as long as possible to give Alec time to figure out a way to end this. "At what cost? Do you think I'll be happy knowing a child of mine was born in blood?"

His lips tightened, then his head canted. His eyes filled with sadness. "You won't have to settle for being a Weir's whore, Stasi. You can have your pick of mates."

The front door of the town hall opened and all eyes and weapons turned on the man entering the room.

Alec strode in, a thin smile curving his lips.

No, no, no! God, Todd will kill him, too! Stasia glared at him for being so stupid, walking into a room filled with men holding weapons. What was he thinking?

"Looks like we've got ourselves a mess of trouble here," Alec drawled. "Why am I not surprised you're at the bottom of it, Todd?"

A scraping sounded from the opposite end of the building and before Stasia had a chance to turn, all hell broke loose.

Gunfire erupted and Stasia hit the floor, pulling down the people in the seats nearest her. "Stay down. Cover your heads!" she shouted. Then she belly-crawled toward Max and draped her body over his.

This was all her fault. If she could give Alec one gift, this was it—the bastards wouldn't get his brother. If she died from one of the stray bullets ricocheting around the room, so be it.

Max shifted beneath her. "Get off me, Stasi," he muttered. "Take cover!"

"Shut up, Max." She crawled over him. With her breasts cradling his head in between, she peered up to see what was happening.

Dark-clothed creatures spilled through the back door and crashed through the windows all along the hall. Their protruding brows and jagged fangs made them a terrifying sight. One, two, three…no, five! "Vampires!" she whispered.

Max grunted beneath her. "Well, halleluiah—the cavalry's arrived."

Alec rolled behind a pew and came up with his weapon in his hand.

"Use this!" Joe Garcia tossed him a revolver.

Alec raised his eyebrows in question.

"Silver bullets—only thing that's permanent, right?"

He holstered his own weapon, and crouching low, sped down the aisle toward Todd where he'd taken cover behind the laird's upended table. He ducked behind the first pew and peered around the corner. Max and Stasia lay in the center of the floor. Max bucked beneath her, but Stasia's thighs straddled either side of his shoulders and she'd bent low to cover her head with her arms. The woman's ass made a tempting target.

Around them, the vampires traded gunfire with the masked wolves, some of whom had partially transformed. Fur sprouted, fangs bared and growls filled the air while they clutched their weapons with lengthening claws.

A wolf fell to a bullet, screaming as the silver entering his system forced convulsions and he foamed at the mouth.

Amos Hughes reached for the dying wolf's weapon and jerked it from his arms as the creature stiffened, his back arching in the final throes of poisoning.

"I take it the vampires are with you?" Amos shouted above the din.

Alec shrugged. "Looks like it."

The old man winked. "I'll try not miss what I'm aiming at." Then he crawled to the opposite end of the pew and bobbed up to aim his weapon and fire.

Weaponless, most of the people huddled behind the pews while the battle continued to rage around them. A few of the men, including several of the elders were tearing at their clothing, letting the change overtake them so they could join the fight. But one by one, the masked men were taken down by the vampires' bullets, their horrible screams echoing like demons from hell in the close confines of the room.

Alec tore off his uniform shirt and raised his weapon above the pew to fire three blind shots well above the heads of anyone behind the table, and then tossed away his weapon. He leapt up on the pew and launched himself, transforming in midair. He landed on two feet, still sentient, behind the table and lunged at Todd McGwyre who rounded on him with his weapon raised.

However, something knocked Alec sideways and an explosion of light and gunpowder, so close the sound rang in his ears, jerked back the body that had barreled into him.

Another explosion, this time from over the top of the table, happened so quick, Alec only had time to roll against the table and hope the bullets stopped.

When the powder cleared, there was a deadly silence. At his feet lay Joe Garcia, gasping and holding his side—but alive.

He glanced up and found Stasia standing above him, a revolver dangling from her fingers. Following her frozen gaze he saw Todd, his back arching as spittle and foam spilled from between his gaping lips, a long wheezing breath sucking into his lungs while a rose of blood bloomed on his chest.

Alec's bloodlust faded and he stepped between her and the sight of her brother's dying form to take the weapon from her hand. "Stasia, don't watch."

Her stare lifted to meet his gaze. "I killed him. I killed my brother."

Around them, the vampires gathered and lifted the elders to their feet, setting the tables upright and dragging the bodies from the room. Max walked up behind Stasia, rubbing his wrists. He slipped an arm around her back and leaned close to whisper in her ear. Then he planted a kiss on her cheek and met Alec's gaze.

Stasia blinked and her gaze narrowed for second, before her gaze finally seemed to focus and she launched herself into Alec's arms.

"What the hell did he just say to you?" Alec said, as he squeezed her tight.

"He said you were going to buy me a collar."

* * * * *

Much later the overlaird's gavel pounded the old oak table, ending the meeting. The townfolk spilled out of the building and headed to their vehicles.

Alec waited for the vampires. Despite their aid that night, he still had to escort them out of town. The law was the law.

Max walked beside his Pia holding her hand, followed by Joe Garcia, who was walking on his own already, despite the wound to his side. Navarro and Dylan O'Hara were still making nice with the overlaird—or at least as nice and as vampires and werewolves could ever be. They didn't shake hands at their leave-taking, but all fangs were sheathed.

"I still want to know how you guys just happened to be here tonight," Alec said to the group.

Emmy O'Hara curved her arm inside his and giggled.

Fighting his natural instinct to recoil from the curvy blonde, Alec took a deep breath and relaxed—concentrating on the lively color in her cheeks and the light glittering in her eyes. Max had been right—vamp or not—Emmy's effervescence was hard to resist.

"Well, it's the funniest story ever," she said. "You know, Pia and I thought we were being so clever. We'd fly in to rescue Max and Joe and fly back out, and the rest of the guys would never know. I mean, we had a cover story and answered our cell phones when they called—"

"Emmy…" Pia rolled her dark eyes. "They met us at the airport. Your overlaird called them here for a meeting. He'd gotten wind of Darcy's murder by the boys in the Nantahala clan and wanted to let the vampires know he had matters in hand."

"The guys were shocked to their boots when they saw us walk into that airplane hangar." Emmy rubbed her bottom. "Have to tell you my Dylan was mad as a hornet. Not that that's a bad thing," she said with a saucy smile.

Alec shook his head. "I still can't believe Navarro's willing to lend us the services of Dr. Deats and his team."

"Navarro's deep," Max said. "If he's willing to share technology that will help our population thrive, he must have a long-range plan in mind. Don't you think for a minute this is the end of it—or that there won't be some pretty long strings attached."

Alec raised his eyebrows. "You sound like you like him."

Max scowled. "He's a damn vampire…but I respect him."

"Well, I guess that's good enough for me, too," Alec murmured. "Man, I'm sorry for the rash of shit I gave you about—" he halted when he realized who was still clinging to his arm, "um, them."

Emmy lifted a finely arched brow and grinned. "Didn't think you'd like any of us, did you?"

"You saved our asses. It's hard to hold a grudge in the face of that."

"Yeah, we did. And believe you me, you'll be reminded about it every time we see you."

Alec faked a growl. "Plan on visiting often?"

"Hell, no!" Her laughter tinkled like tiny bells. "But I had you worried, didn't I?"

Max lifted his chin toward Stasia who was standing near the edge of the gravel parking lot with Amos at her side. "So, what are going to do with her, little brother?"

He sighed. "I'm not sure. She betrayed me."

"Think you can get past that?"

Alec's gaze swept over her body, remembering the offering she'd made when she'd laid her trap and felt his lips twitch into a grin. "Maybe, after a little more training."

Chapter Nine

🙠

Alec turned off the faucets and stepped out of the shower, feeling a little less tense than when he'd entered the stall. Hell had come pretty damn close to setting up shop on Dark Mountain tonight.

He toweled his hair and rubbed the terrycloth across his chest, shifting his attention to the little problem awaiting him in his bedroom. What was he going to do about Stasia?

With the resolution of the problems between him and Max behind him, he thought he understood how she'd gotten herself deeply ensnared in Todd's dangerous plan. Blood ties could wield a strong sense of loyalty and duty.

But could she ever feel as tightly bound to him?

Remembering what he'd learned about the key to unlocking her passion, he thought perhaps the same lessons could be extended beyond the bedroom. Was the application of structure and control the answer?

Whether it was or not, the thought of the lesson was having an invigorating effect on his cock. Already it lifted from between his legs, filling, tensing—aching for the silken warmth of her cunt.

Wrapping the towel around his middle, he opened the door and strode into the darkened bedroom just as Stasia lowered the telephone onto its cradle.

"Your sister okay?" he asked.

His weresight adjusting quickly to the absence of light, he saw her nod. "That was Amos. He said she's already in bed and she's welcome to stay all night."

"Good. We have a few things to straighten out." He kept any inflection from his voice, unwilling to give her a hint of the direction of his thoughts.

She shivered inside his robe, rubbing her arms as though racked by a sudden chill.

"Take it off, Stasia."

Her breath caught, but she didn't bother to ask a clarifying question. Instead, she unbelted the robe and stood, letting it slip to the ground to puddle at her feet.

Alex grabbed the front of his towel and tore it away, bracing his feet apart. "It's the right time, now."

"What?"

He didn't answer, letting her search her mind for the thread of this conversation. When she found it, her back straightened.

"Crawl to me on your hands and knees," he commanded.

For a moment, she looked as though she'd refuse. Her mouth tightened, her hands curled into fists. Then her gaze dropped below his waist.

Knowing she was staring at his stiffening cock, Alec waited for her to make up her mind which course she would take. He was ready for disobedience, but he hoped she'd choose to comply with his command. He really wanted her mouth on him tonight—and he needed to trust she wouldn't sink fangs into anything important.

Swallowing loud enough he heard the gulp, she slowly knelt, then fell forward on her hands.

His thighs tightened and he tried like hell to suppress his delight as she slowly crawled across the carpet toward him.

When she reached his feet, she sat back on her haunches and waited for his next instruction. Her jaw was tight, her gaze wary. He couldn't read her thoughts in either.

Was she giving him obedience because she feared the consequences of her actions earlier, or because she truly wanted to submit to him? Only him.

"Suck me off, Stasi. Make me forget every other woman I've ever known."

Her hands fisted on her thighs. "Have there been so many?"

"Does it matter?" Would she give him honesty? Or would she continue to guard her heart?

Moisture gathered in her eyes even as she narrowed her gaze. "It does if you plan to seek any of them out...ever again."

"You asking if I plan to be faithful to you, Stasi?"

She bowed her head. "I'm sorry. I don't deserve that any longer. I just want to know how long you're going to keep me here...with you."

Alec drew a deep breath, relaxing. He'd heard the sorrow in her voice and knew she regretted endangering their relationship. It was enough for now—enough for him to work with. "I thought we talked about this before," he said quietly. "I chose you for my mate. Your disobedience was as much my fault as yours. You lack discipline. I plan to rectify that...starting now."

Her face came up and she blinked away her tears. "What do want from me?"

"I already told you."

A little mewl broke from her throat and she reached trembling hands to his thighs.

She made delicate glides up and down his thighs, her fingers combing through the sparse hairs covering his skin. First his outer thighs, then inside, the touch so delicate he shivered.

"Don't be afraid to handle me," he whispered.

Her hands burrowed between his legs, scooping up his balls. She leaned close, her hot breath brushing his ball sac. Then her tongue reached out and stroked over them.

Alec tunneled his fingers into her soft hair and curved around her head, not guiding, just caressing. He wanted her to decide where to go from here, wanted to learn how much she knew about pleasing a man.

Stasia groaned and opened her mouth to suck on one ball.

With her tongue laving it inside the hot cavern of her mouth, Alex squeezed shut his eyes. Her tongue continued to lick all around while her mouth suctioned softly.

"That's it, baby," he couldn't stop the praise from spilling from his lips.

When she swallowed his whole scrotum deep inside her mouth, his fingers fisted in her hair to hold her there so he could savor the start of the buildup to his release.

Suddenly, her teeth pinched the skin at the back of his balls, stopping his momentum cold. His eyes flew open and he stared down at her where she knelt. "Stasi?" he asked, his voice betraying his worry.

Her gaze was narrowed, and he didn't have any doubt in his mind she was capable of munching on his oysters if she so chose. What the hell was she doing? What did she want? He'd expected total acquiescence, but he really should have known better. He'd all but spilled his guts a moment earlier. Stasi knew he still wanted her.

Good thing he knew what she wanted, too.

"Don't even think about it or I'll beat your ass until you can't sit for a week."

Stasia's eyes widened and he didn't miss the scent of her arousal wafting thick and delicious in the air around them.

"When you're done sucking me off," he said, keeping his voice cold and mean, "I think I'm going to warm your ass with my hand. So much more intimate than a belt, don't you think?

Just worry about that for the next few minutes. Enough with my balls, suck my cock, she-bitch!"

To his relief, she let go of his balls and kissed and licked the skin she'd abused with her teeth, before smoothing her lips up the side of his shaft.

He widened his stance and set his hands on his hips, assuming a more powerful posture when he was swearing up a storm inside. *Fuck, yeah!*

As she reached the plump mushroom-shaped head, she paused and met his gaze. "May I suck you off, now?" she asked, a little smile curving the corners of her lips upward.

"Add a 'master' to that request and I might just let you have that privilege."

Her eyelids dropped, and her head tilted to the side. The look she gave him next had his toes curling into the carpet. "May I suck you off now, master?" she asked, her eyelashes batting innocently.

Alec growled deep in his throat and felt his muscles tense and hair sprout from his were follicles as the beast inside him roused. "Hell no," he rumbled with his beast's voice, "I'm going to fuck your mouth. Let me show you the difference, baby."

Stasia quivered at his feet as his flanks were clothed in golden hair. He'd halted his transformation, probably to keep his ability to order her around, but she didn't care. The beast was the one she wanted to play with tonight.

Her relief that he still wanted her as mate made her want to tempt the animal inside him. She wasn't naïve enough to think all their problems were resolved, but once they lay spent in each other's arms she could give him the softer words she yearned to share.

She tugged the thickening hairs surrounding his enormous cock and wet them with her tongue, ruffling against the direction of growth to tease him.

Then she gripped his cock hard, to let him know the dutiful bitch still had claws, and guided his cock to her mouth. She knew he loved her lips—he'd sucked her upper lip so many times moaning about watching it close around his cock. She took her time doing it now to tease and inflame him past control.

She guided his plump head into her mouth and let her upper lip drag around the crown, peeking beneath her eyelashes at him to gauge his approval.

His lengthened snout quivered and flared, sniffing her scent. His fangs were bared in a wicked grimace. She hoped those gleaming white incisors would chew on something soft of hers later.

But now it was her turn to tempt the beast into exploding all over her in a frenzy of fucking.

She widened her jaws and sank on his cock, taking him as far into her throat as possible, then bobbed on him, suctioning hard as she drew off his long shaft.

His chest rose and fell, his breath gusting, panting. Her hands slid around the base of his satiny cock and squeezed as she sucked. She sighed, content for now to tongue his shaft and suction hard on his cock as she built his release.

However, his hands fisted in her hair to control her movement. He growled, flexing his hips to drive his cock inside her throat, and she remembered what he'd said about fucking her mouth.

She braced herself, her hands sliding over fur to clutch the notches of his hips, her jaws widening, achingly, to accept his deep thrusts. Gagging each time he rammed deep, she accepted his domination, remembering to breathe through her nose. Her own body ripened, juices sliding from her cunt to slick her thighs, her nipples drawing to stiff, aching points.

"Are you wet for me, bitch?" his deep, growling voice bit out.

Murmuring her assent, she squirmed her hips.

"Think I need to see for myself." He yanked on her hair, pulling her off his cock. "Present your ass to me."

His fingers let go of her hair and she turned around on her hands and knees, lifting her quivering bottom into the air.

The golden wolf knelt behind her, and his claws dug into her cheeks. Then his hot breath washed over her moist folds.

She couldn't help the sucking sound her pussy made as it convulsed—her sex begged for him to fill her. Stasia bit her lips to prevent voicing the same desire.

Then his long tongue lapped her from clit to asshole, and then burrowed into her folds, seeking the cream of her delight.

His growls vibrated on her pussy, his facial fur chafed delicate flesh and she gasped and squirmed again, trying to encourage him to lick deeper.

When his body covered hers, the coarse fur abrading her bottom and back, she widened her knees, waiting for his huge cock to find her center.

But he drew away and nipped her ass.

Before she had a chance to complain, an open-palmed swat landed on her rump and Stasia howled. Another, harder than the first, struck the other cheek. "Oh Christ, fuck me now!"

He rolled her to her back and climbed onto her, straddling her thighs and she thought she'd never seen anything sexier than her golden wolf. The shining gold discs of his eyes stared down at her, and Stasia moaned. She brought her hands to her breasts and lifted them. "Please, they ache."

His head canted, and she wondered how much of the man remained within the beast. She arched her back to lift her chest higher and plucked her nipples to tempt him.

His snout descended, and he nuzzled the soft center of her breast, then his teeth latched on to her nipple and tugged.

Stasia's feet curled as he chewed and lapped her sensitive areolas. When the one breast had taken everything she could stand, she nudged his head toward the other and suffered his sweet torture until her cunt pulsed with need. "Fuck me, Alec. Fuck me," she whined.

His heavy body slid farther down her legs as his head licked a tantalizing path down her sternum, across her flexing abdomen, dipping into her belly button, then lower. When he reached the fur covering her mound, a rumble rocked his chest and he lashed out his tongue to spear between her wet folds, grazing her swollen clit.

She arched off the floor and tried to part her legs, but he didn't seem to understand she needed to open herself, spread her legs for his exploration and her pleasure.

She shoved at his head and wriggled, but he just growled and licked at the top of her pussy.

Her clitoris grew impossibly engorged, and she sobbed her frustration. She didn't want to come this way. She needed him inside her. Needed him to overwhelm her senses and her body with his powerful frame and thick cock and mark her forever with his scent.

She didn't realize she'd voiced her need aloud until he crawled to the side and urged her to her knees again. He kissed her pussy, licked it until her delicate inner lips quivered. Then he drew back. "This is the only cock that will ever fuck you again. Say it!"

Stasia's heart burst with joy. "Your cock's the only one I'll ever fuck again. Master."

He nuzzled her cunt with the soft fur of his snout. "Open for me, baby. Let me make you mine."

Stasia couldn't halt the sobs that racked her chest as she leaned forward on her arms. Moans, one on top of the other, broke free while his furry thighs rasped the tender insides of her thighs and his chest warmed her back.

As his cock nudged into her inflamed pussy, she hiccoughed and tilted her hips just so, aiding the straight thrust of his cock as he sank into her silken depths.

The first raw flexes of his hip, drove him deep into her clasping cunt, butting her womb. Each stroke dragged his thick shaft along her inner walls, building a friction that threatened to erupt in a raging fire, but every time she drew close to bursting into flame, he slowed his motions.

"Alec, please fuck me hard," she keened, trying to slam back on his cock.

"Tell me you love me," the wolf growled.

Stasia sucked in a shocked breath and shook her head. "I...can't."

He stopped moving. "Because you don't?"

Stasia closed her eyes. "Because you've never said you love me," she whispered.

His teeth nipped her shoulder. "That's not the way this works, baby. You have to take the chance. You have to break free. Go for broke."

Her body trembled, close to ecstasy while her heart broke. "But that leaves me naked. Totally in your control. You want everything from me."

His muzzle rubbed her neck. His hips circled once, screwing her deliciously. "Trust your instincts, Stasi."

Still she fought him though the tension building along her channel rippled on the verge of something wonderful. "It's not hard for you," she gasped. "You're not giving anything up. All you want is my obedience, my devotion."

"Sweetheart, if you haven't noticed, I already have that," he said, the wry note sounding sexier than it ought to in his beast's voice.

"You'll hold all the power," she said, her voice thin and high.

"I won't abuse it, I swear," he rumbled in her ear.

"I love you," she blurted out.

His tongue licked her jaw and shoulder and his hips drew back, pulling his thick cock out until only the swollen head remained inside. "Hold on, I can't stop now."

Disappointed he hadn't given her the words back, nevertheless she couldn't resist the heat that built with the powerful thrusts he delivered, each one harder and sharper than the one before. No one had ever fucked her like this — controlled, precise power — all of it directed at her pleasure.

His domination was his gift to her. He'd sensed her need and given her what her body and soul craved most. That was real love.

That he'd also discovered a wicked delight in torturing her, was just an added benefit — and incentive to keep him torturing her until they were old and gray.

His strokes scooted her across the carpet, but she welcomed the hot, stinging burns growing on her knees. She'd beg him to lick them better later. As his hips hammered faster, her cries built into howls that intertwined with his as they both crested the wave.

Her last thought as she drifted into a faint was she couldn't wait to wear his collar.

* * * * *

Quentin woke as the sun slipped beneath the ocean snuggled next to his beloved's naked body. His hand cupped a small breast, his thigh rode her slim hip. He kissed her shoulder and fingered the rosy-brown nipple until it spiked.

Her flesh remembered him. If he slid his hand between her legs, she'd cream and he could take her like he'd been dying to do so many nights. But the release she'd bring him would be hollow.

He pulled away his hand and sat up on the side of the bed, bowing his head as he gathered the strength to do what he must. Then he turned back to check the manacles that kept her limbs chained to posts on the floor at both ends of the bed.

His sleeping beauty was healed — in body. The gruesome wounds the wolf had left in her belly and skin had closed, not leaving a single scar to mark the change. Even her belly, that had swelled so with child, was flat — no trace of her pregnancy to mar her pale skin.

He picked up the razor blade on the nightstand and made a thin, but deep cut down his wrist, piercing the throbbing vein beneath the skin. He held his hand above her mouth, pleased she drank without him having to resort to manipulating her throat. She really was getting better.

By the time his wound closed, her mouth stopped moving, her hunger assuaged. Now he needed to find a meal to replenish what he'd lost. He dressed slowly, always listening to the sounds of her breathing, hoping for some little sign she'd waken — and dreading it, too.

Her injuries had been so extensive she might never wake up. He almost hoped she wouldn't, because he feared what he'd find in her eyes. A revolver rested in the drawer of the nightstand, a bullet chambered in the awful event she woke…changed.

He wasn't sure he could do it. He hoped he wouldn't have to. She'd remained in a coma since the night of the attack, had barely survived as he'd held her torn skin together with his hands and licked her wounds over and over to help her heal and fed her his blood to save her life.

But she could very well carry the werewolf's poison in her blood. There was a chance, when the next full moon rose in the night sky she could awaken a beast. A nightmare. A maddened rogue with a vampire's strength.

Perhaps Navarro had been right. He should have let her life slip away that night, but he couldn't bear the thought. If there was one chance on earth that she could be saved, he'd give it to her.

Without her he was a shell of man. If he was forced to use the silver bullet to end her life, he'd greet the sunlight and join her in death.

The glass door slid silently open and he stepped out onto the sand. Two days until the full moon. Two days left to try to save her.

There was only one person on the planet who might possess the magic to awaken her and prevent the werebeast from rising.

The witch who'd sired him.

He'd bundled Darcy into a bloody sheet and carried her to the private plane he'd paid a fortune to acquire. With her slack body strapped into the passenger seat he'd flown her to his birthplace in the Caymans on the blind hope *she* would help him.

Following the curve of the familiar shore, he felt the breeze lift his hair and plaster his shirt against his skin. The palms creaked as they bent to the rhythmic gusts.

A little farther, his heart beat faster. But where a crude wooden shack with the palm-frond roof had once stood was a whitewashed villa with an iron gate. Maybe this journey was for nothing. The past he'd sought to leave behind was really gone.

Maybe there wasn't any hope left for Darcy…or him.

Pushing through the creaking gate he stepped onto a tiled patio and caught a whiff of an elusive fragrance, like honeysuckle and mint. Hers. Already he braced himself for the sight of her dusky skin and the sound of the island patois in her whiskey-rich voice.

She'd seduced the human man, made him a slave to her passion, until the day she'd taken his life and pulled away the gauzy curtain that had hidden the true darkness in her heart.

A footstep sounded behind him and he stiffened, closing his eyes to steel himself against her *glamour*.

"'Bout time you come home, husband."

Why an electronic book?

We live in the Information Age—an exciting time in the history of human civilization, in which technology rules supreme and continues to progress in leaps and bounds every minute of every day. For a multitude of reasons, more and more avid literary fans are opting to purchase e-books instead of paper books. The question from those not yet initiated into the world of electronic reading is simply: *Why?*

1. *Price.* An electronic title at Ellora's Cave Publishing and Cerridwen Press runs anywhere from 40% to 75% less than the cover price of the exact same title in paperback format. Why? Basic mathematics and cost. It is less expensive to publish an e-book (no paper and printing, no warehousing and shipping) than it is to publish a paperback, so the savings are passed along to the consumer.

2. *Space.* Running out of room in your house for your books? That is one worry you will never have with electronic books. For a low one-time cost, you can purchase a handheld device specifically designed for e-reading. Many e-readers have large, convenient screens for viewing. Better yet, hundreds of titles can be stored within your new library—on a single microchip. There are a variety of e-readers from different manufacturers. You can also read e-books on your PC or laptop computer. (Please note that Ellora's Cave does not endorse any specific brands.

You can check our websites at www.ellorascave.com or www.cerridwenpress.com for information we make available to new consumers.)

3. *Mobility.* Because your new e-library consists of only a microchip within a small, easily transportable e-reader, your entire cache of books can be taken with you wherever you go.

4. *Personal Viewing Preferences.* Are the words you are currently reading too small? Too large? Too… ANNOYING? Paperback books cannot be modified according to personal preferences, but e-books can.

5. *Instant Gratification.* Is it the middle of the night and all the bookstores near you are closed? Are you tired of waiting days, sometimes weeks, for bookstores to ship the novels you bought? Ellora's Cave Publishing sells instantaneous downloads twenty-four hours a day, seven days a week, every day of the year. Our webstore is never closed. Our e-book delivery system is 100% automated, meaning your order is filled as soon as you pay for it.

Those are a few of the top reasons why electronic books are replacing paperbacks for many avid readers.

As always, Ellora's Cave and Cerridwen Press welcome your questions and comments. We invite you to email us at Comments@ellorascave.com or write to us directly at Ellora's Cave Publishing Inc., 1056 Home Avenue, Akron, OH 44310-3502.

erridwen, the Celtic Goddess of wisdom, was the muse who brought inspiration to storytellers and those in the creative arts. Cerridwen Press encompasses the best and most innovative stories in all genres of today's fiction. Visit our site and discover the newest titles by talented authors who still get inspired - much like the ancient storytellers did, once upon a time.

Discover for yourself why readers can't get enough
of the multiple award-winning publisher

Ellora's Cave.

Whether you prefer e-books or paperbacks,

be sure to visit EC on the web at
www.ellorascave.com

for an erotic reading experience that will leave you
breathless.

Made in the USA
Lexington, KY
30 January 2010